FINDING SIGNS

FINDING SIGNS

SHARLENE BAKER

Alfred A. Knopf   New York   1990

THIS IS A BORZOI BOOK
PUBLISHED BY ALFRED A. KNOPF, INC.

Owing to limitations of space, all acknowledgments for
permission to reprint previously published material may
be found on page 243.

Library of Congress Cataloging-in-Publication Data

Baker, Sharlene.
Finding signs / Sharlene Baker.—1st ed.
p. cm.
ISBN 0-394-57912-7
I. Title.
PS3552.A43455F5 1990
813'.54—DC20   89-39696
                                              CIP

Manufactured in the United States of America
First Edition

To my mother and my father

To Juanita Herrera, wherever she is

And to Paul
anyway

This story would still be in,
had it not been wheedled, kicked,
coerced and charmed out of me by Daphne Athas,
Doris Betts, Max Steele, Judy Hogan,
Sally Pont, Mike Stanley,
and last and most, Gloria Ribet Cash.
I thank you all,
from the bottom of my heart.

HIGHWAY 5, NORTH

1 ◫ IT'S ONE OF my favorite parts of being out here
... when the headlights keep streaming past my thumb, and
I'm weary from the cold and the dust and the stares, I wait
until between cars to slip away from the roadside. Behind the
lone puddle of light at freeway exits, if there's no gas station,
it's always black. I like stepping blindly into the darkness,
stomping out a sleeping spot in the crunchy cold grass. Big
enough to lie down? Good. Sleep here. No one in the world
knows where I am. Not even I know where I am.

I'm asleep and then I'm awake. Between the two, I open
my eyes. Never before has it been so simple.

I find myself in the gentle morning light nestled down in
thick fog and tall yellow weeds stiff with frost; at my feet a
small gray field rabbit is sniffing my sleeping bag. Our eyes
connect; he stops sniffing, but doesn't stiffen or tremble; he
takes his time hopping away. Propped on my elbows I see
that I've slept within a field of toppled one-room concrete
buildings, maybe a dozen, slab broken crazily on slab in the
yellow grass in the quiet fresh fog. Last summer's shriveled
vines cling to the slabs, brown and golden.

I unzip the side pocket of my backpack, pull out my water
bottle. Al's letter slips out along with it, to the ground. I take
a slug of water filled with ice chips, then lie back and unfold
Al's letter, again. "September 10th," I read. "Brenda! I've
passed the bar exam at long last and I'm ready to start living
again. Visit me. Visit me. Visit me. Al."

Sweet Al. His brown eyes, the line of his jaw, his smooth lips.

I refold the letter, return it to the pocket, then start rummaging for the raisin bread I know I have somewhere, probably smashed. Suddenly I see the rabbit again, nearby, nearly camouflaged. He is nibbling on a frosted tuft of grass. I watch to see just how he nibbles, then I gingerly lean over, smiling, and bite off one long tough brown stalk. Very chewy. Delicious.

2 🏵 ON THE ROAD you belong to the world. You depend on strangers to take you places, and often to feed you and take you in; you depend on the weather not to be too cruel to your highly vulnerable self; you depend on your own body not to betray you with sickness or depression. I'm always a little hungry and a little cold. I like it that way: lean and ready.

On a freeway entrance that looks like every other freeway entrance, I meet up with another hitchhiker sitting next to his pack. We're heading in different directions, so we won't be hitching together.

He looks supremely content. I ask him, "You been waiting a long time?" That's a standard question among hitchhikers.

"No," he answers. "Only about four hours."

Now, four hours is a long time to me. I tell him that I would be despairing after four hours.

He shrugs. He grins up at me ever so slightly. With one hand he is playing a kind of solitaire game with bits of roadside gravel.

"Where'd you start from?" I ask. That's another standard question.

He looks puzzled. "Well ... I had a job, oh, about six months ago, in New Orleans. I guess you could say I started there."

If I were a man, I would be that man. It isn't that I admire him so much. It's just that I know that's how it would be.

I lope over to my own entrance, and right away a man in a yellow Pinto stops for me. On his tape deck is Janis Joplin: "Get It While You Can." *Hold it, need it, want it, want it ...* I loved Janis. Janis isn't around anymore; she tried to get it while she could for too long.

I know a woman can't make it for long, out here. I really do like the road, but I'm only out here for as long as it takes me to get to Al's. Probably.

"You're headed to San Juan Capistrano?" the driver asks.

I answer "yes," because that's what my sign says. It's safer for me to look like I want a ride for a hundred miles instead of over a thousand. But after we've been driving together for an hour and he's talked about his girlfriend and his ex-wife and his kids that he misses and his job he can't stand, I mention that I'm really going to Spokane.

"Spokane." He whistles. "That's a long way for you to be traveling alone. Not too many girls that'd go that distance alone. Hmm. Spokane, Spokane, that's up there in central Washington. In the desert, right?" He flicks a new tape into the deck. All he has is Janis Joplin. This tape starts off with drunken hooting. A concert tape.

"*Is* it desert?" I ask. "The only time I drove up there was five years ago, and I drove into town and out of town in the dark, so I never noticed, really. It seems strange for there to be desert in a state like Washington."

"Shit. More desert around this country than anyone realizes. Deserts everywhere," he says, then suddenly reaches forward to turn up his stereo, yelling, "I love this part."

Janis pleads out to us in her gravelly voice, *Now you only gotta do one thing well to make it in this world. All you gotta do, is be a good man, one time, to one woman, and that'll be the end of the road babe, so come on, come on, come on, come on, come on . . .*

3 ◨ I T W A S A L who got me out here on the road, without his even knowing. Or maybe it goes back further, back to when I first met MaryEllen Keen.

MaryEllen had wanted my body, no doubt about it. I never wanted to mess with hers, even though MaryEllen was the sort of woman I would have gone nuts over if I were a man. It's nice to know, for sure, that you haven't got homosexual interests. Just to know.

MaryEllen had saved me from cashiering my life away at a Safeway. About nine months ago, at a Valentine's party, I'd been bitching about my job and she came over and introduced herself and told me I ought to try getting on where she worked. A week later I was doing landscape construction—building decks and benches, and laying concrete and such. MaryEllen and I were the only women on the site. We used to show up for work on those hot, dry, Southern California days dressed in bikini tops and cutoffs and big black steel-toed boots. MaryEllen was deceptively lean, and muscled, with a long brown ponytail that stuck to the sweat on her back between sharp shoulderblades, and with long brown legs, and sinewy arms that could hit a nail blam! once to set it, and blam BLAM! to knock it flush, just like that. The men were afraid of her. Our boots crunched in the sandy soil as we wheeled heavy wet cement around the site in wheelbarrows—I just barely, MaryEllen effortlessly—and no one messed with us.

Her skinny short-haired boyfriend Sean had gone to Harvard and now was a welder at a shipyard in National City, afraid the other welders would find out he'd gone to Harvard. He was trying to make enough money to pay off his school loan.

"Ask me *anything,*" he would say, "about the writers of the Constitution. *Anything.* Their wives' maiden names. *Please* ask me. It cost me fifty thousand dollars to learn that stuff."

What he'd discovered was that he really liked welding. At least he liked being around welders more than he'd liked being around his Harvard classmates.

Most nights after work I'd go to their house and we'd have tremendous feasts—always something we could get our hands in: dripping, sweet watermelon, or artichoke leaves topped with mayonnaise, or long asparagus tips we'd dip in lemon sauce. Sometimes we'd try out some new drug that Sean had picked up at the shipyard, and we'd lie around with our heads on each others' stomachs while we waited to see what would happen, and we'd talk lazily about what we'd do if we ever hit it big at the racetrack.

Before Sean and MaryEllen went to bed, one or the other often tried to talk me into joining them, but I knew it was always MaryEllen's idea. They'd stand there with their arms around each other, MaryEllen's eyes glowing, her pupils huge and black, her cheeks blazing, and she'd have this smashing smile on her face. I'd tell her, no, thanks, I'd see her in the morning; and she'd laugh and say, "You're afraid."

"Naw, I'm just saving myself for the love of my life."

"How do you know *I'm* not the love of your life? Me and Sean, both. The loves of your life."

"Because the way I see it is, someday, when I least expect it, I'm going to run head-first and full-speed into him. Him," I reiterate. "I'll get knocked silly; stars zinging and reeling around my head. I'll pick myself up with a giddy smile on my face, in time to see *him* pick *him*self up with a giddy smile on his face. And then, bingo, there he'll be."

"And you'll fuck like bunnies. Come on, Sean-boy. And by the way, Brenda, as for 'saving yourself,' you can only do that once."

I smile, shrug. "I'm saving the best stuff."

I'd stay lounged on the floor while they giggled in low tones in the next room. I'd lie and eat asparagus tips for a while. Sometimes I'd hear Sean moan, but I never heard MaryEllen make a sound.

We lived in a beach community, rickety two-room beach cottages lined up closely together. I loved the walk home through the salty warm night air, running my fingertips along the weathered picket fences. I'd walk past open doors—loud card games going on under blazing lights, surfboards lining the wall. Couples holding hands would pass me on roller-skates; wild-haired beach kids out late raced by on their skateboards. And in the dark distance I'd hear the ocean's roar, waves pounding the shore, waves I couldn't see.

4 LAST SPRING Sean and MaryEllen and I took trips out to the high desert east of San Diego once or twice a week. It was a two-hour drive. We'd leave right after work, not even bothering to wash up or change, just so we could get there at sunset, spend the night and wake before sunrise to get back in time to start another workday.

I carried water in a plastic quart milk jug that I tied to my beltloop with a shoestring. I liked zwieback then—the stuff babies teethe on—so I'd put some zwieback in a plastic bag and tie it to the beltloop on my other hip.

Sean would ease his heavy Rambler off the pavement, then

drive through canyons, washes, until we'd decide to stop. I'd tie on my water and zwieback and take off, usually in a different direction from Sean and MaryEllen. MaryEllen was hooked on expectorants that spring. She really dug coughing. I could always count on hearing her cough in the distance. I'd be standing alone among boulders as huge as houses, among stands of prickly pear huge as buses, and think: they're down in Dead Miner's Gulch, or, they're up on Squaw Tit.

In my pocket I had a USGS map that Sean had picked up. It was worn smooth like cloth from frequent fingerings and foldings. I didn't look at it much in the desert; Sean and MaryEllen and I liked to study it back at home, at the beach. We wanted to know the names of everything, the way the railroad tracks, unused now, blocked by tons of fallen boulders, wove through the ragged canyons. We walked those tracks sometimes. They had been built by Chinese, a never-ending string of Chinese, a man always coming along to replace the last one killed off in the big flu epidemic that year, 1918. We'd follow the tracks winding down, down across impossibly high, impossibly long wooden trestles, down layers of canyons dusted, in the spring, with belly flowers. We knew the switching station as small as a phone booth, where there was penciled inside: *What the big red rooster did to the little red hen, Herbert Hoover is doing to the railroad men.*

There was a crane out there, trapped between landslides. We packed in gallons of gasoline one Saturday, and spent all day puttering on the thing, trying to get it to run. We wanted to play with it like you play with a toy crane at an arcade, but with big boulders instead of stuffed animals. We couldn't get it started, though. That dusk, two border patrol men with binoculars hanging on their chests came strolling down the tracks. "You tripped some sensors we've got planted out here," one of them explained. Then they stood around, arms dangling, as if hoping we might start a conversation. We didn't.

It wasn't that we didn't like them—they had their job to do and looked decent and goodhearted. It's just that their desert wasn't our desert.

"Seen any aliens?" the other finally asked. We shook our heads. "Well, see you around, maybe."

All that night, as I slept fused to the cool hard desert floor, I dreamt of aliens, green aliens with oversized, veined heads, plodding down the ramp from their pulsating disk, not the aliens we occasionally saw: small groups of people half-running, half-walking, through the black desert night, bringing with them their paper-sack homes.

Sometimes there were lightning flashes on the far-off mountain ranges. Sometimes I walked to one of the oases surprisingly tucked inside narrow canyons, lush with date palms, birds, jackrabbits, and that amazing puddle of water, buzzing with lazy bees. Once it even hailed, pellets bouncing so high off the hard desert floor that they seemed to be shooting up out of the ground as much as shooting down from the sky. Sean and MaryEllen and I ran miles back to the car, yelping all the way, while the hail pellets stung our naked arms and legs.

But usually there was just the silence so solid I felt I could touch it, and the occasional wind rushing like a moaning ghost from a far canyon until it came in a hot blast, pelting me with sand. I'd just stand there, while the dusky sky turned black, I'd stand without moving for an hour or more, in my own two boots on the desert floor, while the Milky Way spun slowly above the cholla, above the ocotillo. I'd stand until I couldn't stand anymore, then I'd take a slug of water, good old tepid H-two-O, and eat some zwieback, and lie down just like that, in my t-shirt and cutoffs and boots, flat on my back on the earth's floor, my hand for a pillow. I'd look around at that huge busy sky and feel I'd have to grip the earth to stay on it. This was the desert, then: coyotes and tarantulas, ocotillo, cholla, wind and stars, dried bleached bones. And new bones, strong and growing. I could feel them growing, there. They were mine.

5 🖾 MARY ELLEN AND I got laid off. We had seen it coming so we weren't devastated. We made good enough money on unemployment, and had a lot of free time to body-surf. The floor of my cottage was always gritty with sand, my towels always damp and salty.

I started skateboarding every morning until about noon, then again for an hour or so around sunset, doing hotdog stuff on the sidewalk near the pier. The seawall near the pier was always covered with young transients, whom I finally got on a nodding relationship with. No small accomplishment: they really kept to themselves. It wasn't that I wanted to be friends, but I would have liked to talk with them a little, find out where they went from season to season. They must have slept on the beach, or maybe up in the cliffs; there were all kinds of niches and caves up there.

There was a dwarf couple who had matching tattoos, and rough skin, and tough looks on their faces that showed they'd been kicked around a lot in life. And they had the most angelic little daughter, normal sized, a lovely slim-limbed beach girl of about four. All morning she ran like the wind back and forth between the sparkling surf and her dwarf parents, who sat on their jackets on the seawall, dressed in their dark winter clothes, scowling.

At dusk, when I'd head back out to the beach, they'd be gone. I don't know where. The affluent crowd started showing up then, the plumbers and lawyers and realtors, sandy-haired tanned boys of thirty-five or forty-five who worked short days so they could still bike the boardwalk on funky banana-seat bikes, dressed in holey surfer shirts and Op shorts and cheap thongs, a beer in the plastic drink-holder attached to their handlebars. Others walked out the door of their beach houses straight across the warm sand into the orange ball of the sun, and threw themselves and their boards onto those cool dusk waves that they shared with surfing dolphins.

I'd sit on the wall and watch them and think about how I was twenty-three years old and owned nothing; all I was doing was being a person, the same way a seagull is a seagull. Then I'd ride my skateboard along the length of the fishy-smelling pier, past all the new Vietnamese kids who knew how to fish over the edge with a piece of old string and a safety pin, and when I got to the end of the pier, way over that deep black ocean, I'd start to spin on my board, my arms stretched out like wings, my stringy hair flying away from me like windblown sand.

Almost every night I'd have dinner at Sean and Mary-Ellen's. After a few months of unemployment, MaryEllen started talking up a scheme of hers for the three of us to move to Arizona to work at her friends' apple orchard. Miranda and Marty and Juan lived there; it was called the Juan-of-a-Kind Apple Ranch. MaryEllen showed us one of their box labels: an apple wearing a sombrero and spurs, lassoing a saguaro.

MaryEllen would wait until sunset, when she and I were itchy with dried seawater, and Sean came plodding in from the shipyard, greasy and grinning, and food was popping on the stove, then she'd woo us with names like Dragoon Mountains, and Cochise Stronghold. "Cochise!" she would yell, as if he were Lincoln or Gandhi. And she'd tempt us with the promise that the nearby town of Tombstone had the hottest swingdance bar in the U.S., and that Miranda sang there. I couldn't help noticing the way that MaryEllen talked about

Miranda. It wasn't exactly what she said about her, it was all in the way she said her name, Miranda, the way it lingered in her mouth, and that shine in her eye. I recognized that shine.

I wasn't so sure about going. I had promised my brother I'd go to the track every day, and place bets for him. That's what I did every afternoon, getting up to Del Mar by the third race. Will paid me to play his system; he needed to place bets every day. I would remind him on his down days that all the tracks in the world are supported by people's systems, but he knew that already, and it didn't stop him from following the circuit religiously, from Hollywood Park to Santa Anita to Del Mar.

On weekends we'd often go together to the track. He was seeing this woman named Cassandra, who worked near the navy docks at a place called Titillation—she called her job "dancing," not "stripping"—and she went along most of the time too. Will had been dating strippers for a while. I wasn't so crazy about them. They had names like Calypso and Slash and Honey. Cassandra was okay, though. I went to Titillation a few times with Will, and she was right; all she ever did was dance. She didn't stand on her head with her legs spread and vibrate her hips in men's faces like DeeDee, and didn't fuck candles like Dorae. I appreciated that. I told Cassandra if she ever started doing floorwork I'd never speak to her again.

Cassandra, like me, bet on jockey's colors, or horse's markings, or mostly, on horse's names. Will bet straight system. His system was based on the theory that the track was crooked, that races were thrown. He spent a lot of nights on his living room floor, racing forms spread out, taking notes in his neat, small handwriting, and highlighting the forms in three colors, until he thought he could tell what circumstances meant that the race was going to be thrown. It was never the Daily Double—that's why I didn't have to get to the track until the third race.

I liked that life, ambling through the track gate in my t-shirt and ragged cutoffs, a couple thousand bucks rolled in a wad in my front pocket, scuffling around the vast hot ticket-littered blacktop, studying the toteboard, following Will's formula until all the signs would point to it: this one. This is the crooked one. I'd look up at the tinted windows of the Thoroughbred Club, perched high above the finish line, and feel like I was a partner in crime with someone up there.

I'd stand in line at the hundred-dollar window behind the rest of the regulars, pencils behind their ears, dog-eared racing forms clutched in their armpits, and at the window I'd lay down one, two, maybe three hundred dollars on one horse, three hundred dollars in exchange for three thin tickets. It would all be over in three minutes—a three-hundred-dollar, three-minute thrill. Too much of a thrill; my heart would just about beat out of my chest when I had Will's three hundred dollars on the line. He did ok, though I tried not to keep track of it dollar-wise, because I had a sneaking suspicion that on top of paying me, he was pretty much breaking even.

Then I'd check in with Will. He lived alone in a faceless part of town, in a little apartment in the middle of a huge complex. He lived like a monk. He'd decided he didn't want things, didn't want anything around him that he didn't need or love. He had a few cups and plates in his kitchen, one pot. His living room was furnished with a couple of big pillows, a lamp, his pile of marked-up racing forms, a half dozen photos in frames placed around the floor and windowsills. One picture was of me that he'd taken when I was about eight. I was grinning wildly, wearing a borrowed tutu, arms held over my head, leg out. Right after Will had snapped it, I'd kicked my leg high the way I'd seen ballerinas do, and even now, I remember what it had felt like to land on my butt in the grass.

Often when I got back from the track, Will was asleep on his mattress on the bedroom floor, even though the sun was still up. He was doing renovation work downtown, and since he'd bid on his own jobs he could work at his own pace. He liked to work like the absolute devil, then come home and sleep like a dead man. That way he could stop working for a week or even a month every once in a while.

Sometimes when I found him dead to the world like that, I stayed for a while, sat on the floor next to his bed and thought about things. Will had an old wind-up clock that ticked loudly; that was nice. Propped on the wall next to his mattress was a picture of him and his old best friend, Kirby Renfroe. In the picture, he and Kirby are in their fatigues and big black boots, sitting on a couple of ammunition boxes somewhere in Vietnam. Under their helmets, their smiles: Will's broken-toothed beam, and Kirby's heartmelting grin. Man, Kirby was handsome. Will and Kirby are mud-splashed and sweat-soaked, but spread on a taller ammunition box between them is an impeccably clean lace tablecloth, three lit, white tapers in a silver candelabra, a crystal vase with a rose, and spread around it, their hacked-open green tins of rations. I've never been able to ask Will about that picture because I've never been able to ask him about what happened to Kirby.

I'd leave Will's racing form and his cash beside the bed without waking him, then go back to the beach to mess around on my skateboard for a while before sunset. I kept telling MaryEllen that I was going to get gutsy enough or foolish enough to make a run down Mount Soledad, over where they were putting in new houses and there wasn't much traffic yet. I had dreams of plummeting downhill at fifty miles per hour, blissfully balanced and centered.

Then one day, out of the blue, Sean announced he was moving back to Boston at the end of the month. He was tired of the Southern Californian lifestyle, and he said that after Boston and the National City shipyard, Dragoon Mountain fresh air would kill him. I thought he and MaryEllen had been getting along all right, so I was surprised at how well they seemed to be taking their imminent splitting up.

About the same time, Will was having a rash of losses that I couldn't ignore. It got to where I couldn't stand to look at his worried face, and worse, couldn't stand the way he'd shrug off the bad news like it was nothing. I was afraid things were going to start happening with him again, like they did the winter before, when I'd been living with him over on Front Street. I was afraid he was going to start listening to his Crystal Gayle album again.

The racing season ended at Del Mar, and Will wanted me to start going to Agua Caliente.

"You're in the hole now," I argued with him.

"Come on, Brenda, it's all part of my *system*. It's part of my *system* to lose for a while until I win really big. *We* win really big."

"But Agua Caliente! It's nighttime, and it's Mexico, and most of all, it's dogs. I don't do dogs."

"You've got to play this system through. Look, you can't run out on me like this."

Occasionally at Del Mar I'd bet two bucks of my own here and there. The night I finally went to Agua Caliente, pushing my way through the teeming masses of Mexican men all shouting in a language I didn't know, I bet on a Trifecta: Candida, Desert Sun, Vagabonda, and damned if it wasn't one of the purtiest sights I ever did see, those very three sets of sleek muscles and long bones streaking their way over the finish line ahead of all the others.

I gathered up $560 at the payoff window, pocketed it, and without even laying down a bet for Will, turned right around and went to his house. I told him I was sorry, but I just couldn't keep on losing his money for him anymore. I tried to give him half my winnings, but he wouldn't take them. He only wanted me to keep betting for him.

"You promised me you'd help me," he called after me as I went out the door. His voice sent a jitter down my spine, but I pretended I didn't hear him, and kept on walking. Those words reminded me of something that happened when we were kids, but I couldn't remember what the incident was, or even if it had been me or him who had said, "You promised me you'd help me."

I went to Sean and MaryEllen's, busting in with the $560 in my fist.

"Great!" MaryEllen said. "Go to the Apple Ranch with me. Sean says he'll drop us off on his way to Boston."

So there it was. And there we were, Sean and MaryEllen and I, heading to the Dragoon Mountain fresh air, heading to where apples wear spurs, where Miranda lives. We were sailing in Sean's old Rambler, sailing past saguaro. I was singing out the window, and trilling, and hoping like hell things were going to be okay with Will.

6 WILL'S FRIEND Kirby Renfroe had been a stupid-looking kid, all elbows and nose and teeth and giant, dirty Keds with perpetually broken laces. He had a world-weary shrugging way about him that made adults forget to treat him like a kid, and he had the most ready smile and the sweetest nature, seemingly blissfully unaware of his awkward looks and stumbling ways. Kirby's father had been in the air force like our dad, though he hadn't been a pilot. Somehow, by chance, Kirby's dad was transferred three or four times to the same bases where we were, so Will had something that was a rarity among military kids: a childhood friend.

Somewhere, oh, when I was about ten or so, Kirby changed. Over the summer, he grew into his knees and voice and teeth and nose; out of the blue, he was a knockout. Girls from my school who'd ignored me all the year before suddenly wanted to come over to my house to play, on the chance that they might get to see Kirby Renfroe. They knew he was always there, his fatally handsome self draped out along our couch. Through his transformation, he'd kept his same smiling sweet nature, and just as he'd walked around ignorant of his ugliness as a kid, he walked around just as ignorant of his new-found good looks.

Dear Brenda, Kirby was killed last week, said Mrs. Renfroe's letter. *You may already know of this from Will, as he was with him when he died. We expect his body tomorrow. We are having him cremated along with some articles that were dear to him. Could you please send a small item of Will's to be burnt along with Kirby?* That's the way she'd put it: to be burnt along with Kirby.

I was seventeen years old, then. I'd sat on my bed, my heart in utter confusion, and read the letter over and over. Then I went in the garage where all of Will's things were. The garage wasn't cold, but I was shivering the whole time I opened boxes, looking for the item that would be just right. In one of the boxes I found a yellowed envelope, folded in thirds. Inside was the little chip of Will's tooth that he'd broken off when he was eight years old. I had to smile at that; I had no idea he'd saved it.

I brought it into the house, wrote, "From Will to Kirby" on the envelope. Then, "Personal," and sealed the flap.

Will wrote several times between then and when he came home, but he never once mentioned Kirby.

A month later, they took down the plaque in my school lobby that was engraved with names of graduates who'd been killed in wars. They needed to add more names. When it came back, there was his name: KIRBY RENFROE. I stood on the dirty linoleum of the hallway and thought, in just a few years after this war ends, if it ever ends, this plaque isn't going to mean any more to the people walking past it than a Civil War memorial means to me. Someone'll stop by chance and read the name KIRBY RENFROE and they won't have any idea that he used to be this really great guy with a ready smile, this heartthrob kid. Kirby's name wasn't even the last name on the list. There were already a lot of names below his.

7 WILL, TWENTY YEARS AGO, on the "Howdy Doody" show:

For months he had been badgering our mother about wanting to be on the show. We'd moved to downtown Boston then, and used to pass the studio building all the time. Every few days, after my brother came home from school, our mother would bundle us up, and she'd hold Will's hand and he'd hold mine, and we'd run down the Boston sidewalks and across streets through clouds of exhaust toward what she said was an employment agency. We were really on our way to her appointment at the city mental health clinic, but Will and I didn't find that out until years later. We were always late. My feet were never underneath me—always flying around somewhere behind. My brother's hand was the only thing holding me up.

One slushy Boston day when all of our noses were running, and we had all been slipping on the icy sidewalks in our clear rubber overshoes, my mother suddenly turned and brought us into the TV station building. I think she mainly wanted to get out of that slicing wind. We took the elevator right up to the "Howdy Doody" office where the receptionist took one look at my brother's beaming smile and broken front tooth, the tooth he'd broken trying to fly off the roof in a cardboard box airplane, and signed him up for the following week.

"Howdy Doody" was live then. Almost everything on TV

was live then. The next week we dropped my brother off at the station, rushed home, and there he was, Will, in the front row of the Peanut Gallery. Clarabell the clown was standing right beside him holding a giant Tootsie Roll. "Now boys and girls," Clarabell squeaked, "when you want that special after-school treat . . ." Suddenly he dropped the giant Tootsie Roll. It bounced and rolled across the stage while Clarabell gagged, and clutched his left arm and grabbed at his big ruffled collar like he couldn't breathe. "Heart," he gasped. The camera swung wildly, then focused on the Peanut Gallery where a man with a puppet on his arm was jumping around getting the kids to cheer. The kids were all squealing and clapping, except for my brother. He was pointing offstage with a look of horror on his face, his mouth dropped open wide. The camera swung again, and when it came back Will wasn't in the Peanut Gallery anymore.

We found out later that they'd dragged him offstage along with Clarabell, and somehow Will had gotten swept along the corridor to the back exit where he'd watched them pull off Clarabell's nose and wig while they waited for the ambulance.

When my mother and I showed up, no one knew where Will was. The studio people looked like they were mad at my mother, that they had enough to worry about without having a missing kid on their hands.

Someone walked us backstage and down hallways, and then there he was, huddled on the floor by the exit sign, crying. He had been crying the whole time.

I looked down at him and thought he looked younger than me, though he was five years older. I looked down at my saddleshoes and noticed that they were on the wrong feet. My brother's still the kind of guy who's not afraid to cry.

8 ◫ LAST WINTER lasted forever. Last winter was damp drafts, a leaky roof, lousy part-time work at Safeway. Last winter was when Will went on five-day drunks, and listened to Crystal Gayle like a madman.

I had moved in with Will and his seven roommates in their twelve-bedroom Victorian on Front Street, in uptown San Diego, across from Par Liquor. We weren't *under* a flightpath, we were *next* to it. The house hung on the edge of a canyon that 727s dipped down into in rapid descent toward the landing strip that blinked below us, down by the bay. When we sat in the living room, the jets screamed by the windows in profile.

It rained like crazy. We had pots and pans and bowls and buckets and trash cans all over the house to catch the leaks—seventeen in the living room alone. We had three old couches covered with Indian bedspreads that we lounged around on. Everyone worked sporadically or part-time. We all got cabin fever. There was always a pot of tea on the table, another pot brewing, the kettle boiling, simultaneously; there was always a card game going on.

Will was working, though, at his renovation jobs, fourteen hours a day, coming home just to sleep. He was making a lot of money; he'd bought a brand-new pickup with cash. One Sunday morning I went with him to marinas to price boats; in the afternoon he bought an open-dated airline ticket to Hawaii, saying he'd use it soon.

Then one day he came home early holding a Crystal Gayle album still in its cellophane, a full bottle of rum, its seal unbroken. He wanted to use my stereo, in my room. He didn't have a stereo.

He closed the door. I sat with our roommates drinking tea. The same side of the album played over and over, until I got to know what songs were coming up next, I got to know a lot of the words. *It's been too long a time, with no peace of mind, and I'm ready for the times to get better.* Crystal's voice had become like breathing.

"He must have fallen asleep with the turntable arm up," I finally said. "This is driving me nuts."

I opened the door of my room and my heart dropped. Will was lying on his back crosswise on the bed, eyes wide open, filled with tears. His glass of rum was resting on his diaphram, his fingertips playing on its rim. He didn't look up at me; he didn't seem to even know I was there. I backed out of the room and shut the door.

I slept on one of the couches that night. The album played on and on. I wavered in and out of sleep; I heard Crystal's voice, I dreamt it, I curled around it, rubbed it into my skin, clear and sad. In the night silence I could hear the turntable arm lift up, drop down again. *I've got to tell you, I've been wracking my brain, hoping to find a way out.*

I woke to her voice. I didn't need to get into my room to dress for work; the room was tiny, only enough space for my bed and stereo, so all my clothes were in a closet in the hallway.

When I came home, the album was still playing. My roommates shrugged, drank tea. They were playing poker, betting quarters.

I went into my room and shut off the stereo. Will woke up. The bottle was on the floor, empty. The glass was tipped over on the bed. He rolled off the edge of the bed onto all fours, then pulled himself up and walked into the bathroom.

I was bluffing with an empty hand when the front door opened and Will walked in with three more bottles of rum, and went straight into my room. The stereo started up again. *You seem to want from me what I cannot give. I feel so lonesome at times.* Her voice flowed like liquid into the room. We looked at each other over our poker hands. "Poor Will," Eddie said. "Fifty cents and call."

When I went to work the next morning I heard snoring from my room.

The third day, the album stopped. It had been stopped for a while before we all seemed to notice it at once. "Thank god," someone said, but just then, it started up again. At least it was a new song, the other side of the album.

I went into my bedroom and found him like before, lying flat on his back, his eyes so teary and bloodshot they made my own eyes sting just to look at them. I stood there and took a deep breath and just tried to say the name, Kirby. It was funny how it wouldn't come out.

"That year, 'sixty-eight, that was the worst," I finally said. My voice sounded loud. Will jumped a little, but didn't look at me. "You know, when Bobby Kennedy was shot? Where we were living, in Westchester, his hotel speech was live on TV. I saw Bobby Kennedy get shot in the head, live, on TV. You didn't know that, did you. It was late . . . Mom and I were both watching. The announcer was yelling, 'The gun is pointed at me! Grab his thumb! Grab his thumb!' "

My heart was pounding like mad, like it always does when I remember this, my head shaking back and forth by itself, no, no. "I was eating a tuna fish sandwich, and I dropped it on the rug. I grabbed big handfuls of my hair, like this." I showed him, but he didn't look up. "I was actually trying to rip the hair right out of my head. I was screaming. And you know what? Mom, Mom was sitting right there. And she said, and she said, 'For God's sake, Brenda, it's only TV.' "

Will snorted softly. "She was pretty out of touch by then," he whispered. He sounded really drunk. I sat down on the edge of the bed. Will stunk of old sweat and rum.

"You know, to this day, I can't eat tuna fish? Just the smell of it depresses the hell out of me. You wouldn't think . . ."

"Y'know what, Bren?" Will slurred. He never called me Bren. "Sometimes," he said, "you get your face too close to my face."

I jumped off the bed as if I had been stung, put the needle back on the record and left the room. I stood in the corner of the front hall where our roommates couldn't see me and cried and cried. When I stopped, there was Crystal's voice filling up the room again.

For five days Will came out of the room only to drag himself down the hall to the bathroom or across the street to Par Liquor. He turned the volume down on the stereo. It was worse in a way—it was like I was imagining her voice. A jet's scream would drown it out, then I'd have to strain my ears until I could be sure she was still there.

Will went back to work for a few weeks, then went on a drunk again and again. I don't know what he did with his money, but somehow he was always broke, always borrowing. I got used to it after a while: the shut door, Crystal's monotonous lilt, the streetlight shining through the window into my face when I slept on the couch. It didn't seem like a big price for me to pay toward that lousy war.

What finally happened though, was that Will and I had to move out. Will had to, that is, and I moved out soon after. Our roommates pitied him and pity can last only so long before it turns into disgust. Will finally did something to tip that balance: he broke 250 fluorescent light tubes in the backyard.

On one of his renovation jobs he'd had to haul a bunch of junk from a basement, and among the stuff he found the light tubes. They were still good, so he hauled them home and unloaded them in the backyard. He was so excited, with that particular type of excitement: easy money. When he wasn't on a drunk those days, he was absolutely obsessed with money.

No one wanted the bulbs. They were obsolete. He called

all around, but no one had those odd-sized fixtures anymore. Damn, they laughed, you're just fifteen years too late. Try Mexico, they laughed. The bulbs sat stacked in the backyard, turning brown with dust, gathering leaves.

One afternoon I came home from work to a shattering in the backyard. I found Will sitting crosslegged on a tree stump, his jacket pockets bulging with stones, and all around him, like a world of ice, glittered broken bulbs. The back door was open; I leaned against the doorframe watching him. The sun was piercing the eucalyptus leaves high overhead, flashing and sparkling off the glass like diamonds. Will took a single stone from his pocket and studied it calmly, tested it for weight and size and shape, then winged it so powerfully and true that it made a singing sound before shattering a bulb in an eerie popping way, not explosion, but implosion.

Maybe if what he was doing wasn't so pretty, I would have stopped him, but it was beautiful destruction. I stood in the doorway for a good half-hour, until he had hit every last one. Then he sat there on that stump, uplifted above his whole shattered world, calm and quiet. He was chewing gum—I remember that. I said, "Will?" and he stood up and without looking at me crunched across the yard past me through the back door, walked through the house, out the front door, got into his pickup, and drove away.

I was really worried then, but as it turned out, I didn't need to be. He told me later that he'd just gone down to the docks and watched the sailboats going in and out of port. I don't know why that did the trick, but it did; he stopped drinking his way to self-destruction for a while.

I tried raking up the glass that afternoon, but it was impossible, it was so thoroughly shattered. When I finally came inside I heard our roommates talking in the living room. "Wish he'd broken that goddamned record," one of them said, and they all laughed.

I went into my room, and sure enough, there was the album on the turntable. The needle was off it, but the stereo was on, the album spinning smoothly around and around. Propped next to it was the picture of him and Kirby, and beside that, the album cover. Will and Kirby and Crystal were staring out at me, and all three of them had smiles sweet and soulful and sad sad sad.

9 MARYELLEN, of course, lost the directions to the Juan-of-a-Kind Apple Ranch, which she'd written on the back of an envelope. She figured she left it at the Circle K in Yuma where we had to stop so she could stock up on chocolate bars. MaryEllen was off expectorants and onto chocolate. She'd read in a magazine that there was a chemical in chocolate that was the same chemical your body released into your system when you were falling in love. She said she was going to live on chocolate from then on.

She and Sean kept staring at each other flush-cheeked on the whole trip so I figured there was something to it. I wasn't so certain that Sean would go to Boston. But then, maybe both he and MaryEllen would, or maybe they'd stay and I'd go to Boston, or maybe I'd go with either MaryEllen or Sean to Boston. Or Baltimore, Brooklyn, Brazil. Whenever I get a set of wheels underneath me, every situation, every possibility seems to make sense.

MaryEllen thought she could remember the way, even without directions. She had been following this local religion in San Diego—I could never remember the name of it: Earth Love Alliance Church or somesuch. The minister was a woman named MaryEllen, which I think was most of the reason MaryEllen followed her. The church's theme was "trust thyself." MaryEllen trusted she would remember the way.

So we were riding past apple orchards that were perched all up and down the rocky hillsides, when MaryEllen said, "There it is. I was supposed to look for that." At the entrance to a gravel drive in a field of weeds behind a mailbox was a car seat. On the seat sat an inflatable life-sized lady. She was wearing a lace slip and a straw hat, and her red vinyl mouth was opened in a big surprised "Oh."

MaryEllen got out of the Rambler, leaving the door hanging open, crossed the road and riffled through the mail in the box. "Yeah, this is it," she yelled to us. She checked out each piece of mail, turned over letters for return addresses, paged through a catalogue. Then she put it all back into the box, and picked her way through the weeds to the inflatable lady. She took off the lady's hat, put it on her own head, sat on the seat next to her with one arm on her shoulder, and posed, smiling at us. As she was putting the hat back on the lady's head, she jumped up suddenly. "Gross!" she yelled. She pointed to the lady's vinyl mouth. "Used! She's been used!" She started running to the car, then stopped and with great resolve walked back to the inflatable lady. She picked her up, turned her upside down, looked at her back and her front, then set her upright on the seat. Back in the car, MaryEllen slammed the door, hard, and stared at the both of us, steely-eyed. "Just as I thought," she said. *"Every* orifice."

Sean looked at me as he nodded his head toward MaryEllen. "My little shrinking violet," he said, as we bounced down a badly rutted drive to a crazily shaped farmhouse. There was no telling where the main body of the house was; every part of it looked like a tacked-on afterthought. We couldn't decide which door was the front door. MaryEllen just picked one, and walked on in.

We found ourselves in the kitchen, which had a sloping floor and smelled of fermenting apples. A woman walked in a doorway.

"Miranda!"

"Well now, don't y'all just look like the Three Caballeros," she deadpanned. Then she and MaryEllen hugged and rocked for a while.

"I love your scarecrow at the top of the drive," MaryEllen said.

"That's our mascot. Marty and I found her out in the orchard after we bought the place. I kinda identify with her, if you know what I mean. Y'all thirsty?" She poured us cider in jelly jars. I walked across the kitchen, sat in a chair, leaned my elbows on a counter. It seemed like every table, every chair, counter, floor, every surface in the house was sticky.

Miranda was about thirty, delicate yet sturdy, with long brown hair that fell smooth like a slow waterfall, all the way past the bottoms of her cutoff jeans. Then long brown thighs, and high fringed suede Indian moccasins.

"You look like Crystal Gayle," I told her, and she leaned onto the counter, laughed in a tired voice and drawled, "Honey, you're just about the thousandth person who's ever told me that."

Sean left, he actually left that dusk after dinner, gravel crunching beneath the old Rambler wheels. MaryEllen and I could see the dust he was kicking up for a long way. Then all that was left was the mountain silence that made my ears ring with the sound of my own blood. Planets started appearing— evening stars. MaryEllen just smiled bravely at me and shrugged.

"Mars should be coming out about there," I said, pointing into the sky. Will taught me about the stars.

"Mars isn't coming *out*," MaryEllen said. "It was *there* the whole time. The whole time we were crossing the desert, it was there. We just couldn't see it."

Miranda had a gig that night in a bar in Tombstone, so MaryEllen and I went along. Marty and Juan, who we met only briefly, stayed home. It was close to harvest, and they were putting in long hours, getting up at dawn.

Miranda's speaking voice was sweet and lilting, with a Scarlett O'Hara accent, but her singing voice was loud, gravelly, raunchy. It filled the inside of my head, the inside of the room, overwhelmed it, slipped between the sweaty bodies that were spinning in pairs, dancers so drunk in the dark that only centrifugal force was holding them up.

And I was downing beers and sliding off the bar stool at the start of each song into this man's hands and that man's arms, fine-tuning myself to each one's style and rhythm, submission as a fine art, and I saw MaryEllen dancing almost every dance with a thin, short-haired guy who reminded me a little of Sean, and Miranda, on her breaks, was hanging onto a guy, large, bearded, with a cowboy hat. She was smoking cigarettes and laughing loudly. Half the men in the bar were looking her way and quite a few were looking mine, and normally, this was where I'd be flashing a smile in some lean heartbreaker's direction, but I don't know, just not that night.

When Miranda laughed lustily into the microphone and announced that the night was over, started singing, *Well, the girls all look purtier at closin' time,* I slid drunkenly from my chair and weaved between people in the dark into the side room. I started playing pinball with great concentration; the machine spoke out in a monotone electronic voice. "No one escapes the black hole," it said. "No one e-scapes the black hole."

The next morning I was eating Cheerios in the sticky kitchen when MaryEllen and the skinny guy shuffled in, then Miranda and her guy, still wearing his cowboy hat. I wondered if he'd ever taken it off. We were sitting around the table, not saying anything, crunching and slurping on Cheerios. MaryEllen and I and the two guys were checking each other out, trying to figure where we each fit in. Miranda looked like she knew just where she fit.

"Hah! Listen to this!" Miranda read off the milk carton, " 'American Facts: People who are not citizens of the country in which they live are called aliens. There are nearly five million permanent resident aliens in the U.S. today.' Can you imagine that? It'd be bad enough to be called an alien, can you imagine being called a *permanent alien?*"

We all shook our heads dumbly.

Then the men were leaving, walking toward their separate cars. Miranda's guy said, "Had a nice time," and she answered, "Sure enough, Rob."

He stopped, stared at her, confused. "Ron," he said.

"Ron?"

He nodded his head.

"Really? All this time I thought it was Rob." She laughed and shrugged her shoulders, her laughter sweet and sad.

10 PICKING APPLES was hard work, good work. I felt like a midwife, laboring long hours, birthing the heavy-hung trees of their fruit. I was good at picking, at positioning the ladder, at not being afraid to stretch those last precarious inches. When I would descend the ladder for the last time at a tree, after emptying my heavy bag of its musky fruit, I'd take a minute to step back. The tree always looked so wonderfully grateful: lean, and independent, reaching to the sky instead of bending over its own trunk.

Sometimes MaryEllen was the only other person in the orchard, and I would even forget she was there, or that there was anyone or anything in all the world but bark, limbs, apples, leaves, and the heightened rhythm of my own breathing, my own two hands. Most days, though, Mexican farmworkers showed up in old schoolbuses, some days whole families pouring out, the kids running around, screaming, happy for the open-air freedom. Then MaryEllen and I drove the apple-filled trucks around the orchard or into Tucson to the distributor. Mostly, though, we worked at the press, making cider. I was working cider, drinking cider, breathing cider, my pores were infused with apple cider.

At night, I was always so exhausted that right after dinner I'd go to my bedroom, lay my work-weary self into bed, and slam right down into the deepest of sleeps, sleep that felt so good to drop into and so good to lift out of the next morning. Then I'd head outside for another day of work in the clear mountain air and the rows of trees that rolled over the hills off into the blue sky.

Nothing developed between MaryEllen and Miranda. I guess Miranda wasn't interested. We rarely even saw her; she and Juan and Marty liked to keep to themselves. The apple ranch wasn't at all like the house on Front Street, with the six or eight or however many there were of us playing endless card games there. Miranda did the phone work and the dollar-and-cents work, and went off to other band members' houses to rehearse. MaryEllen and I still went to the Swing On Inn to hear her sing, but only once every week or two.

Some nights MaryEllen and I hung out in my bedroom. The room was crazy, tacked onto a separate hall that was tacked onto the back corner of the farmhouse. It had windows on three walls that looked out on endless rows of apple trees, and two doors, one to the outside, one to the hall. I had a tall shaky four-poster bed that sat right in the middle of the room. I'd curl at the head of it reading, with MaryEllen on her belly crosswise at the foot. She was really taken up by Cochise, reading all she could find about him in the books she picked up on our trips to Tucson. She wrote long, fact-filled letters to Sean, who was working as a welder in a shipyard in Boston.

"Wow!" she shouted one night, looking at a book. "Brenda, god, listen to this, what Cochise said: 'I was going around the world with the clouds, and air, when God spoke to my thoughts and told me to come in here and be at peace with

all. Why is it that the Apaches wait to die—that they carry
their lives on their fingernails? They roam over the hills and
plains and want the heavens to fall on them.' Jesus, Brenda,"
and already she was copying furiously onto Sean's letter, "I've
got to send this to Sean. 'I was going around the world with
the clouds and the air, when God spoke to my thoughts . . .'
Jesus."

Slowly the whole orchard was becoming an even color of
green, no longer speckled with apples. Each morning was
colder.

"Go with me to Boston!" MaryEllen said one afternoon.
We were alone in the orchard, sitting on the ground, leaning
against trees, eating sandwiches for lunch. Sandwiches and apples. "I'm going, right after the harvest party. We can get
work there, easy. Some kind of work. I'm trying to talk Miranda into driving; she's never been to the Northeast. Maybe
she will."

"Naw, MaryEllen. Boston sounds so crowded to me. I was
thinking I might go find a job someplace like Santa Fe. Or I'd
like to live in the Northwest for a while, Oregon or Washington. There's an Oregon Coast Trail I've been dying to do.
It's hard to decide. There's so much stuff I want to do."

"When in doubt, make a list. Write something like: What's
Important in Life. Then list what's important in life."

"I already made a list, when I was ten years old. I was really
sick for a long time. Death's door. I was in bed for weeks.
Then when I finally got better, one of the first things I did
was go to the library, walk in, pick up a magazine, open it,
and like magic, there was an article about a man who'd been
deathly ill when *he* was ten years old, and while he was sick,
he'd made a list of a hundred things that he would do if he
ever got well. And he'd made a solemn oath that he would
do them all. I think he'd done about eighty, when the article
was written. He'd piloted a blimp, won a ribbon in a rodeo,

pitched for a minor league team, been in an earthquake . . .
you name it. I think he even climbed Mount Everest. So I sat
down in the library and *I* made a list of a hundred things and
swore I would do them all, too."

"That's the problem," MaryEllen said. "Excess. Disorder.
Moderation and order is what you need."

"So sayeth MaryEllen Keen. I'm supposed to listen to ad-
vice like that from *you?*"

"Anyway," MaryEllen continued, "you ought to at least
revise your list every thirteen years. And be more concise this
time."

That night, alone in my bedroom sitting crosslegged on the
bed, I wrote *What's Important:* on the top of a piece of paper,
and without pausing, listed underneath: *1) Adventure.* This is
easy, I thought. Under *Adventure* I listed: *2) Love.* Then I
decided that love was encompassed in the word *Adventure,*
that love was just a most amazing adventure, so I scribbled
out *Love.*

I sat for a while, alone on that tall bed staring at the words
What's Important: 1) Adventure. Then I got down, walked
down the hall to the kitchen and called my brother.

"Will, hi, it's Brenda. Want to take a trip?" He laughed.
"The harvest party is coming up next week, and then I'm out
of a job. So let's go somewhere."

"I was actually just thinking I needed a vacation. I *really*
need a vacation. But jesus, Brenda. I lost all my savings. At
Agua Caliente. I'll win it back, but I have to stop for a while.
Dogs are different, and Mexico's different. I've got to come
up with a new system."

"How about if I send you some money? Not to bet with,
but just to pay your bills so you can adventure for a while
with me."

"I don't need *some* money, I need a lot. If I don't hustle,
I'm not even going to make rent. I'm really in a bind, Brenda.

I wish you hadn't left. I don't think this would have happened if you hadn't left." He waited, but I didn't say anything. "Cassandra dropped me, too."

"God, Will, I'm really sorry about that," and I was, from his point of view, though not from mine. "Please let me send you some money. I can even send a lot of money. I still have my winnings from the racetrack, and I've been earning here and hardly spending any, except for beers at this bar in Tombstone called the Swing On Inn. I've been thinking of going to Oregon, or Washington. I want to see some big trees and big ocean, and islands."

"Oh, Washington! Some guy sent you a letter a couple of months ago. From Spokane. It got forwarded to the Front Street place and then to the beach, and finally landed here. Hold on a second, I've got it around somewhere," and I could hear him shuffling papers. "Al Righetti."

"Al! I bet it's been five years since I've heard from him."

"Well, it would have been another five if I hadn't finally remembered. I'll send the letter to you. What have you been doing there?"

"Picking apples. Driving trucks. Working at the apple press. MaryEllen and I were just talking about how we're not ninety-eight percent water anymore, we're ninety-eight percent apple cider. I've been living on apples. MaryEllen's been living on apples and chocolate."

"And expectorants," Will said.

"No, she's off expectorants. You know what Cochise said?"

"*Cochise* said something about *expectorants?*"

"No, no. Talking about MaryEllen made me think of Cochise, because he's all she's been talking about for the last two months. He said, 'Why is it the Apaches wait to die—that they carry their lives on their fingernails? They roam over the hills and plains and want the heavens to fall on them.' "

"I feel like that, too," Will said and I was afraid he was

going to start talking about waiting to die, but instead he said, "I'd like the heavens to fall on me." Will spent so many nights standing outside, head tipped back, drinking in all the stars, that I knew he meant something good by that.

"Will you come out here?" I asked. "Then you can bring the letter with you. You won't have to spend all that money on postage." Will laughed, because he always laughs at my jokes.

"Shit . . . ," Will said, and paused in a way that made me think he was considering the idea, so I held my breath and didn't say anything. "Yeah, okay."

"You will?"

"Yeah, sure, I will. All right? I will."

"You're really going to do it? I'll send a check right away. If you'll come here right away."

"Brenda, for god sakes, I promise, okay? As soon as I can, I'll be out there, I promise."

"I promise," he'd said, and I hung up the phone and laid my tired self in bed, and dreamt of that big Northwest, of islands and whales, of volcanos, and of waterfalls that crash down, right in the middle of cities.

11   FIVE YEARS AGO I'd called Al and he'd said "Come Visit" so I did, drove for sixteen hours to Eureka, slept in the car before driving sixteen more hours to Spokane. I was still in high school then, Al had been in college for a couple of years. My father was retired and my parents were away as they usually were, this time for a week in Las Vegas.

It was after midnight when I finally reached Spokane. I was dead and dreary until I drove over the waterfall—a crashing waterfall right in the middle of the city, and suddenly I was awake and alive, singing, swinging down this street and that street, standing in the buzzing fluorescence of a closed gas station checking out the street map taped to the inside of its window, feeling wildly tragic and romantic and solid, like a fast-talking woman in a late-night movie. Then there was Al, standing in the doorway of his basement apartment looking at me with his brown eyes, saying, "Jesus, Brenda, I can't believe you got here so soon, god, it's good to see you, come in." Behind the cinderblock kitchen wall, a scratchy record started up, as if we were in a movie, this, the opening song, some crazy fast wailing Tex-Mex stuff, *No te he visto, hace mucho tiempo* ... Al stood smiling at me, holding both my hands in his, drinking my bedraggled self in. "So," he asked, "wanna dance?"

I fell easily into him, his step; we swung into the next room, the only other room in the place, where a portable phonograph was stacked high with dusty 78s. Al had told me about those records on the phone; they had been given to him by a friend who had bought a 1940 Wurlitzer jukebox out of a bar in Nuevo Laredo, Mexico, still stocked with the original records.

We spun to the nasally, whining, heart-rending voices, we slugged down Dos Equis, bottles dripping cold on each others' shoulders, beer sloshing down each others' backs and we never stopped dancing, Al spinning me away from him, and back, away and back, even as the next record dropped, with a crash, onto the pile waiting for the needle, still we swung and swayed, panting, spinning into tables, walls, ... *mis lagrimas son como un rio* ..., leaning on each other with half-closed eyes, whirling round and round, my heart slamming into my ribs, the music slamming off the cinderblock walls, and we were in that bar in Nuevo Laredo in 1940, Al and me, we didn't smile or laugh or talk, we were the mysterious gringos hanging onto each other's sweaty arms and never letting go, never stopping, singing softly in each others' ears, words we didn't know, words and beers, . . . *te pido, pido que no me olvides* . . . , my knee giving way, panting, leaning and sliding and slipping until I thought I would die, die of dancing, die of never stopping, die of spinning dizzy and being young and never never stopping until our knees buckled beneath us and we made a blithering, desperate love rolling over and over, the whole room the whole world spinning beneath above around us, until I half-woke to Al asleep stretched long and heavy on me, me a glowing sweaty mass pressed into the rug, the phonograph needle bobbing on the spent stack of 78s, clickety click, clickety click, clickety click, clickety click.

We both woke later, the sky glowing soft gray through the basement windows high on the walls above us. Dawn, I thought.

"Let's not move yet," I said to Al. "It's still early."

We lay quietly for a while, then Al sat up sluggishly. "No," he said. "It's late afternoon. Look, four o'clock," and he began handing me my clothes, as he found them, tangled in with his on the floor. "Let's get up. We can drive somewhere to get a good view of the sunset. I haven't gone to look at one since I left San Diego."

He grabbed a quart of milk from the refrigerator as we left the house, which we drank sitting on the car hood a few miles outside of town. The air was icy, the car hood hot. Milk never tasted so good and cold before. The sun blinked out on the horizon.

"Well," Al said, later, as we turned down his street, "I guess it's bedtime again already, thank god. I'm exhausted."

"This is crazy." I shook my head. "You're not going to believe this. I have to get back. To San Diego. I should have left this afternoon as it was. I've got a couple of big tests, finals, and I'm going to get back just in time to take them. And my job; I've got an after-school job a couple of days a week."

"Please tell me you're kidding."

We had just pulled up behind his apartment house. He unlocked the door and we went in, but no farther than the doorway. I reached in my coat pockets, pulled out my keys and wallet, a comb, toothbrush, and my birth control pills.

"I guess I don't exactly have to worry about repacking." I went in his bathroom and peed, combed my hair, brushed my teeth.

When I walked out Al was still standing by his open door.

"Marry me," he said.

"Al," I started. I was looking down at the linoleum pattern, because I knew his eyes would be so sweet and wanting. "I'm still in high school, you're busy with college; you don't want to marry *me*, you want to marry *someone*. That's just you, Al, that's always been you. You probably would have been happiest in life if you'd been *born* married."

"I want to marry *you*."

"Or someone else. Anyway, I can't. I made this list of a hundred things I have to do in my life, and I forgot to put 'marriage' on it."

"Let me see the list," Al said, holding out his hand.

"You don't think I really made one, do you? But I did. When I was about ten years old, after I'd been really sick for a long time."

"Rolly was always sick as a kid," Al said. Rolly was Al's twin brother, an unidentical twin, who still lived in San Diego. "I always remember him with a thermometer sticking out of his mouth. But don't change the subject. Where's the list?"

"Al, I don't exactly carry it with me everywhere I go. In fact, I wrote it at the library when I was ten, and I think I lost it on the walk home. But I remember it, mostly. I've done some of it already. I've been in an earthquake, for instance."

"Everyone in California's been in an earthquake," Al said. "So, are you going to marry me?"

I just kissed him and shrugged and got in my car.

"Put me on the list. As a hundred and one. Put me in as fifty. And we'll do the next fifty together."

"I thought you wanted to be a lawyer," I said. "That means a paneled office and a ton of law books. When you're a lawyer you can't exactly be a hobo."

"I'll *be* a hobo," he said. "I'll be the world's first rail-hopping lawyer. Just imagine it, Brenda, can't you? There we'll be for the rest of our lives, coupling and uncoupling like two boxcars in the moonlight on a legendary, neverending stretch of great American railroad."

My mouth dropped open. "You keep composing like that and you're going to be a great lawyer, Al."

He smiled wryly.

"Just because I won't say I'll marry you doesn't mean I won't love you madly, always and ever."

Al shut the car door, then I started the engine and pulled slowly away from the curb. When I glanced back to wave goodbye, he had his hands cupped around his mouth. "Brenda!" he shouted. "Put me in as twenty-five! Put me in as thirteen!"

I drove back, singing along with all the love songs on the radio. I almost turned around a dozen times before I got to Eureka, but I wouldn't cry. I slept for a while, started the next sixteen-hour stretch. Just as I drove under the banner that said, Welcome to Castroville: Artichoke Heart of the World, the tears started. It felt so good just letting them roll down my cheeks and drop onto my shirt. I opened the window so all the cows grazing in the hills could hear me wailing, and could look up, surprised.

I wrote Al as soon as I got home. I didn't know what to say; I wrote a chatty letter about nothing, about school. He wrote me back, a chatty letter about school. Then I didn't hear from him for five years, until Will brought me his letter: "Visit me. Visit me. Visit me. Al."

12 WILL SHOWED UP about ten o'clock the night of the harvest party. Things were already hopping, the hour being exotically late for all us agricultural types. A stereo was blasting rock 'n' roll next to a bonfire that raged just short of out-of-control; silhouette figures were flying and flinging around the leaping flames. It was a freezing night, a teeth-chattering high-desert-in-late-fall night, so everyone had to either be dancing wildly or hanging out by the bonfire or numb drunk, just to stay warm. Most people were all three.

I was just another silhouette to Will, I could tell, by the way he got out of his car and stared right in my direction, grinning at the goings-on, but with no look of recognition on his face.

"Will!" I shouted, and ran to hug him, just as Miranda and her band mounted the makeshift stage for another set.

Will saw her right away.

"That's Miranda!" I shouted over all the noise, before he had to ask.

"She lives here?"

A big bruiser of a guy came up suddenly out of the dark, running right into Will, spinning him off his feet, around and down.

"Oh, hey, bro', so sorry, so sorry. Here, here, my apologies," he said as he helped Will up, then handed him the bottle of Scotch he was holding. "My apologies," he said again, backing away, tipping his cowboy hat. It was Ron—or Rob, whichever.

He clumped up to the stage. "Mirandy!" he bellowed. "Sing it sweet for me, darlin'."

Miranda smiled out in her usual seductive stage way. "This is dedicated to the one I love," she sang, "... whose name is what ... Rob?" She shaded her eyes from the lights, but couldn't seem to find him in the dark. "This goes out to you, Rob." She'd gotten it wrong again; even I remembered then that it was Ron.

Will started slugging down beers at twice my pace, with an occasional slug at the Scotch bottle. It was easy for me to see Will was going to lay one on. I showed him around the farm, the farmhouse, MaryEllen's room that had Cochise stuff, drawings and photos, all over the walls.

"Where should we go?" I asked Will, in the den. We had atlases and maps and magazines spread all over.

"I think here," he said, plopping down beside me on the sofa. He threw a magazine article in my lap: San Juan Islands.

"See, we can meander up the West Coast, oh, through L.A., up past Point Concepcion, Big Sur," he was sliding his finger up a map, "San Francisco, take in some redwoods, go a round trip on the Skunk train at Willits, then on up to Eureka, Coos Bay, Cape Foulweather, then up here in Washington, see, follow the edge of the peninsula, make a great big turn around Mount Olympus, home of the gods, see it from all angles, swoop around Seattle, oh, stop at a fishmarket, pick up a goo-ee-duck, then keep driving, keep driving," he was zeroing in now, with his finger on the map, "there! Anacortes. Take the ferry to the San Juan Islands. See some whales, sea lions. Go ocean kayaking. Anyway, I heard about some hippie-run resort there, where we can stay free, if we work. Repairing. Building cabins and stuff."

"Exactly!" I said, and I could feel my own cheeks blazing, my own eyes shining. "I don't have a lot to spend." Then I felt bad for having said that. It was true, but I didn't want him to think twice about all the money I'd sent him. "I can't wait to get on the road. You know a term I heard someone use the other day? An open-ended adventure. I love the sound of that: an open-ended adventure. Hey, you want to see the orchard?"

I walked him around the outside of the farmhouse to point out the extent of the orchard, in all directions, and also the crazy shape of the house.

"They're thinking of raising llamas," I said. "Miranda is, anyway. She's talking about building a fence all around this area," and I pointed it out. "Miranda thinks llamas'd do well because it's a lot like Peru in these mountains. I don't know if that's true or not."

We were nearing the front of the farmhouse; Will suddenly snapped open his jeans jacket, ran his fingers through his hair, hooked his thumbs in his pockets. Miranda was standing on the front porch in the glow of the porch light, a cigarette in one hand and a long-neck beer in the other. It's a funny feeling, to see your own big brother turned on by a woman. Miranda had her eye on Will, too. As we neared, she dropped languidly down the steps toward us.

"Brenda, gal," she said, though she was looking at Will, and was speaking in a public kind of voice, "roommates are supposed to share, now, don't cha know?" She apparently didn't know that Will was my brother. She flung her head, her thigh-length hair swaying, drifting this way and that, and laughed, and went back to the group at the doorway.

Then Will did something I would never have imagined him doing in a million years. He walked up the stairs to Miranda, plucked the cigarette from her hand, and took one long drag. I'd never in my life seen him smoke. He blew the smoke into the glow of the porch light, eyeing Miranda all the while. He smiled a seductive smile at her, eased the cigarette back into her mouth, tapped her on the jaw, then, without a word, turned around and returned to where I stood in the darkness.

"Let's take a walk," he said.

We walked and walked, up and down steep hillsides of apple trees. Will and I were each walking down different rows, so a tree passed between us every few seconds. I was beer-drunk, and cold, my collar up and my arms crossed in front of my chest. Will was slugging down the Scotch. I'd had Scotch once before; I couldn't stand the stuff. We kept walking, and talking about how great our trip was going to be, but after a while, I didn't care about the trip anymore. I was just cold, cold to the bone, and exhausted. I felt like we had been walking all night, my legs moving woodenly below me; I was expecting at any moment to see the sky glowing pearly with sunrise.

"Come on, Will, let's turn back," I said for the fourth time.

"Naw. Let's run!" he shouted, and pounded away into the pitch-black night.

"Goddamnit, Will, slow down! Stop! You're going to hurt yourself!" I yelled after him as he flew, a shadowy figure, down the hill between rows of trees, and sickeningly, dropped out of my sight. Then came the undoubtable sounds of a body tumbling downhill.

I stumbled in the direction I'd seen him disappear. It was so dark I was afraid of running into a tree, or dropping off an edge into blackness myself. "Please, Will, answer me. Will you? Come *on*, Will." I'd started crying, when I heard a cough nearby, and his voice, dropping comically, "*I'm* ok."

I almost stepped on him. He laughed, a little. I could only hope he was all right; he was so drunk I knew he couldn't feel a thing.

"Can you walk?" I don't know if it was fear or the cold, but my teeth were chattering like mad. "It's freezing, I'm freezing, please can we go back now?"

But he wouldn't go back. "It's too late," he mumbled, "just let me sleep." He rolled over, shoved me when I tried to pull him up. He took his jacket off and balled it up to use as a pillow. He was going to freeze right there in the orchard if I didn't get him home. I kicked him, his arm, his side; he grabbed me by my leg and pulled me down, hard, bruising my hip. We got into a shoving match, a rough and rougher shoving match, him laughing all the while.

"Freeze, then, if you want to!" I finally ended up shouting at him, tears flying. "You can be so goddamned stupid sometimes!"

I turned and started the long walk back to the farmhouse. All I wanted was warmth and sleep, and I was pissed off as hell that instead I was going to have to find someone to follow me all the way back out there to drag my passed-out drunk big brother home.

It seemed hours when I finally, gratefully, climbed the porch steps, my fingers hard and numb on the railing. There were still quite a few people around. Juan was in the bathroom, someone said when I asked, so I sat on the couch to wait for him. Someone threw another log in the woodstove; the fire glowed hot yellow on my face while the stove door was open. And then, just for a minute, just while I was waiting for Juan, I lay down on the couch. And then, just for a second, I closed my eyes. It was so warm and comfortable inside. Just for a moment, I told myself. Just for a second.

13 THE FAMILY STORY about Will's chipped tooth, the one Will and I still tell because it's the one we've told for so long in front of my parents and their friends, is that Will, at the tender age of eight, had been so awestruck by a little girl named Barbara Dallas St. John, that he'd run full-speed smack into a telephone pole while trying to show off in front of her. He'd broken his arm and chipped his tooth. The arm got repaired, but the chipped tooth was always around as a reminder to my parents to ask Will and me about the Barbara Dallas St. John story, again.

This is the truth of the matter: Will came home from second grade one day awestruck by Amelia Earhart. He read me some parts of his *Weekly Reader*, showed me her picture.

All the next day while Will was in school, I cut and pasted an airplane out of a couple of cardboard boxes. "You can boost me up on the Amatos' shed roof, and I can scoot off the edge and fly all over their yard."

He shook his head. "It's not gonna work, Brenda."

I cried long enough, big fat tears rolling down my three-year-old cheeks, that Will finally said, ok, then, but *he*'d take the maiden flight in it, just to test it for kinks. We brought the plane down the street to the Amatos', and I boosted him up on the shed. I was to stay below to catch him in case of trouble.

I was pretty far away when he dropped like a rock.

"I'll catch you!" I screamed, running for him. But of course I didn't. And he made an awful sound when he hit.

We ran home, and all the way to the doctor's office in the taxi I told our mother the Barbara Dallas St. John story. She was holding a bloody towel over his mouth; he just sat there cradling his purpling arm and nodded his head at her. To this day Will and I have never said anything to each other about the real story. I bet Will and I have told that other story fifty times. I don't even know what it is Will believes anymore.

As it turns out, that chipped tooth serves him well. The second he smiles at anyone, they know him: he's a little bit vulnerable. And a little bit reckless.

14 ✺

I WOKE to Miranda's voice. "Where's that sweet-smilin' brother of yours? You didn't tell me you had a brother. I *do* hope he's sleeping alone."

I jumped up off the couch, almost knocking Miranda over. "Oh, jesus, Miranda. I left him in the orchard. What time is it?"

It was four a.m. Probably three hours, passed out in the freezing weather, I was thinking, as I sat in the bed of the pickup, curled into my coat, icy air whistling around me. Will was in the cab with Miranda, Juan driving. Three hours, passed out alone in the freezing cold. Not even knowing his way back if he did manage to come to. And me inside, asleep and cozy by the woodstove.

At the house, Miranda pulled Will gently out of the cab onto his feet, supporting his weight with his arm over her shoulders. His legs were shaking and buckling, but at least he was moving them underneath himself, and Miranda managed to get him up the porch stairs and through the front door. She was being good-natured as hell about it all, singing out "Whoa, Nellie!" when they swayed together, threatening to fall, and "Oh, excuse me, Willy honey, did I get my toes under your foot?"

Will was shivering, pale, his teeth chattering, with a look on his face as if he was about to puke. I expected it, any second, and thought Miranda would handle that in her sweet Southern Belle hospitable way, too.

I thought she'd drop him on the couch right inside the doorway so he could warm up by the woodstove and sleep it off there, but she kept walking him right for the stairs. She was every man's sickbed dream, a warm sensuous cooing Florence Nightingale, and I was the bumbling baby sister, standing flatfooted, slack-armed in the living room, watching her take him away.

Just as they disappeared from my sight on the landing, Miranda's voice sang out, "Lord-y, what ever made you drink yourself dead like that, anyway, Willy honey? You another one of them screwed up Vietnam vets? You guys are crawlin' all over this country like maggots these days . . ."

I actually cried out, right there in the living room. A woman sitting on the couch turned to the man next to her and said, "Tact," but no one else seemed to have heard Miranda, or the noise I made, or thought I must have made. I took two steps toward the stairwell and stopped. Will was a man, twenty-eight years old. And about to spend the night with Miranda.

I spun around, and there was MaryEllen. She had been taking it all in.

"Oh, hell, Brenda, it's ok. Jesus, if it wasn't for Miranda, you would have woken up in the morning and found him out in the orchard like a Swanson's TV dinner."

"Is that supposed to make me feel better?"

"Oh, hell, Brenda." She put her arm around my shoulders and started strolling down the hallway to my bedroom. "Just catch some sleep. All's well that ends well, yes?"

I wandered around my cold bedroom alone in the dark, then finally crawled into bed, where I lay exhausted, wide-eyed and shaken. My bones vibrated, my eyes stung. There were still party noises down the hall, laughter, a stereo. Outside, car doors slammed; engines started and drove off into the distance. Finally, all at once it seemed, everyone was gone.

I woke to pitch black, and Miranda's voice, soft and soothing, drifting down to me from somewhere above. I could tell that her song was a spiritual. But I couldn't make out the words.

15 In the morning Juan, Marty, MaryEllen and I, and a couple of people I'd seen at the party but didn't know, were all eating oatmeal in the kitchen when Miranda came down, alone. "Mornin'," she greeted, without looking at anyone, lit a cigarette, then pulled a kitchen chair over to a high cupboard and began fishing around in the back of it.

She pulled out a package of Twinkies. "Must be five years old," she explained to us, sat on the counter, pushed a lock of her impossibly long hair behind an ear and began unwrapping them, carefully, slowly, cigarette in her mouth, one eye squinting.

I saw Juan shoot a glance across the table to Marty; he screwed up his mouth, and we all went on eating oatmeal. Before Miranda had come in we'd been bantering about the party, though no one, I noticed, mentioned the incident with Will. But as soon as Miranda had walked in, we'd quit talking, not a sound but spoons scraping bowls.

"How's, uh," Marty cleared his throat, "how's, uh, y'know, Brenda's brother?"

"Will," I said.

Miranda didn't look up. She went on unwrapping the Twinkies with relentless care, as if something deathly would happen if she tore the paper.

"You driving back East with James?" Marty asked MaryEllen. James was a guy who worked at the apple distributor's. He was from D.C. and for his vacation week was planning to drive out there and pick up his girlfriend, move her back with him to Tucson.

"I don't think so. Naw. He's not leaving for a few weeks, and I'm anxious to go now. How about it, Miranda? Are you going to drive me to Boston, or not?"

Miranda had a mouthful of Twinkie and a sick look on her face.

"That man," Miranda said suddenly. She was glaring right at me, pointing at me with her cigarette; she dropped off the counter and took a couple of steps toward me. Her cigarette was almost in my face, and her hands were shaking. "That man up there just spilled his guts out to me."

I could feel that my eyes were round as moons. I don't know what other people thought she was talking about, but I knew: Kirby. He had spilled his guts to her about whatever it was that happened to Kirby.

Miranda flung her cigarette and Twinkie into the sink. "What the fuck am I doing in this kitchen eating a goddamned Twinkie?"

Miranda stormed from the room. I looked around the table. Everyone was keeping their eyes on their oatmeal bowls while Miranda was running up the stairs. Then, when she got to the end of the hallway, I heard her open her bedroom door, gently, and close it, gently, behind her.

I went over to the downstairs bathroom but someone was in it; a voice I didn't recognize said, "Just a minute," when I rapped on the door. "That's ok, there's another john upstairs," I answered. At the top of the stairwell, a sudden laugh came out from behind Miranda's door. I stopped, waited.

"She was always that way." Will's voice. "She was a second mother to me." I didn't know Will had a second mother. I took a step closer to Miranda's door. "All dressed in orange and all. But it was fun, and there was some chanting and dancing. I was glad she'd waited until I got back. Then that Prem Baba Frijole, or whatever his name was, opened up the urn at the water's edge and dumped Kirby's ashes out. But you know what?"

"No, baby, what?" Miranda's lazy drawl.

"It wasn't just ashes. I always thought ashes were ashes. But they're not. I waded into the surf right after Prem Baba. Ol' Kirby would have been proud of me being curious about what was left of him. And guess what was there? Teeth!"

"Teeth?"

"Yeah, little charred bits of bones and teeth rolling around in the waves." He laughed, delighted. "I guess those chambers can't get hot enough to burn up everything. So I went over to Mrs. Renfroe and brought her over and showed her. And she just started laughing and I started laughing, and we laughed until we had tears in our eyes. Maybe we were crying. I don't know." There was a long silence and I started to back away, trying not to make the old floorboards squeak, when I heard Will chuckle and add, "Kirby would have done the same for me."

16 ◫ I ENDED UP on a Greyhound bus, going back to San Diego, alone. Will and Miranda had wended their way around the Apple Ranch for two days, plastered together like one human being, then finally Will had announced to me that he was going to stay on for a while, build Miranda her llama fence.

No open-ended adventure. Almost no money; no job. The trees were picked bare; Marty and Juan had been talking about pruning trees, but neither mentioned needing my help. MaryEllen was planning to fly to Boston, to be with Sean. Will had Miranda. And a llama fence to build.

I sat in the Greyhound, watching the saguaro fly past. Outside of Yuma were the dunes, then the ocotillo surrounding the town of Ocotillo, then after the 6,000-foot climb to the high desert, the moonrocks of Jacumba. I wanted to be furious with Will, but I wasn't. For one thing, I was too embarrassed about having left him in the orchard.

For another, all the while that I sat in the netherworld of Greyhound-bus-ride-through-the-desert, the sun baking me through the window, I was daydreaming heavily, reliving a story my friend Catherine had told me.

Catherine was raised in Switzerland. When she was fourteen, on a trip to Paris with her family, she fell in love with a soul-eyed curly-headed boy named Jacques. And Jacques fell in love with her. They wrote letters to each other for a couple of years, then, on school holidays, she started taking the train to Paris to visit him. Jacques's sister, Monique, let them stay at her apartment whenever Catherine was in the city.

They were shy with each other. It was a holy love, an adoring infatuation, and every night they stared starry-eyed at each other until they couldn't keep their eyes open anymore. Then they bumped awkwardly, trying to kiss, and finally Catherine climbed up into the bed, and Jacques curled up on the floor. And of course, she could never sleep, not with her darling her dear her precious soul-eyed Jacques lying so close to her all night.

One night, late, they went to a cafe. It was as if all the people in the cafe were old friends, all kinds of singing and dancing going on. An old man, a distinguished drunk, joined them at their table.

"Ah, youth, ah love, ah, young love," he crooned to them. "You are so beautiful, there is nothing so beautiful in all this world as young lovers. Look at the girl's full lips, at the curly-headed lad's yearning eyes. And tell me now, how old are you?"

Sixteen, they told him.

He threw himself back in his chair as if in pain. "Ah, to only be sixteen and with my sweet lover on this warm Parisian night. You are lovers, yes? . . ."

They both blushed furiously. "No, monsieur."

"Ah . . ." He looked perplexed, then smiled. *"But,"* he said, "you *want* to be?"

They were horrified. They stole glances at each other, eyes

fiery, cheeks blazing, then both looked at the old drunk and nodded yes.

He moaned loudly, he stood up and reeled in ecstasy. Then he stepped on his chair, and stood on their table. "Everybody!" he called. He rang his spoon against his empty wine bottle. "Everybody!" The crowd laughed, looked up at him. "This . . . couple . . . here . . ." and he held out his hand toward them, "they are sixteen years old, and *they are in love!*" He beamed down at them while the cafe crowd hooted, clapped. "AND—" he continued, with great enunciation and fervor, "they . . . are going to go home now . . . and make love . . . ALL . . . NIGHT . . . LONG!"

The cafe crowd cheered, gathered around Catherine and Jacques and, with songs and congratulations, hurried them out onto the warm Parisian sidewalk.

"So . . . ," I'd asked Catherine, when she'd told me the story, "tell me . . . what happened that night?"

"Well, we went back to Monique's apartment. It was a special weekend; Monique was gone all weekend."

"And?"

"We went home . . . and we made love . . . ALL . . . NIGHT . . . LONG!"

The dream dissolved away, and there was my own reflection, smiling, in the Greyhound bus window.

We hit the outskirts of San Diego, and the scenery became faster and dirtier and more crowded minute by minute, until I was dumped out at the grungy Greyhound depot downtown.

I had the key to Will's apartment in my pocket. I didn't feel like calling any of my friends; instead I walked uptown, through an old gay neighborhood, past the mission, down past a boatyard, a nursery, then a long haul uphill to Will's faceless apartment complex, where I locked myself in for three days trying to decide what to do next.

I drank beer. I ate pretzels. I drank more beer. I ate Cheetos.

I read: *Candide, On the Road, My Life Among the Sioux Indians.* I counted my money: $280. I read Al's letter.

I emerged early, yesterday morning, unlocked Will's storage room where I had my things stored, pulled out my backpack, and packed it, neatly.

Then I walked down the road to the first freeway entrance going north, took a deep breath, turned face-first to the rushing traffic, and just like that, stuck out my thumb.

17 THIS IS the worst freeway entrance I can imagine.

Middle of L.A., on a hot winter afternoon: grime, acid air, hot car after hot car kicking up gravel, parents pretending they don't see me and my pleading thumb, and their kids bouncing around in the back seats pointing and screaming "a girl!" The cars are leaving Disneyland; the parents have bloodshot eyes and wrinkled foreheads and they can't stand the thought of one more goddamned attraction.

After two hours of this I walk to the nearby Howard Johnson's. They don't like my backpack. No, they have no place for me to put it. I finally leave it in the vestibule. A thin, harried man wearing a tiepin reading MANAGER moves it behind the cash register. I eat all I can afford at these prices: a cheese sandwich and a glass of milk. The white bread has been squashed paper-thin and is transparent with oil; the cheese is tasteless American that sticks to the roof of my mouth. I leave a good tip for the bouffanted waitress. I always leave a good tip.

Back into the foul air, back onto the entrance. Fifteen minutes later I hear a truck horn blaring on the overpass. The driver is giving me a big howdy-do wave, and he is pulling over.

I run up the entrance road. Because of my boots, my pack, and the loose gravel, I feel like I'm moving in slow motion up the length of the truck, which is painted with a large yellow triangle, red word: RADIOACTIVE.

I swing into the cab. My apprehension about the driver dissolves instantly. A friendly looking young Mexican guy sits, grinning from ear to ear.

"Man," he says, "Am I ever happy to see *you*. I been looking for company for a hundred miles. Can you imagine? Not one hitchhiker in all of Southern California. I'm going nuts. I'm not much of a truckdriver." He stomps on the clutch and slams the truck into gear after slow low gear. His name is Tony.

"You know what's back there?" He motions with his head to the load behind us. "You'll never guess . . . laundry. *Laundry.*" He laughs out loud, a big hearty, healthy laugh. He shakes his head. He has beautiful teeth. "Radioactive *laun*dry. You ever think of that? I never did before I got this job. But all those workers . . . like at San Onofre? They wear those special clothes and then *some*one's got to wash them. We're the only company on the West Coast that washes radioactive laundry." Tony smiles through all of this. A sudden static breaks out over the CB radio.

I can never make out the words on CB radios. I've watched truckers listen to that static and talk back to it and listen to it some more and talk back some more. It impresses the hell out of me. To me it always sounds like: Fffff . . . eeoh eeoh eeoh eeoh.

Tony picks up the mike. "Rubber ducky," he says, "Rubber ducky . . . Fffff . . . eeoh eeoh eeoh eeoh . . . ten-four ten-four . . . over and out." He snaps off the microphone. "I can't make out a word on these things," he says to me.

Every ride I get is with one or two men. If there are two men, the driver talks about his car, his job, and his wife. In that order. His car he talks about something like this: "Got it for a pretty good price. Hasn't given me too many problems. Well, I had to fix the transmission a couple of months ago." His job he talks about something like this: "Make pretty good money. Hours aren't bad. Don't get much cooperation from management, though." About his wife he says: "She's got a pretty good job, but she doesn't make what she's worth." A lone driver speaks tenderly about his wife, ponders his past, and rues his broken dreams. In that order. And immediately.

Tony has an ex-wife in Florida named Juanita. He misses her, he says, he misses her something awful. He likes the West Coast, knows they could do good here, but she won't come out. Sudden tears fill his eyes. He says in a choking, dramatic voice, almost like a child whose feelings have been hurt, "I ain't never going back. Too much needle there. Too much needle." He shakes his head. I look at his arms. All I can see is a tattoo: a palm tree, and the words BORN TO BE WILD.

"I'm lucky to have gotten this job. I almost feel ashamed at how much money I make. And they *like* me there. They really *like* me."

I want to say to him, "Tony, it's no surprise," but I know that if I just sit quietly and listen, he, like every other lone driver, will unload all of his troubled soul.

"They like me so much, they want to send me to Hawaii to start up a new branch office there. Hawaii! They like me *that* much. They trust me *that* much."

He bites his lower lip. "She won't leave Florida," he adds.

Tony is insistent that I stay awake. He needs me awake so he can stay awake. We have to haul over the Grapevine in the moonlight, a tiring hour-long grinding to lower and lower gears, engine growling, gears chattering enough to shake my teeth out, the dizzying stench of diesel exhaust. Out the window in the headlight beams I see individual blades of grass and bits of gravel, we're going so slowly. I could be walking faster.

Then we finally make it to the top, and start the giddy ride down, pressed by all that weight that seems to want to push us on a free-flying plummet off the edge; and I see occasionally, through all the twistings and turnings of the ink-black hills, the spread of city lights like stars below.

At four a.m. we pull over at a truck stop. I buy a stamped postcard of desert animals, and on the back write: "Al! Congratulations! I'm glad you're ready to start living again. Yes. Yes. Yes. Brenda." Then, because it's been over two months since he wrote the letter and probably doesn't remember his triple request, I add: "p.s. I am on the road to you now, and I hope to arrive before this postcard."

I leave the card on the pile of others next to the cashier, who has said she always drops them off in a mailbox after she gets off work in the morning.

Then I join Tony at the counter where he insists on buying me a big-Western-truckstop-at-four-a.m. Mexican dinner, and lots of coffee. He pulls out an aluminum foil packet of amphetamines as the waitress clears away the dishes and the tip. She doesn't notice, or more likely, has seen it all before and pretends not to notice. Tony takes two and offers one to me; when I don't accept, he raises his eyebrows.

When I come out of the bathroom he is gone. I race to the door, heart pounding, thinking of my pack, yet the truck is there, under a towering humming yellow light: RADIO-ACTIVE.

Down the hallway, I see Tony at a pay phone. Coins lie in a mound on the shelf beneath it; he is feeding them in one by one.

He clutches the phone with both hands and waits. A sudden surprise floods his face; he hangs up quickly without speaking, as if the phone receiver has stung him, then stands with both hands on his hips, breathing heavily, staring at the phone. I wonder whose "Hello?" he has just heard that has stung him so: Juanita's, or a man's.

When he looks up and sees me, he smiles shyly, embarrassed. "Come on," he says. Later, in the truck, "I think I'll take that job in Hawaii," and later still, as the sun rises on the straight, flat freeway, "I wish Juanita would come out here."

18 ⊠ MY MIND has a habit of getting all crazy mixed up with lingo and jingles, words and phrases and spits of songs that reel around inside.

Sometimes, particular lines stick with me for years. I remember when I was about ten, two songs: "Somewhere Over the Rainbow" and "Climb Every Mountain." I used to sing them in the shower . . . not the whole songs, just those phrases, repeated over and over. Since we were Catholic, I interspersed them with the words, which I belted out in baritone: "A-VE MA-RRRRI-A . . ." I was a very dramatic kid. I thought a talent agent was going to drive by, hear me, and make me into a big star. It didn't matter to me that I lived in such an unlikely place for this to happen as an air force base in Hawaii, with our bathroom window butted up against the barbed wire fence that separated us from Pearl Harbor. I was convinced beyond the shadow of a doubt that those few lines could change the course of my life.

Right now I've got a couple of lines that swoop around like Halley's Comet, streaking by from time to time. One is from my friend Judy: When the sacred moments loom, be ready to be in them. And there's one from my brother . . . this is what he'd said just before he went off the Amatos' shed roof in the cardboard airplane: "Schemin', I'm always schemin'."

19 ◪ THE TIP of the sun is just showing over the cool gray horizon.

At the freeway entrance I find a hitchhiker's abandoned sign. SACRA, it says, meaning Sacramento. My friend Pam lives in Sacramento. I walk down the road with the sign to a gas station, fill my pockets with coins, and call her.

"I'm on my way to Spokane," I tell her. "To Al's."

"No kidding. Al. I hope you two have your timing better this time." She is almost whispering, to not wake her husband and baby. "You know, I was always rooting for you two back in high school. It just seems like you were meant for each other. You were so comfortable together, like you knew each other through and through. I haven't seen that too often in my life."

"We *were* the best of friends. I don't know why we were never in synch. Whenever one of us was available, the other of us had always just fallen in love with someone else. We were always going to each other for a shoulder to cry on."

"Maybe you two can finally get it together."

"Well, to tell you the truth, Pam, I really don't know what Al wants. I don't know what I want, either. Just to visit him. He wrote a couple of months ago asking me to visit."

"Come here along the way," she says. "How *are* you?"

"Filthy," I answer. "Really."

"I don't care if you've got mud in your hair. I don't care if you've got mud in your *teeth*. I want to see your face. Bruce wants to see your face. Bear wants to see your face. Zen the *cat* wants to see your face." She pauses. "There's this guy I want you to meet . . . Roger. He reminds me of Al. If you can manage to get here by Saturday, you'll get to meet him. We're having him over for dinner."

I ask what's been going on with her.

"Bear doesn't spit up anymore," she says.

"Oh. That's good."

"That's *great*. You have *no* idea."

"Maybe I'll come visit. Now that Bear won't spit up on me anymore." She laughs. "How's Bruce?" I ask.

"Fine, fine. He's asleep now, you know. He's fine."

"That's good," I say. There is a long comfortable silence. We both sigh.

"What's that mariachi music in the background?" I ask.

"It's the new people that moved in downstairs. A Mexican family with seven or eight kids. I've never been able to count. The mother does all their laundry by hand in a washtub out in the parking lot and hangs it all over the fence. She has a parrot that sits on her shoulder and swears in Spanish. I guess it's swearing. It sounds like swearing. They play that Mexican cantina music constantly. I don't think they ever sleep. I feel like we're living in a little flat above a bar in Tijuana."

"I think I'll come visit," I say. "I mean, probably. I'll probably come visit."

I hang up and get the key to the restroom from the gas station attendant. The place is wonderful: heated, a bar of soap, real paper towels. I give myself a bath from the sink, smiling when I pull the plug and watch the scummy water swirl down the drain. I wash my hair. It's early yet; no one knocks on the door. I put on my cleanest clothes and return the key to the attendant. He is America's favorite hardworking son with a heart of gold, sleeves rolled up, sweeping the front of the gas station in early icy air.

He glances at my pack. "Going a long ways today?" he asks.

"Meaning to," I answer, return his best-of-luck smile, and walk back down the road with the sign under my arm.

20 ⬛ THE GUY in the back seat says they're on their way to a wedding reception but why don't I just come along, what the heck. The driver looks back at me, says, "We missed the wedding because Rhonda took so long to get ready," and the girl next to him smacks at him and says in a whining voice, "Bullshit. Weddings are such bullshit anyway. Receptions are great, though ... except for that garter and bouquet bullshit. All the free food and booze is great. I hardly knew her anyway. She was just in my sorority." She has her bare feet on the windshield and is making a careful pattern of smear-marks on the glass with her toes.

We are driving on a flat straight highway and suddenly slow down to turn into the gravel parking lot of a VFW hall, sitting inexplicably alone in a ragged field. The three of them wait while I hide behind the open car trunk changing from my jeans into the one skirt I have brought along, the skirt I plan to wear when I finally get to Al's. I've had to fish it out in a wad from the bottom of my pack. There is riotous music and drunken singing coming from the hall. I look into the rear-view mirror and comb my fingers through my hair; then we walk in together.

The bride is standing flush-cheeked and wobbly atop a chair surrounded by what looks like an entire fraternity, who are singing up to her, with great gusto, "The Sweetheart of Sigma Chi." Misty-eyed parents line the walls. One of them rushes to us.

"How nice you could make it! I'm Frannie's mom. And you're ...?" She is holding my hand a little too tightly, as if afraid she might fall over.

I myself am feeling drunk just being in this drunken room. The singing has gotten louder for the final verse. "Brenda Bradshaw," I shout.

"Oh, how *nice,*" the bride's mother answers. A man, his

face flushed like the bride's, joins us. "This is *Mr.* Fitzgerald," she says to me, and to him, "Honey, this is Brenda Bradshaw." She pauses, then prods him, "You remember . . ."

"My daughter has always had such nice things to say about you."

"Yes," I answer. I'm almost bowled over by his Scotch breath.

"Well, Brenda, name your poison." He claps his hands and rubs them excitedly.

"Scotch," I answer.

"Ah, a girl after my own heart." He leads me by my elbow ahead of him awkwardly and formally to a linen-covered table piled with napkins printed, in silver lettering, "Frannie and Tim."

"Tim's a lucky man," I say to the bride's father.

"Yes, he is, Brenda. Straight up? With a little soda . . . ?"

When a waltz begins, he suddenly sets the drinks down. "Little spin around the room? I could show you some things. You kids today don't know how to dance."

But I do know how to dance, how to foxtrot and rhumba and cha-cha and especially how to waltz, and as I think a good waltzing partner is one of the better cheap thrills in life, I decide that I like this bride's father, this giddy-at-his-daughter's-wedding Scotch-breathed flush-faced bride's father, who, gaining confidence in my dancing by the end of the song, is throwing in double turns and dips and smooth as smooth Scotch spins, and introducing himself to me as "Ed." We end the dance and go back to our drinks, but as another waltz starts, Ed sputters, "Oh! Down the hatch, young lady! Gotta catch this one more waltz," so I do, quickly, down the hatch, and that is my only Scotch, which I follow with champagne and champagne and more champagne, and I waltz and foxtrot and rhumba and even, after a quick lesson, samba, dancing with every father in the room, but mostly with Ed.

Trying to make my way to the restroom I realize that this

is the drunkest I've been in a long, long time. The frat boys by now are clapping their hands chanting "Rock 'n' roll! Rock 'n' roll!" more to each other than to the band, and a girl's shriek turns into a drawn-out giggle. Somewhere in the smoke I bump into Rhonda, grab her shoulders and shout at her, "Best kept secret in the world, Rhonda, I swear to god, best kept secret in the world. Middle-aged people, man, they really know where it's at."

In the restroom I meet up with the bride's mother who is fixing her makeup in the mirror above a pitted sink. Gold and pink cherubs surround her, and she is making a mess of herself, drawing uneven lines around her eyes with black eyeliner. "Nice reception," I say as I head toward a stall, but she stands in my way.

"Frannie told me all about you, a long time ago, Brenda," she states dramatically. The brash lighting makes me feel I'm in a soap opera. I notice lipstick on her teeth. I feel absolutely stunned, I can't move, and the two of us stand staring at each other for what seems like forever. I almost fall over as I turn to leave, grasping onto the doorframe.

I still have to pee, so I wait outside the door for the bride's mother to come out, but she doesn't. I think about going back with her still in there, I'm so desperate by now, but decide instead to pee outside. I always have been partial to peeing outside. I push through the drunken mob, which is in a frenzy dancing to a painfully loud version of "Light My Fire."

Outside the back door the night air is fresh and cool and quiet. I start across the field toward the highway, surprised there are no cars, though I can hear a faint whine of tires in the distance. By the time I get to the road's edge, even the whine is gone. And here is the road: a quiet throbbing moonlit straight-arrow band of silver left and right. I step deliberately onto it, one foot at a time, and discover with surprise that I'm barefoot. Barefoot, with a full glass of champagne in each hand.

"Down the hatch," I say out loud, drain one, and toss it into the grass behind me. Then I whirl like a discus thrower and fling the other glass, which miraculously bounces once before it shatters musically into a thousand moonlit splinters. I look down the long quiet road in both directions, take a deep shaky breath. "I marry *you,*" I say.

I manage to make it back to the VFW hall, though now that I know I don't have my shoes it's slow going, and I also have to be extra careful when I stop, halfway across the field, to pee. Inside, the hall is smoky and loud loud loud. My eyes can barely focus as I start searching for my shoes. I think of calling Al to tell him about this, about how I've lost my shoes, but decide that in the morning it might not seem as hysterically funny as it does to me now. And it does seem hilarious—especially the way that I'm managing to crawl around under tables looking for them while holding two more glasses of champagne. When I finally locate my shoes, I stay under the table laughing. One of the fathers grabs playfully at another's tie, and they both fall onto the table I'm under. The band starts playing "Girl from Ipanema," and the bride's mother calls, "Ed! Eddie! Come dance! It's that girl from impamima song. Impaninna." She laughs while Ed hugs her saying, "Impanimpa," and the last I remember is leaning against the wall under the table, hearing myself say out loud, "Man oh man, best kept secret in the world."

I wake up lying on a couch, covered with a brown blanket. It's daytime; the two guys I vaguely recognize as the ones who drove me to the reception are asleep on the rug, rolled in blankets. I seem to be in someone's upstairs apartment. There is a shuffling in the kitchen, cabinet doors opening and shutting. The two guys wake up, one rolls over, sits up, holds his head, groans, and lies back down, pulling his blanket over his head. I don't know where I am and I don't know anyone's name.

A woman—I recognize her—Rhonda, walks out of the

kitchen slopping down cereal. She looks embarrassed to find us awake and watching her. She shrugs. "There was only enough milk for one bowl," she whines. I fold my blanket and sit for a while. No one has anything to say. The three of us watch Rhonda eat her cereal. "Some wedding reception," she says. My stomach growls.

I slog flatfooted down the hall, finding my pack leaning against the wall just outside the bathroom door. I brush my mouth, tongue and all, three times, trying to rid it of the dry Scotch and champagne taste. I look in the mirror and pinch my pasty cheeks, comb my fingers through my hair, lean against the sink looking longingly at the shower. What the hell, I decide, strip, and take a crashingly fresh shower, forcing myself to make it a short one, and dry off with my own damp towel from my pack. Under the sink I find an unopened can of Ajax, and scrub what must be a year's worth of brown grunge from the tub. As I put on my socks I notice that my feet are covered with scratches.

I sling my pack over one shoulder and carry it through to the living room. "Thanks for the ride," I say. They all look up bleary-eyed and manage slight smiles and nods, but no one says anything. I head down the front cement steps and to the street corner. Second Avenue and Main Street, my god, *Main Street*, and I laugh out loud. I haven't the faintest idea what town I'm in.

Suddenly I remember last night, shattering the champagne glass on the highway. 'Stupid,' I think. Broken glass for all those car tires to drive over. And anyway, I don't want to be married to the road.

21 ⬛ THERE'S A THEORY that my brother and I have had since we were kids; only when we were kids, of course, we didn't call it a theory, we called it a game. The theory is this: that everyone has a spot in space, a spot where the very core of you lives, your home. Nothing can knock you out of that spot, not even dying. It's like the opening line in my old catechism book, "God always was and always will be." I spent hours staring at that line. I can even see the style of print. I think it's burned into my retinas.

As to the game: when you think you're walking down the sidewalk, propelling yourself through space, you're not. You're in your spot. You're pulling the sidewalk beneath you with your feet. And there's this: the earth is buoyant. It's a lot easier to pull the earth up behind you as you walk downhill than to shove it down when you walk uphill.

I love crossing bridges. I love the sensation of pulling the railing posts past me one by one, moving the whole damned river, the earth spinning slowly beneath me.

My brother's favorite is pulling things to him that he needs. As a kid when my father would ask him at the dining table to go get the salt and pepper, Will would lean close and say, "Watch me pull the kitchen toward me." Then he'd walk with exaggerated effort. I thought it was hysterical. As far as I know, no one else knew what we were talking about.

So when I'm just outside of Sacramento watching the endless rows of tomatoes flash by, and the driver keeps complaining that he feels powerless with his girlfriend, whom he is on his way to see, I have to answer, "Nonsense. You're pulling her toward you at sixty miles per hour." I had just been mulling over this very thing while I was tuning out his whining, that I was pulling Pam toward me at sixty miles per hour.

I don't think he gets it, or maybe he does. He had been

focusing on me a lot, even taking his hands off the steering wheel to gesture, but now he just fixes his attention straight ahead on the road. I say, "We're sitting in this cubicle, and with one foot, you're making these wheels spin, which are pulling the road beneath us, and yanking your girlfriend toward you at sixty miles per hour."

I don't know if he brushes me off as crazy, or just wants to think about it, but he reaches out and punches on his radio, loud. I yell over it, "With one finger, you're causing a band to play ten years ago."

He gives me a wry sneer. "Real cute," he says, and I'm sorry that I pushed it so far, because I really did want him to get this spot-in-space theory. The rows of tomato plants shuffle past on both sides of us like cards, and there's nothing for me to do but shrug at him, nestle down in my own warm safe spot, and go to sleep for a while, until I have brought Pam all the way to me.

22 It's just like Pam said—a half-dozen kids running around the front of her apartment complex. One kid is pushing another around wildly in a grocery cart, laundry is hanging everywhere, and in the middle of it all stands the mother scrubbing jeans on a sudsy washboard. Turning and scrubbing, turning and scrubbing. The parrot sits clucking on her shoulder. She is Indian, and looks more dignified here, scrubbing laundry, than I could look anywhere, doing anything.

A jet screams overhead, painfully low. The bay doors are open, landing gear down, and I can see the tread on the tires. I walk through the kids, around all kinds of junk, past a cracked aquarium, to the concrete steps that lead to the second floor.

At the steps is a nativity scene. Two-foot plastic figures kneel around a shoebox manger in which an orange cat sleeps. One angel is facing the wrong way. Worm-shaped styrofoam is scattered around, like snow, and lying flat, a piece of mirror, like a lake, surrounded by tiny plastic buffalo. The three kings stand in a line going up the steps, an electric cord running between them.

I climb to Pam's apartment and see her through her window, leaning over a counter writing, the baby balanced on her hip. I rap on her door.

"Nice nativity scene," I say when she opens it.

"Brenda!" She and Bear are fused in a mass of tangled hair, tears, drool, and wet cookie crumbs. I kiss them both on their gooey cheeks. Pam glances downstairs. "See how they set the kings going up our steps? I think they did it for our souls. Because we don't go to Mass. It's nice, the kings lighting our way home at night. Well, two of the three kings do. And the manger. There's a lightbulb in the manger, in some Easter grass. Like Zonker says in 'Doonesbury,' 'Jesus is a forty-watt bulb.' "

The phone rings and she stays on for a long time—something about Bruce and some tools of his that had been stolen, some insurance thing. I've had to walk about five miles from where my ride dropped me off, so it feels good to just sit. Bear has fallen asleep in her arms, and he looks heavy, but when I make hand-signals to take him from her, she whispers, "He'll wake up."

After a while I go outside and sit on the steps. Below me, a girl of about eight sits splay-legged in the middle of the ruckus patiently weaving a potholder on a toy loom. The youngest, a girl about four, is pedaling around the yard on a Big Wheel, dusty legs pumping furiously under a faded dress. When she sweeps by too close, her sister shouts, "Teeny! Cut it out!"

Teeny pumps to where I am, gets off her bike, and stomps

over. She is a pretty little Mexican angel, and I am sure that she will always be poor, and will have lots and lots of children.

"Do you live here?" she asks.

"No."

"*I* do. Here." She points to the apartment below Pam's.

"I can see that."

"That's my ma*ma*." She points.

"She's working hard."

Teeny looks at the manger. "My cat threw up last night."

"Oh. That's too bad."

She stomps over to the shoebox. "Scat!" she screams, windmilling her arms. The cat opens one eye, stretches lazily, then steps delicately out of the box. In the Easter grass, like an egg it has just laid, is the lightbulb: Baby Jesus. Teeny picks up one of the buffalo and tosses it after the cat, then runs back to me, knocking over an angel without noticing.

"Do you love Jesus?" she asks.

"Yes," I hear my voice say, with surprising conviction. "Yes, I do." It startles me.

"Oh, I do too," she announces passionately, mounts her Big Wheel, and starts pedaling around the yard again. I watch her go around and around. Eventually the cat steps back into the manger, and another jet screeches low overhead.

"Off the phone!" Pam yells. Bear is on her hip, yanking at her hair, and I go back up the steps.

"I don't know," Pam says. "I don't even know if the insurance company is going to pay for all of Bruce's tools, and there we went last night buying a dishwasher. From Montgomery Ward's." She sets Bear down.

"Up, up, up," he wails, arms stretched straight out toward her. "I want moo." She picks him up. She gets him a cup of milk which he sucks down like a desperate teary-eyed puppy.

Pam collapses on the couch. "Remember when you and I

used to smoke dope back when you got twenty years for it? And now you just get a small fine for it, right? I don't even know anymore. And Bruce and I were having such a hard time finding a place to rent because we weren't married, then suddenly nobody seemed to care anymore if we were or not, then we thought, well, why not get married, after all?" She shakes her head, smiling. "And why not file insurance claims, and have a baby and nickname him Bear, and buy a dishwasher from Montgomery Ward's? Ka-plowee, Brenda, when did I get so goddamned respectable?" She laughs.

Bear drops his empty cup to the floor, toddles over, puts his hands on Pam's knees, his head tipped. "You happy, mama?" he asks, delighted. "You happy?"

"Um huh," she answers, " 'cause I'm gonna eat some bear toes for dinner."

He squeals, runs on fat baby legs into the bedroom, screaming all the way.

"And you know what?" Pam asks me. "That little guy in the next room needs me. And that big guy out there needs me. And all I can say is, what's so wrong with that?"

Bruce comes home. "I hope you'll stay for a while," he says. "I know Pam will enjoy the company."

"Well, maybe a couple of days." I shrug.

Bruce is standing beside Pam, absentmindedly fingering her hair as if there is some new, wonderful texture in it that he has just discovered. He needs her. There's nothing wrong with that.

23 I DON'T KNOW what it is about this guy, Roger, that reminds Pam of Al. She's invited him over for dinner, and he sits on the couch across from me, large-boned, dark, and brooding. He's brought along a girlfriend, a large-boned, dark Italian beauty. They are both quiet in a compelling, mysterious way.

"Roger works with me," Bruce explains. We are all sitting around the coffee table, putting together tacos, eating tacos. The apartment is too small to have a dining table. "He just got back from spending a year sailing around."

"Six months sailing, six months in jail," Roger states casually, to no one in particular.

"In Mexico," Bruce fills in for him. "For having guns on board. See, *everyone* carries guns on board their boats, protection against modern day pirates, drug runners, you know, but in Mexico it's against the law."

"Just an excuse to confiscate boats they like," Roger says in that same strange way, to no one in particular. "Lucien's trying to get that boat back, but I'm afraid he won't pull this off. She was a nice boat, too, real nice equipment, that's why they wanted her. Oh, well, Lucien'll get to the point where he'll laugh it off. Buy himself a new one."

I ask his girlfriend if she sailed with them.

"No, I model," she says, as if that answers the question. She glances at Roger, and they both half-smile at each other. Energy fairly crackles in the air between them. Sexual energy, I think at first, then decide, no, it's that sweet exotic energy of mystery.

"What's Mexican jail like?" I ask Roger.

"Ok, I guess. They're actually pretty nice to you. They don't make you work or anything. Lucien set up these classes, taught all these guys English, had them teach us Spanish. He takes advantage of every situation, ol' Lucien." He shakes his head. "I called him 'Fagin.' And the food was actually pretty good."

"Oh, Roger, not as good as these tacos, surely," kids Pam.

I am about to ask him what he meant by Fagin, when he looks me point blank in the face for the first time. I'm silenced, off-balanced.

"You wanna sail?" he asks. "West Indies?" He's not kidding.

"Sure," I answer. I'm not kidding.

" 'Cause I left, so Lucien's looking for someone. Last time I talked to him, he told me to send him someone. He's going to Jamaica, first, I think he said. I'll drop him a line and tell him to keep an eye out for you. That you'll be looking him up. Sometime in the next few weeks. You can ask for him at Marijack Marina, in San Diego. They'll have an idea where he is."

"All right," I say. I look around. Everyone is crunching on their tacos, as if all of this were an everyday occurrence.

Later that night, while sleeping on Pam's living room floor, I wake up in mid-dream. I try to remember what I could have been dreaming that disturbed me so, then suddenly I do remember, and sit up in shock. "Sail to Jamaica" had been on my list. My list of things to do in my lifetime. When I'd been sick, I'd read *A High Wind in Jamaica* ... *Or, The Innocent Voyage*, it was subtitled. I'd put "Sail to Jamaica" first on my list.

All the rest of the night, lying flat on my back on Pam's living room floor, I dream of sailing to Jamaica, I dream that I am lying flat on my back on the deck of a boat that is sailing to Jamaica. I dream that I am pulling Jamaica toward me slowly, in a watery way. I have to dream that there is a tape player on below deck, because of the mariachi music booming beneath me.

I don't get around to leaving until late in the afternoon the next day. I kiss Pam and Bear as I head out their door.

"I hope things go well with you and Al, Brenda," Pam says.

"They will," I say. "I should be there by tomorrow, probably. I'm going to shoot back over to One-oh-one, to San Francisco first, head up the coast from there."

Or down the coast from there. Because it could only happen just like that. To sail the West Indies with Fagin.

24 ■ I TRY LOOKING at it from the spiders' point of view. For all they know, I'm a rock. Or a leaf, a twig, a trashed refrigerator. I lie on my side, hands over my face, fighting the hysterical urge to jump up and swat the spiders off me. They aren't hurting you, I say to myself. Just go to sleep, I say to myself. I feel the spiders run, whisper-soft, across my hair and down the backs of my hands.

I think they're spiders. It's too dark to see, but there are hundreds of these tiny things, thousands of teeny legs scurrying over me, and by the way they seem to be dropping on me from overhead, I figure they're spiders that have just hatched, now floating along on the breeze until they encounter me. I'm just an obstacle to them, I tell myself, just *be* an obstacle: a mute, deaf, sleeping obstacle.

It had taken me forever to get out of Sacramento; all my rides had been short ones. Before long, it was dark, and I wasn't going to hitchhike to headlight beams, though I felt itchy to keep moving, to keep watching that silvery highway slide beneath me. I wasn't sleepy, but there was nothing else to do but go ahead and burrow in for the night. The problem, I noticed as my last ride pulled away, was that there was no place to burrow; all around me were eight-foot chain-link fences, and barking dogs. I was getting close enough to San

Francisco to be within the suburbia that has spread right up to the freeway's edge.

I slung my pack over one shoulder and checked out the length of fence along both the entry and exit sides of the freeway, then fully shouldered my pack and crossed over the freeway bridge, only to find it identical there. I stood shifting my weight from one leg to the other, wishing I could just start hiking down the freeway, but that was illegal, of course. Up both lengths of the exit boulevard stood the tightly enclosed suburbia: twin sets of frosted bathroom windows lined up into the distance. An uncommon number of California Highway Patrol cars began pulling past me, and I could just see, in the streetlight, two pairs of eyes in each one, looking my way. I stood stupidly in limbo, being examined, unwilling to stop, unable to go.

Finally I waited for a break in the cars and ran down smack into the middle of the cloverleaf circle, unrolled my sleeping bag in the dark and lay flat on my back in the center of the freeway universe. No stars, but headlights spinning around my head. I dozed until this: the spiders.

I finally sit up, untie my pack, fish a t-shirt out and drape it over my face. Better. My eyelashes brush against the shirt with every blink. I listen to myself breathe.

What wakes me are the sprinklers suddenly chucking on nearby. I should have known, I had tripped over the irrigation control box on the way down into the circle. The water's not hitting me, but I expect the system near me to turn on soon enough. The sky is barely glowing pink, and my eyes feel puffy, my mouth like mud. I'd like to sleep longer. I think about searching around for the box and shutting down the system, easy enough for me since I used to install the things. But instead I roll up my bag. No spiders on me. Not a spider in sight. I almost wonder if I've dreamt them, or if I'm going crazy.

Miraculously, a compact pickup truck comes swinging past

just as I make it to the exit's edge, and stops even though I haven't had time to put out my thumb. The driver motions with his head for me to jump in the back. He's a window washer, and the back of the truck is filled with neatly stacked ladders, buckets, squeegees, long-handled scrubbers, all clean, clean, sweet-smelling and clean.

I settle in as best I can atop the ladder rungs, then shift my pack around until I'm comfortably lying back, my pack for a pillow. Through the window, past the driver dressed in bleached-and-ironed white, I see his dashboard clock: 5:20. What I can see of his face looks neither tired nor animated, grateful nor bitter, simply that it is 5:20 and he is on his way to wash windows in San Francisco, and he is ready.

We take an exit and wind through a maze of suburban streets where he stops twice to pick up two more men, younger, but also dressed in white and wearing the same expressions. Each barely nod toward me as they step up into the cab, and none of them greet each other. And then I have one of the most amazing rides of my life: the sunrise blazing orange, invading the blue-gray sky, the city of San Francisco slowly approaching, until we slice right into its heart, it looking shiny and orderly in the morning light, and me lying back there, the queen of window washers, the queen of clean.

They stop at North Beach where there is an open cafe, tiny and filled with smoke and people looking as if they've been up all night and have just gotten off from the late shift, or just starting the day, like the window washers, purposeful people, all speaking Italian. I can't seem to get the attention of the counterman, and have to say "Espresso, please," three times before he understands me.

I amble over to the table of window washers and thank the driver again for the ride, but he barely acknowledges me. There is no place else to sit, so I stand near the door sipping the dark brew which is scalding hot and good, tasting like clean black earth on a riverbank. Around me, people are sitting in twos and threes, smoking, talking rapidly in Italian, bodies bent toward each other with the importance of their arguments, their worries and theories, arguing, then laughing, and I am alone propped up on my pack in the corner when I notice the hordes of ants crawling from my pack down my pants leg. Ants. I hate ants. I gulp down my espresso, pause for just one second to savor it, then lug my pack outside where I throw its contents onto the sidewalk. There it is: a half-filled bag of raisin bread, teeming with ants. Ants going up my arms as I beat my sweater onto the sidewalk, ants tumbling from my pack to the ground where they crawl in wild confusion in all directions; all my belongings now scattered in public, a pitiful jumbled pile of necessities. I see legs stepping around me as I squat there shaking and picking and rubbing and beating ants.

After a while I decide I've done the best I can do and jam everything back into my pack, even though I'm usually methodically neat about packing. I toss the bag of raisin bread into a nearby trash barrel.

Immediately a thin man wearing only one shoe fishes it out. He beats a slice of the bread on his pants to knock off most of the ants, then crams it into his mouth, smiling at me and chewing with great relish, open-mouthed. He salutes me with the loaf of bread. "Here's to you, girlie," he says, then walks down the sidewalk singing.

"Win-ter-ti-ime," he wails, "and the livin' is ease-aaa . . ."

25 🔲 I SPEND the day in San Francisco, puffing
my way up and down stepped sidewalks, passing kite stores,
crazy street musicians, and Chinese grocer windows hanging
with strings of pale ducks. I beat these streets that Kerouac
knew so well; I go to City Lights Bookstore. The clerk looks
like a bored Allen Ginsberg—in fact, I decide he *is* Allen Ginsberg, bored, a little bit flippant with the customers.

I wake from a nap on the panhandle of Golden Gate Park
knowing that I need to finish this journey, that I need to get
to Al's. I take BART north as far as it goes, and pick up a
ride from a man who is just leaving the parking lot for the
Park N Ride, who had seen me, he says, earlier, on BART.

He is a nice-looking father of two young children and he
brags about them and about his wife. It is a wonderful counting of blessings, and at least for right now, here, in this car
on the road, he seems as content as a man can get.

"I hitchhiked when I was younger, too. I'm glad I did it
then. I'm so glad I don't have to wonder why I never did it.
It was fun. Well, pretty fun." He glances at me and I suppose
he sees my questioning look because he laughs and says, "I
don't think I was very good at it."

"How could you not be good at it? Didn't get rides?"

"Oh, no. I got rides, all right. I just never felt right. I felt
. . . uncomfortable."

"I never want to feel comfortable," I say, and I believe it,
but he smiles at me like I am just young.

"I felt too public," he says.

"It's something, isn't it? There you are, just a private person
thinking private thoughts, walking down the street, then you
turn and stick out your thumb and you're suddenly public
property. That moment when you cross the line from pedes-
trian to hitchhiker . . . It's weird."

We are in the middle of Santa Rosa now, and he asks if I'd like to be dropped off somewhere around here for the night. "We live outside of town, you know, in the suburbs."

I tell him I'd much rather be outside of town.

"Well, I don't understand. Where do you sleep?"

"Just on the side of the road. In the bushes. In my sleeping bag. It's usually quite comfortable . . ." I keep adding details because he looks so shocked, then finally he gets a lightbulb look on his face.

"Well, I'll be damned," he says, "I'll be damned. Do you know that it never occurred to me to do that? Why didn't I ever do that? I always stayed at scuzzy YMCAs in downtowns. It was awful. They had public showers and there would always be old men around watching me shower with their mouths hanging open. And to think that I could have camped out all the time. I don't believe it."

He lets me out at his exit where in the early dark of winter shine the lights from a McDonald's and a 7-Eleven. I go into the 7-Eleven and buy a loaf of raisin bread—my staple—but then opt for a little of that comfort that I dismissed so easily a few moments before and hike farther down the road to a Sambo's, not because I like the food, since I know it will be awful, but because I want to sit on a cushy seat in an overheated place and have someone wait on me in that great American way: sloshing black coffee into my cup after every few sips I take.

All the booths are full so I sit at the counter. It's just as I thought, overheated, and the waitress immediately tips my cup upright and pours so quickly that coffee spills into the saucer. I am feeling quiet and comfortable and lazy. A man two seats down starts a how-about-this-weather kind of conversation, and I put in a few responses to be polite.

"I saw your pack. Are you hitchhiking?"

"Yes."

"Aren't you afraid?"

"I get asked that by *everyone*. I guess if I were really afraid, I wouldn't be doing this, would I?"

He shrugs. "You ought to be afraid. Lot of kooks in this world. Better for a man. I used to hitchhike when I was younger. It was cheap for the traveling, but then it was expensive for rooms for the night. I think it would have worked out cheaper to take a bus. At least on the bus you can sleep for free."

"I just sleep on the side of the road."

"No kidding. Just right there?"

"Yeah, just off to the side of the exits, there are always bushes. Just right there."

"Isn't it noisy?"

"It's noisy. You get used to it. There are cars rushing right past your head, and not a soul knows you're there."

"You're brave doing stuff like that. Don't you get, you know, scary rides?"

"Almost every ride I get is with a man who has a daughter my age and is worried sick about me. Look," I say, and pull, from my wallet, odd scraps of paper, penciled with names and addresses. "These are all the people I'm supposed to write to, saying that I made it safely."

"Made it safely where?"

"To Spokane, eventually. To visit a friend. I've been getting a little sidetracked, though."

"I live in Eugene. I work for the phone company. I have to travel all over the Northwest teaching people how to use the new systems we're installing."

"You get to travel."

"I *have* to travel. It's lousy. I get these lousy efficiency apartments. I'm a constant transient; I never stay anywhere long enough for anyone to know who I am. And my old friends in Eugene never know where I am or what I'm up to. It's lonely as hell. It isn't just that either . . . it's a lot of things. I hate my job."

"Then why don't you quit?"

"Too much trouble to quit a job. And then you have to look around for a new one. Besides, there's pretty good money in this one."

I want to take him by the neck and shake him until his teeth rattle, yelling, "Half of your life! You're talking about half of your life! Pissing it away!" but instead, I stab into a tomato and ask the waitress for more coffee, please.

"Um, I was thinking," he starts, and already I don't like it. "Look, I'm no pervert or anything, really, I was just thinking, you'd be a lot more comfortable at my place."

"No," I say firmly. "Thanks for the offer." And I stab into another tomato.

"Really. Just on my living room floor. On my rug. It's warm there. I keep my place really warm. I keep it hot."

"No. Honest. Thanks."

"But it can't be comfortable sleeping out there. Where're you going to sleep? Out there?" He points toward the exit, right toward the bushes where I had planned to sleep.

I pause uncomfortably. "Around there, I guess. Maybe on the other side. I think on the other side."

"Look," he says, "you need a place to stay. I have one. I don't like having to sound so desperate."

"No," I say, getting up, dropping a dollar for a tip. I struggle into my coat. "Thank you. Very much. You don't sound desperate. I'm sure you're a nice man. I like sleeping outside, I really do." And then I am outside in the dry cold stinging air, running across the parking lot aware of every streetlight I pass under, my back prickly, trying to glance over my shoulder without looking like I am. My heart is pounding furiously. He is leaving the Sambo's now, I'm sure, standing in the parking lot lighting a cigarette, one eye squinted; sucking and blowing, and planning.

Stop it, Brenda, I tell myself. He's a goddamn lonely telephone company worker who tried to pick up on you. Big deal. I push into the bushes. Even though I'm in the pitch dark, I am sure he has seen just where I have gone.

The bushes are thick and tangled. I get down on my hands and knees and crawl into their convoluted mass, shoving my pack awkwardly ahead of me. I crawl deeply into the maze. Still, I can imagine him finding me, following my scent, tracking me down like an aboriginal hunter with a poisoned spear. Hunted. Just him against me. "Cars rushing right by your head and not a soul knows you're there," I hear myself say to him. I stop and listen. I tune my ears from the nearby traffic to an even closer sound, but there is nothing there in the bushes but my own fast breath. Don't be ridiculous, I tell myself, he's home in his own hot lonely efficiency apartment right now.

I know I can scare myself . . . I can scare the bejesus out of myself. Nothing has ever scared me as much as my own self, but knowing that doesn't help me now, here, lying on my belly in my sleeping bag, shivering in the cold air, propped up on my elbows, eyes stinging and dry. I feel my blinking getting heavier, and shake myself awake. I try to guess at the time. One o'clock, maybe only midnight. Car after eternal car swings past. That would be his plan, I decide, to wait until three or so. When he thinks I'm asleep.

I imagine I'll see his shoes first. I won't hear their crunch on the leaves until they appear suddenly along the very edge of the bushes. Twelve feet away, I estimate. Just the shoes, and then . . . a flashlight. I almost scream at the thought of it, of being hit with a sudden blinding light, and him getting to see my confusion and panic, my hands shielding my eyes, him laughing long and low, or maybe one of those feverish high adolescent laughs, a laugh that only I would hear. Outside of the bushes, dozens of people would pass obliviously, their car windows shut up tight, their stuffy heat blasting on high.

An ax. It would be an ax. I can already imagine my own

thick blood spattered on the undersides of the leaves. Then just my severed bones within my clothes to be found by some unlucky hitchhiker of the future while he is innocently trying to nestle into the bushes for a warm winter's nap. And finding this horror. This horror.

I jolt awake to my own silent scream—*this is it!*—thrashing wildly within my tangled sleeping bag, sobbing in anguish as dust flies, blinding and choking me; I scream, a bloodcurdling scream, until between my gaspings for breath what finally, finally, finally reaches me in my muddled brain is that it is daylight, bright daylight; he's not here, I'm all alone, and only the sharp morning sun stabbing through the branches has wakened me; that, and the jumping of my own jangled nerves.

I'm shivering now, my teeth chatter. I try to pick pieces of bark out of my mouth, but my hands are shaking too much, my tongue and lips are numb, and it's a hard hard cold, a hard and dirty cold. I'm tangled in my sleeping bag on the hard cold dirt, my fingernails black, there is no way to get warm, no way to get clean, and I have no strength to do anything but crawl back down into my bag until it covers my head, and blow onto my icy fingers, try to deep-breathe and calm myself, but it is too late; I cry cold tears for myself alone and lonely, lonelier than the telephone man, pitifully alone in the bushes while dozens of people drive past me, drowsy from just having left their warm marriage beds, and it is true, it is true, what they say: that your own worst enemy is yourself.

26 ◪ THE RAIN made me act so foolishly, the rain and my own dead dreary soul. All day long I had my ear talked off by a slobby truckdriver, a really depressing complainer, who bitched his way from one subject to another,

hour after hour. And now, just over the border, in Oregon, I'm in a car with a man I'm wildly suspicious of, not because he's said anything, but because he's said nothing. I hadn't taken my usual precautions. This car had stopped, and I'd blindly hopped on in.

"What kind of work do you do?" I ask, then sit as the windshield wipers clack back and forth, sweeping sheets of rain off the windshield in both directions. Finally the man looks over at me, at my face, then drops his eyes down my lap.

I force myself to stare back at him in a neutral way, neither afraid nor threatening. A difficult thing to do. We pass a sign: Rest Stop, 2 miles. "Stop there." I point to the sign. "I gotta go." No reaction from him. His eyes slide over me again, and I stare back and begin picking my nose, really digging in there with relish, and he pulls off at the rest stop exit.

As I suspected, as soon as I've stepped out of the car dragging my pack with me, he drives away.

I run through the rain to a covered picnic table, sit for a while. I'm sure a rest stop will be a hard place to get a ride, especially in the rain. I can't stand at the end of the entrance road with my thumb out; most people are uncomfortable about being confronted face on; and anyway, there's the question of how I got to be here to begin with, I mean, who kicked me out? and why? people will wonder.

Even *I* would be wary of picking up a hitchhiker at a rest stop.

The situation turns out to be worse than I imagined. All day I sit beside my pack at the entrance to the bathrooms, on display, hoping someone will offer a ride. All day I listen to the rumble of industrial flushing, and the hum of the hand dryers. I turn down the one offer that comes my way, from a man who has lit and smoked an entire cigarette while staring at me, before asking, "You need a ride, honey?"

Dusk comes on, and then night. I eat the last of my food: four squashed pieces of raisin bread washed down with rusty tap water. Then I sit foolish and hopeless. I can't decide which is worse: all the people walking past, staring at me with their eyes wide, or the fact that the later it gets, fewer and fewer people are walking past me at all.

The night turns cold. I move from outside to inside the women's room, sit on the floor under the hand dryer, and reach up to punch its button again and again. The restroom is unheated, open brickwork on the top, and the blast of the hot hand dryer on the top of my head is the only thing keeping me warm.

Late in the night, when there have been no cars for a while, I hear a truck pull up. Then a man appears at the doorway, with a mop and a bucket of cleaning supplies.

"Oh!" he says when he sees me. "You gave me a scare. I didn't see any cars out there." Then he notices my pack, and starts to put things together. "I've got to lock this place up for the night when I'm done cleaning."

I dash to a picnic shelter, unroll my sleeping bag on the table, and climb into it. After I've heated things up in there, it becomes pretty comfortable, pretty comforting, protective walls of rain on all sides of me.

'Early tomorrow morning,' I tell myself, 'someone nice will stop by here, someone who'll be going at least as far as Seattle. He'll have interesting things to say, and be a good singer, and buy me breakfast *and* lunch *and* dinner. And late tomorrow night, we'll pull into Seattle, and stop at his mother's house. His mother will fuss over me, insist I spend the night; she'll make up the pullout bed in the guest room with sweet-smelling flowery sheets. In the morning after a good hot breakfast, they'll wish me well, and I'll leave her house, and walk down sunny streets high above Puget Sound. I'll feel like a million bucks, and I'll be half a day from Al's.'

Snug in my rain house, I close my eyes, and fall asleep to the patter of raindrops.

I open my eyes to a huge black shadow, jesus, a man-shaped shadow looming above me.

"You a hitcher?" the voice asks. "You alone?"

My heart is slamming in my chest as I fumble for the zipper on my bag, I can't find the goddamned zipper on my body bag, I'm bound up in my goddamned body bag, jesus.

A click: his face lights up. He's got a penlight aimed at his own face. "Look at this," he says, and the small circle of light slides down to a paper he is holding, a newspaper ad for a K Mart opening. My blood is pounding in my neck, my brain, I can't think or move, my breath is coming hard and fast, and now, what the hell is this?

"Look," he says. He keeps the penlight on his own drawn face, doesn't shine it at me. "I'm sorry I woke you, and I'm sorry if I scared you, but you are the answer to my dreams right now. Can you drive? Did you see that ad? Grand opening special: Poinsettias, ninety-nine cents. Saturday morning grand opening, *tomorrow,* and those poinsettias are *here* right now, twelve hundred of them, in the back of that truck over there."

In the parking lot sits a panel truck, behind it, an open trailer piled high and haphazardly with wrought iron plant stands, tangled together like coat hangers.

"I *have* to sleep. I'd given up any hope to make it there on time; I only came into this parking lot to sleep. But I thought I'd check for hitchers first, and god, here you are. If we can drive straight through, between the two of us, we can make it on time. I'd pay you."

"I'm not alone," I say, finally. "My boyfriend's over there. Where's the K Mart?"

"Oh, god, a girl, I'm sorry. I must have scared you to death, coming up in the dark like this. Seattle. And that's wonderful that your boyfriend's here. Great. Three drivers. Look . . ." He still doesn't shine the penlight on me. He shines it on the picnic table, and begins dropping things into its circle of light. "The black one's the ignition, tank's about full, but here's a twenty for gas if you go that far, just, you know, go north. Wake me when the two of you get tired. Or get to Seattle. Thanks." He starts across the lawn. "My name's Steve," he adds, then climbs into his truck, and slams the door.

I wait for my heart to slow, my hands to steady, then I pack up. Halfway across the lawn my good fortune strikes me. Seattle! By morning! and I jump into the air.

Steve is really out of it, melded into the passenger door snoring, when I get into the cold cab. I have no idea how to back this thing up. Its trailer of wrought iron tips precariously when I run it up on the curb, but doesn't fall over. Then I'm off again, heater blasting, pulling Seattle to me. Six hours of sleep I've had, tops, I figure, in the last two days.

I'm the only person I know who doesn't have an asleep-at-the-wheel story, no story of waking to see my bumper sending railing sections over a 1,000-foot precipice, no story of waking in the morning to find my car stopped peacefully in the mid-dle of a field, cornstalks brushing the windows in the balmy breeze. On long boring hauls, half my brain may be dreaming a million dreams, but the other half is brightly awake and watchful. If I get tired I stop and sleep, but I do have an amazing capacity to go and go and go.

Five hours later I give a little whoop when I see the sign: Welcome to Washington. Steve stirs, half-wakes. In the rear-view mirror I see flashing lights, cops, and they must be after *us,* because there's no one else around.

Without a word Steve slides over on me and takes the wheel, and I slide over to the passenger side and let him.

"I don't know what I did," I tell him.

Minutes later I sit in the truck cab, dismayed, watching

Steve come out of the weigh-station office, stuffing his wallet back into his pocket.

"Have a good day now," he says with alarming good will to the cop who'd pulled us over.

"Two hundred dollar fine for not stopping to get weighed," he says as he starts up the truck. "There go my profits from this trip. What an escapade. A man works and works for his family, and just can't get ahead."

"I'm so sorry. It never occurred to me to stop."

"Hey, my fault." He holds his two fingers up like he's taking a Boy Scout oath. "One hundred percent my fault. Don't worry about it." We drive a little farther before he suddenly yells, "Where's your boyfriend?" as if we might have left him at the weigh station without my noticing.

"I never had one."

He looks confused.

"Well, I had to do *something* to protect myself."

He smiles. "You had me convinced. So you're traveling alone. Where're you going?"

"Spokane, to visit a boyfriend."

"What's he do?"

I sit confused for a moment, then I answer, "He's a lawyer."

"A lawyer. That's good. A lawyer. Good pay, nice steady work. That's good."

Then like every other lone driver, he tells me about his wife, his daughter.

"I do everything for them. They're my whole life. Man's got to work himself to the bone for his family, if he loves them. They don't understand that, is all. You know what my little girl said to me before I left yesterday? She said, 'Daddy, why aren't you ever home? Don't you love me?' She said that to me! Of course I love her. That's why I have to work the way I do. You know, I used to be in the carpet business. Trained three other men, everything I knew. They all went off and formed their own carpet business. Said I worked them too hard. I never asked them to work any harder than I was willing to. I try to be a good man, and look where it gets me."

We finally get to Seattle, and speed along on the freeway overlooking the sparkling Puget Sound. In the distance, the Olympic Peninsula looks more like clouds than mountains in the morning mist. Seattle! Seattle, right underneath these wheels, and Al's brown eyes only hours away.

We pull inland, and finally swing into a K Mart parking lot so new that the pavement is clean jet black. The manager almost hugs us, us with our twelve hundred ninety-nine-cent poinsettias, and cheap Tijuana wrought iron stands. Christmas music jangles out of the speakers, and just inside the front door, a man is struggling into a Santa suit, a box of candy canes on the floor beside him.

We are still unloading the poinsettias and wrought iron off the truck and onto shelves on the main aisle when the manager unlocks the front doors. Amazingly, the poinsettias and the stands are disappearing under the surge of people flowing through the door. The crowds are even bypassing Santa and his candy canes to get to the poinsettias.

Out of the corner of my eye I see the manager hustling across the store with a worried look on his face and in an instant I've concocted the exact scene which in a few short moments takes place:

"Hey, uh, Steve, you can get me another load of poinsettias, ASAP, yes? Can do? My whole grand opening leader is riding on these babies. And another load of those plant stands too, yes? Thanks a lot, bud."

And I, weary, guilty I, say yes, yes I'll drive back with him to the greenhouse in San Francisco and load up the plants with him and drive back all night long while he sleeps, a repeat of the night before, but this time stop at the weigh stations, of course. I figure it's the least I can do for him, and anyway, he's going to pay me, he says. Goodness knows I'm time-rich and money-poor.

"But," I say to Steve as we head across the parking lot to the truck and trailer, "look, can we stop first and get something to eat?" I'm giddy, lightheaded from no sleep and from hunger, and the sun reflecting off the blacktop is so dazzling me, filling up my eyes and brain, that it's threatening to spin me to the pavement. Six hours of sleep, and nothing but raisin bread and rusty tap water for the last two days.

"I want to get a couple hundred miles under my wheels first," he says.

I stop walking. I feel ready to crumble into tears. "I'm really hungry."

"I understand that. But I have a contract with that gentleman in there. He's run an ad. He can't disappoint his customers, and I can't disappoint him."

"You know, I bet that manager ate breakfast. I bet all those customers ate breakfast. Believe me, he will not begrudge us breakfast. I'll bet he'll even let us take a few minutes every few hours to use the bathroom."

We compromise by hitting up a Jack-in-the-Box drive-thru, where Steve leans out the truck window and shouts into the clown's mouth that we'd like two Jack Burgers, two Jack Cokes, and two Jack Fries, please. Then we roar up the entrance road to the freeway, me, famished, ripping open wrappings with hands that are actually trembling, and balancing everything on my lap.

Damnitall: Highway 5, South.

HIGHWAY 5, SOUTH

27 ◨ I DON'T KNOW, I don't know, I really
don't know how this happened, that I'm buzzing along alone
all the way back to Tijuana in a rented Pinto, dragging Steve's
empty trailer behind. It had made some sense earlier, when
Steve had explained it all to me in his hyperkinetic way. We
had driven all day and all through the long night—Steve driving, mostly, with me sleeping the sleep of the dead beside him,
though I was the one who eventually pulled the truck and
trailer into the greenhouse parking lot in San Francisco just
as they opened at six in the morning. I hadn't told him that
it was a crazy way to run a business, that the oil companies
were the only ones making out on this deal, us driving eight
hundred miles from Seattle to buy poinsettias, only so that
we could turn around and drive eight hundred miles back to
Seattle, when I was sure we could have found a greenhouse
in Seattle selling them for, ok, maybe a few cents more apiece
than the one in San Francisco. But then Steve came up with
this other idea, that he would rent a car in San Francisco for
me to drive back to Tijuana to pick up more wrought iron
plant stands, while he was delivering the plants to Seattle.

"Now, listen," he'd said, as I was getting into the car in the
Hertz parking lot. "It's now Tuesday, seven a.m. I'll get to
Seattle by eleven tonight, unload my plants, sleep for three
hours and be back at the greenhouse here in San Francisco by
six tomorrow night. I'll load up, then meet you back here at
Hertz by seven. Seven p.m., Wednesday. Leaving now, you'll

get to San Diego by seven tonight. Stop at my place in Chula Vista. Here's the address. My wife will give you directions to the factory in Tijuana, and she'll give you pesos. By the time you get to Tijuana and finish up with all the haggling and loading up—they take forever there, they have absolutely no sense of business down there—it should be about midnight. Sleep at your place in San Diego. Leave by seven so you can rendezvous with me here at Hertz by seven tomorrow night. Then we switch the trailer to the truck, and take turns driving so we can deliver a third load of poinsettias and a second load of wrought iron plant stands to the K Mart in Seattle by Thursday, around noon. All right now, do you have everything clear?"

So here I sit, winding down the coast, south, and these seagulls and islands glistening in the late afternoon sun just off Santa Barbara are a far far way from Spokane, Washington, and Al's brown eyes, and what craziness has brought me here? I finally slow the car, slow down those road reflectors—Bott's Dots—that have been machine-gunning their way past either side of me for hours, for days, and pull to a stop at an ocean-side parking lot filled with humming RVs. When I step out, car wheels still spin beneath my feet. I walk to the edge of the parking lot, the ocean breeze so fresh it brings tears to my eyes. I stop with my heels on the pavement and my toes on the sand. How appropriate for the ocean to be wheeling its way before me, curling, crashing, spreading, and redrawing itself to curl and crash and spread again, neverending. And almost to the horizon, the oil rigs pumping and pumping and pumping and pumping. I sigh and get back into the car, the cage.

I slide on through San Diego without stopping, then follow Steve's directions down dark unfamiliar Chula Vista streets until I finally pull into a gravel driveway behind two rusty vans with flat tires. Painted on one van: Steve's Carpet Warehouse. A spotlight comes on, a dog barks, and I hope Steve remembered to call his wife like he said he would. I get out of the car on shaky legs, squint into the spotlight, and walk gingerly to the front door. In the open doorway is the silhouette of a woman, a baby on her hip. The front porch is piled with rolls of carpeting, mildew staining some of them, and stacks of identical cardboard boxes that have been sitting so long they've discolored and half-collapsed on each other.

"You're Brenda?" the woman asks. "Come on in."

The TV is casting its eerie glow in a living room filled with cheap furniture, but nice carpeting, deep cushy stuff under my every step. Steve's wife is very young, and pretty, with a pretty child on her hip. "Have a seat," she offers.

"No, thanks, I've been sitting for what seems like days."

"Steve's working you pretty hard, I guess."

"You might say that."

"Well," she sighs, "let me get my purse and keys."

She drapes the toddler on the couch while she goes in the other room, and the girl remains draped, staring at me suspiciously, with her thumb in her mouth. When her mother enters the room, the child slides down off the couch and clambers back onto her hip.

"We need to unhook the trailer first, then would you mind following me to the car rental place? Then I could give you a ride home from there if you like."

"No," I laugh. "There's been some confusion here. See, I'm supposed to go down to Tijuana . . ."

"The manager changed his mind. He doesn't want any more plant stands. So Steve says just to turn in the car."

I stand for what seems to me like an eternity with my mouth hanging open. "You don't understand," I say. "I was in Seattle."

"But you live in San Diego?"

"But I want to *be* in Seattle. I went to a lot of trouble to get to Seattle, and I want to be in Seattle now."

Steve's wife stands wearily, her arms curled around her

blond-haired daughter, rocking slightly from one foot to another. I can see that this sort of thing has happened many times before, and I feel overwhelmingly sorry for her, and for myself.

We turn in the rental car and she drops me off at my brother's apartment complex in San Diego, with the promise that we'll straighten it all out when Steve returns from Seattle, in a few days after he's delivered a couple more loads of poinsettias. I know better than to argue anything with his tired wife.

"Brenda?" she calls as I walk away. I turn; she's holding a twenty-dollar bill out the window. "I imagine he didn't pay you." I walk back and take the twenty from her hand. And I know, the moment I take the money, that I'll never end up working out anything with Steve.

I enter Will's cold, unlived-in apartment. The electricity is off, probably for non-payment. I haven't the slightest idea where candles might be. I open all the drapes. The ever present city glow is enough to light the room. TV shows are pounding through the walls on both sides. I go into Will's room, slide into bed. Something slaps on the floor next to the bed, sending my heart pounding—Will and Kirby's picture falling over, I guess. My heart begins to slow, though I notice not all the way back to normal: all the cells in my blood, in my bones, in my ears and fingers and feet are still busy driving down Highway 5, headed south.

I decide to call Al. I feel around until I find the phone in the dark next to Will's bed; I take a deep breath, lift the receiver off its cradle. Cradle. What an odd word, *cradle.* I lift the receiver like a baby to my ear. Silence. Disconnected for non-payment too, I suppose.

I step carefully through Will's dark apartment to the door, then down the stairs to the pay phone outside the rec room. I pull out a handful of change and my tiny address book, and dial Al's number, surprised at the violent reaction this sets off in my body, in my poor, underfed, overexposed body. All the classics: pounding heart, sweaty forehead, shaky knees. The phone rings and rings, and for a moment I hope he won't answer, then when I get to ring number six I hope he does answer, and on ring twelve I give up all hope that he'll answer, and hang up and climb the stairs to Will's apartment.

I go back to the pay phone at midnight. Still no answer. I call at one o'clock. And at two. Then when I'm back lying on Will's bed, I decide, ok, he's either at a woman's house, or he's on Christmas vacation. A week off for Christmas vacation. His mother lives in Tulsa. Maybe he's gone to visit her.

Imagine that . . . I would have gone all the way to Spokane to find him gone. So this whole charade with Steve turned out for the best after all.

Except I'm in San Diego alone, instead of in that big Northwest with Al; Christmas is next week, and I've got no job and almost no money, and what am I going to do tomorrow? Try to get my old job back at Safeway?

I try to settle down to sleep, feeling muddled and dizzy, then I suddenly sit up, laughing. Fagin, of course, Fagin! I'd forgotten all about Lucien. Marijack Marina, that's where Roger told me to go to find news of him. I can go tomorrow. First thing.

I think I'll write a second postcard: "Al, I got a little sidetracked. But I'll visit you sometime soon. I promise. I promise. I promise. Brenda." Maybe I'll be mailing it from Jamaica.

28

BUTTER'S MELTED down into the egg cups, but that's the worst of the damage. Will never kept much in his refrigerator, and I didn't add anything of note the few days I was here. I sponge out the egg cups, then take a paper bag and throw things in: a jar of mayonnaise, a green block of cheese. In the freezer is only one ice tray, water in its cups.

There's almost nothing in his cabinets, either, and I'm famished. I find a can of corn, finally, crank it open, tip it to my mouth, and the corn is so crisp and so sweet that I lean against the wall and slide to the floor and close my eyes as I chomp.

I carry the bag of garbage downstairs to the dumpster, unlock Will's storage room, and pull out my skateboard. The day is one of those wondrous, balmy days with unusually clean air that always seem to show up in San Diego close to Christmas.

I step onto my board. One nice thing about Will's apartment is that everything's downhill of it. It feels good to be rolling along like I've done so many times before. I do fancy jumps at the curbs, all the way to the bay.

Next to Marijack Marina I roll past tourists sitting at tables outside a restaurant. They are lingering over their late brunches, and I know as I breeze past that I'm just another San Diego sight to them, like the sails wafting, and the sleek boat hulls and the blue sky.

I hang out at the locked gate leading to a dock until some boat owners show up, then catch the gate before it slams behind them, and slip in. I head toward a man who looks like he runs things.

"Are you the dockmaster?"

He squints up at me from some lines he's securing. "What can I do for you?"

"I'm looking for someone named Lucien," I say, feeling ridiculous, like I've stepped into a prime-time thriller.

But he answers matter-of-factly, "Yeah. Lucien. He's over at, uh, Kelly's Boatyard. You know where that is? Below the mission, next to that nursery."

It's just down the hill from my brother's apartment. I thank him, and start the trek back, thinking how strange it is that this Lucien character is so mysterious and exotic and sinister, yet everyone's reaction to him comes out casual, common, day-to-day.

I walk through the nursery parking lot, my skateboard tucked under my arm. Everyone in San Diego seems to be here, buying Christmas trees, tying them down on their car roofs. A few couples linger over the trees in the lot, examining them with probably a keener eye than they use for furniture they're going to live with for the next twenty years.

Kelly's Boatyard. The boats are the same types I just saw bobbing lazily at the marina, yet here, they take on that workman's quality, sitting steady and tall on their scaffoldings, like they're getting ready for the job they have to do. Some of them are stripped to bare wood, stripped of their fittings. Still, they emit ocean smells, these landlocked, dry-docked boats. I lock my fingers in the chain-link fence, lean my forehead against it, and drink in the different life enclosed inside.

Blood-red mouths lunge at my face, razor teeth snap, black dog bodies slam into the fence, and only after my stunned body has jumped back do the Dobermans set off their frantic barking. "Jesus!" I hear my own stunned voice say. I stand back, shaken, waiting for the dog barks to produce a person, yet no one comes. I finally walk along the length of the fence, the Dobermans following, jumping and lunging and barking, and at last, high on one boat deck, I see a man working. I almost call, "Lucien?" but instead, yell feebly, "Hey! Hey there! Hello?"

"Hi!" he yells down to me, but nothing more.

And again I put myself in the prime-time thriller. "I'm looking for a man named Lucien."

"Lucien?" He looks over his shoulder, back farther into the shipyard. "Yeah, he's here," and I wonder what has set my heart off more violently: the dogs, or this man's words.

He jogs down a ladder to the ground. "Tina! Victor!" he calls, and the dogs come running, stubby tails wagging. He chains them to the fence, unlocks the gate, and they sit calmly and eye me as I pass, far from their reach.

"That's his boat."

She's a beauty. She takes my breath away. Two-masted, stripped to bare wood, rounded stern, elaborate wooden railing. A pirate's boat.

Then I notice the man working on her. He looks about sixty, though age is hard to tell with sailors. He has the weatherbeaten skin of an eighty-year-old, the honed hungriness of a twenty-year-old. He stands, in cutoff jeans and sneakers, looking wonderfully content, though the job he's doing, tapping oakum in endless rows across the hull, looks horribly tedious to me. As we get closer, he breaks into a song, something bawdy-sounding, I don't know what, in French.

"Lou-she-anne!" the man with me calls out, and Lucien looks up, and smiles immediately. "Your crew is here!"

"So!" Lucien sings out, but in his thick French accent, it comes out: "Zzzo!" "So, so, so. It is, at long last, Brenda." I wonder how such a reputation has preceded me. One moment I'm jobless in a borrowed apartment, then nothing but a tourist sight, and now a crew.

And I wonder if my mouth is hanging open as Lucien walks my way, because what I thought I saw when he first smiled is really there: gold teeth. An honest-to-god mouthful of gold teeth, flashing out of the biggest smile I have ever seen on anyone, anywhere.

"So!" he sings again, and shakes my hand. "Well, you have heard, no doubt, how my last boat, she was lost." Even as he speaks, he grins, his gold gleaming.

He shrugs. "But she," he waves to his new boat, "she is more beautiful. And more trouble." His voice sings, draws. "Trouble, though, is not so bad, it means nothing. Not when you are living the way you wish. And you, Brenda, I think you live the way you wish?"

I keep my eyes steady on him and answer, steadily, "Yes."

He throws his head back and laughs. "Come," he says, and I follow him up the ladder to the deck. Ah, this deck, and I feel like I'm floating, in the air, on the sea, my heart anchored to this boat.

"Thirty-eight?" I ask him, guessing at its size, and he laughs and narrows his eyes admiringly at me. "Very good. She is thirty-eight."

We go down into the cabin, dark and cozy. Lucien slides the hatch closed behind him, latches it, then leans back against the ladder with his arms crossed. His teeth shine between sun-dried lips. A faint light comes in through the portholes. For a long time he just stands there and says nothing, and I say nothing; I cross my arms, too, and stare back at him, and I don't waver.

"Sometimes," he finally says, "in a big storm, we are in here for three, four days, being tossed by the big waves, with no relief, and the hatch, she stays shut, like this. Do you see how small it is in here? You see how dark?" Still, he smiles. We stand there motionless for long enough that for just one brief instant, I get a view of what it is like to sail the way that Lucien must sail. That there is nothing in the world that has to be done in life, but live.

He points to a small berth. "This one will be yours. It is always damp, on the deep ocean. Your bed never dry out, you never dry out, on the deep ocean. You know that?"

"I know that now."

"You have sailed much?"

"Day sailing," I shrug. "Bay sailing. Not much ocean sailing. Just along the coast. No open ocean."

"Not many women want to sail the deep ocean. Not many.
You are a rare one. A different breed." He laughs, a little
giggle.

Finally he unbolts the hatch and slides it open. He steps
back so I can be first to go up the steps. Through the hatch-
way is a precious square of blue, a blue that I have never seen
before, and as I climb I feel as if I'm stepping right up into
the sky.

On the deck, I notice, for the first time, a sullen-faced boy
of about fifteen scraping paint off the gunwale. Lucien waves
toward him. "This is Martin." The boy glances up; his frowning expression doesn't change. He eyes me almost threaten-
ingly, then goes back to scraping. "Brenda, she is sailing with
us, to Jamaica," he calls to the boy, and before I have a chance
to question or dispute, he starts down the ladder which is
propped up against the boat's side. Just as I step to the ground,
he asks me, "Why do you wish to sail?"

"Because I . . . want to." It seems like exactly the right
answer by itself, but I add, "Because . . . I think the ocean is
where I'm supposed to be now."

"Ah, so it is a quest." He walks to the stern of the boat.
"You know, you are one of these wonderful breed of American women." He looks up at the stern, studies it. "Yes," he
says, as if he has just made a decision. "So, of course!" He
holds his hands up, as if framing his words: *"Brenda's Quest."*
He throws up his arms and laughs. "She is *Brenda's Quest.*
And the dinghy, she will be *Brenda's Question."* He giggles.

I hear Martin scraping. The boat curves gracefully toward
the sky. *Brenda's Quest. Brenda's Question.*

"So, then." He claps his hands. "I will be gone, all month,

to Lausanne. Business matters. Family matters. Oh, my brothers," he sings. "They blame on me, their stupidity. That they are chained to the family business, and I escape. So. I let them keep the money, after all. Phoo. I need none. Oh, sometimes a little, to buy a new boat, yes? But adventure is cheap. Boredom, *that* is expensive." He walks me toward the gate. "So I see you next month. In the meantime, you may work with Martin or not. It is your decision. Au revoir, Brenda. You know what means, 'Au revoir'?"

"Goodbye?" I suggest stupidly.

He holds his forefinger up, tips his head. "It means, 'to the dream.' "

He growls at the Dobermans as we pass, giggles, gets on his knees just past their chain lengths and begs comically to them, throws kisses to them, recites something to them in French that rhymes. Then he is up, and before I know it, has me out the gate, is locking it with an "Au revoir, Brenda," and before I have a chance to ask him, "Who is this Martin character? And who are *you*, anyway?" he is strolling across the boatyard, singing a French ditty.

I shake my head and start the trudge back up the steep hill to Will's apartment. All the palm trees lining the streets are barberpoled with Christmas garlands, some of them torn and swaying in the breeze. I stop at the spot on the hill where the view looks like a postcard: freeways criss-crossing, stands of palm trees, the bay in the distance, the river mouth, and that hazy ocean on the horizon, an ocean that is bigger and wider and deeper than I will ever be able to imagine, even if I do sail to Jamaica. And straight out and all above me, all that blue sky, looking just a bit different than I've ever seen it before. Looking just a bit more precious.

29 ⬛ WHEN WILL was six, and I was not quite two, back when we lived in Virginia, our mother had a habit of disappearing into the attic a couple of times a week. Will has told me about this so often and so well that I feel like I remember it myself.

Usually this happened close to dinnertime, when she'd call him in from playing outside. She always looked so tired, right down to the ends of her hair. "Will, you watch Brenda. I have to look for something in the attic."

He wondered why she always said that when that wasn't what she was doing. She'd drag her feet up the steps to the second floor, never looking back, then Will would hear the attic door creak open, the ladder slide down, the creak of each rung, the scrape of the ladder being pulled back up, the slam of the door. And she would be gone.

"Brenda, go play in the kitchen," he'd tell me, to get my baby noises as far away as possible, so he could listen. But once the attic door slammed, there was never another sound.

A few times he went upstairs and sat crosslegged on the floor right under the attic door. He held his breath and stared at that door without blinking, as if that could make her appear, but he could tell there was nothing up there but dead air. It seemed to him that she must go up that attic ladder and keep right on going, up and up into the pale blue sky, until she was higher even than where our daddy flew his airplanes. Until she was farther away from us than he was.

One day when Will came downstairs, I wasn't in the living room; I must have been in the kitchen. Will turned on the "Mickey Mouse Club" show and watched it until the part where the gray bony fingers open the cobweb-covered pirate's chest; then he got goosebumpy all over and went to find me.

I was gone, too. He was all alone in the house. He couldn't

believe it; it was as if I'd vanished into thin air, just like his nightmare of everyone in the world vanishing into thin air but him.

He scrambled around downstairs calling me. He wormed his way into my crawly spaces. He looked up the stairwell; he knew I couldn't make it to the top landing, and I wasn't halfway up the steps. But then he noticed: the front screen door was unlatched.

He pushed his way through it and flew down the wooden steps in his Keds, his breath fast and big. He ran out into the street first, then crawled under the steps and in the bushes, twigs scratching his face and arms. I was nowhere around. There was no one around anywhere in the neighborhood. "Brenda! Bren-DA!" It was getting close to dusk.

Then up in the sky, as it so often did, came the whine of a plane. It dipped over the oak at the end of the block: our father's signal. "Daddy!" Will screamed. The plane wiggled its ailerons, which made the plane waggle in a big "hello." Will ran down the sidewalk after it, screaming up into the sky, "Daddy! Brenda's gone! Brenda's lost!" The plane made a big circle in the sky and came back, dipped over the oak again, waggled "hello," again, then flew off into the wild blue yonder.

Will walked back into the house to search for me one more time. All he could hear was his own fast breath. He climbed the stairs, and stood looking at the attic door. He was scared to call up to our mother. Not because she would be mad at him for losing me—she wouldn't. Not because she would be mad at him for bothering her. But because once before, just once, he'd called for her, and she hadn't come down. Because of course, she wasn't there.

"Ma? Ma . . . Brenda's gone. I can't find her." He held his breath. Then, suddenly furious and terrified, he shouted, "Ma! MAAAAA! Come down! Brenda's lost! I said, *Brenda's lost!*"

My voice came from our parents' bedroom. "Will'am?"

He opened the door, and there, he says, he found me, sitting splay-legged on top of the tall dresser, smiling beatifically at my own self in the mirror. I had pulled the drawers out to make steps to get up there.

I pointed to myself in that big round mirror, which was the only one in the house, then turned to Will with a look of peace and acceptance on my face. Those are Will's words, now, when he talks about this: peace and acceptance. And I said to him, "I see me."

"Yeah, Brenda, you do. You see you." He climbed the drawers to get to me, to lift me off the dresser top, and caught a look of himself in the mirror. And what he remembers most about that day was what he saw on his own face: that same look of peace and acceptance, as he helped his baby sister down off the dresser.

He took me downstairs and made us cream cheese on raisin bread sandwiches. He read me some Little Golden books. It was probably an hour before we heard the attic door creak open upstairs, the ladder slide down, back up, the door slam, and our mother's slow footsteps down the stairs. When she got to the bottom she leaned against the banister for a while with her arms crossed on her chest. Then she held her empty palms up.

"Well, Will," she sighed. "I guess I just couldn't find what I was looking for."

30 ◼ I LIE IN Will's bed and read until it gets too dark, then I lie in the dark, and do nothing. Christmas is a week away. I get a sudden vision of myself alone in the apartment, listening to the kids on the sidewalks below wheeling

around on their new Christmas bikes, screaming, their parents shouting encouragements from the doorways. And me, alone above them, pacing the floor, picking up a paperback and putting it back down.

I get up and feel around in the dark for my address book, and go downstairs. Some gangly boys, thirteen, fourteen years old are playing pool in the rec room next to the pay phone. They're all wearing identical red Santa hats. I put a pile of change on the pay phone shelf, turn to "R" in my address book, drop a dime in the phone, and call Al's number again. As I expect, the phone rings with no answer.

When I hang up, my dime drops with a conclusive clunk. I sigh, finger the coin out of the cup, drop it back in, and dial my parents' number up in L.A.

"Hello?" My mother's thin voice.

"Hi. Mom. It's Brenda."

"Yes?"

"Well. Hi. Um, are you busy?"

"I'm watching my TV show."

"Oh. Well, I'll just be a second. I was just calling to say hi. Just calling to see what you and Dad are doing for Christmas."

"The usual. You know, Christmas luncheon at the club."

I remember those Christmas luncheons at the club, the cavernous banquet hall, the endless talk about the roast beef, whether it was as tender as last year, as red.

"Well," I say. There is silence on the phone. "Well, I was calling to see what you and Dad were doing. Because I guess I won't be spending Christmas with Will. He's in Arizona."

"He is?"

"Yes." There is more silence, and I sigh and finally say, "Well, so I thought maybe I'd come up to L.A."

"When?"

"Oh, you know, for Christmas. For Christmas day."

"Why is Will in Arizona?"

"He's got a new girlfriend there. Named Miranda."

"Oh. Are you going to Arizona for Christmas?"

"No. I thought I'd come up to L.A."

"Will will be here, too."

"He *will?* Did he call you? Is he bringing Miranda?"

"Why would he call me?"

"To tell you that he's coming up there for Christmas."

"He doesn't have to. You just did."

"No, I didn't. I said *I* was."

"Brenda," she says, exasperated, "you just now said Will was coming up to L.A. on Christmas day."

"Well, I was confused, then," I say, and it's true, I'm thrown off balance the way I'm always thrown off balance when I call my mother; there always comes a point where I feel I'm getting sucked into the receiver and down the curly cord right into her whirling confusion. "Neither of us are coming up there for Christmas, okay?"

"Who's Miranda?"

"Will's new girlfriend. I gotta go."

"Yes, me too. Commercial's over."

"Well, bye, Mom. Merry Christmas."

"Bye, Brenda. Call more often."

I hang up and grip the receiver and hang onto it, lean my head against it.

The phone rings beneath my hand. I jump.

"Hello?" I ask, puzzled.

"That will be one-fifty-five for three minutes."

"Oh, yes. Thank you," I say, feed the coins in, and hang up again.

Then I see, out of the corner of my eye, that one of the fourteen-year-old pool players has sidled up to the window near me and is sliding the end of his cue stick in and out crotch-high, to the delighted whoops of his friends. When he turns and sees me watching him, the cocky smile drops from his face, and he blushes. But then he saunters, in cool control, back to his friends.

I'm glad I never have to be fourteen again, and I'm doubly glad I've never had to be a fourteen-year-old boy.

I open my address book to the "A" page, and dial the apple ranch.

"Marty! Hi!"

"Brenda. *Que pasa?*"

"I'm fine. Look, let me talk to Will."

"That Will. He's been gone a while, man. He and Miranda and MaryEllen took off for Boston the same day you left." I suck in a breath. "Yeah," Marty continues. "You know the day Will dropped you off at Greyhound? MaryEllen was back here, meantime, talking Miranda into driving to Boston. And then when Will came back, they were outta here in an *hour*. They kept yelling, 'Open-ended adventure!' out the window all the way down the road."

Open-ended adventure! "God damn," is all I can think to say, as I stand, rooted to this San Diego sidewalk. "Good god damn."

"And another thing. I been meaning to talk to you anyway, about that brother of yours. 'Cause I known Miranda for ten years now, man, and I'm telling ya, I love the chick to death, but she's mean as a rattlesnake to men, and I mean just *like* a rattlesnake; she lets you know right from the start she's there and she means business. Guys know what they're getting into when they get into her. Longest I ever seen her go without striking is half-hour, tops. So tell me what that bro' of yours did, cause for *days* I saw her acting s-w-e-e-t. I can't even say that word out loud, talking about Miranda."

"I think it's his chipped tooth," I say. "God damn. Boston. Do you have a number for Sean? Oh, wait. Forget it. I do. Look, thanks a lot. Say hi to Juan for me."

"Will do. Well, adios. Ciao. Au revoir. Whatever."

I laugh, a wry laugh. "Au revoir, Marty, my man. To the dream."

I make a collect call to Sean's number. MaryEllen accepts the call.

"You sound so far away," I tell her.

"I am. Come to Boston. Well, really, now, it's actually Gloucester where we're living. In a cool little fisherman's cottage. You've gotta see it. Come out here for Christmas. We've got all kinds of things planned. And, hey, Will and Miranda are here."

"Yeah, I just heard from Marty."

"So, when will you be here?"

"MaryEllen, I've got one hundred and seventy-five dollars, no job."

"But James is driving out here. Remember? That tall skinny guy from the apple distributor? He was planning to drive to D.C. to move his girlfriend back with him. Don't you remember? I was going to drive with him, but I couldn't wait that long to get to Sean. He must be leaving just about now. Oh, please please please. Call him. You don't need money, Brenda. You got friends and guts and wits; you don't need *money*. Just get here, and Sean and I can keep you fed. Hell, we'll get you *fat*. And then you can drive back with Will and Miranda." She starts singing, "Dashing through the snow, in a one-horse open sleigh . . ."

"It's an idea. It might work. I'd like to be with Will for Christmas. We're usually together. And I'd like to be with you and Sean, too, of course. *And* I need to do something for a month or so. Then I might be sailing to Jamaica." I smile to think of it, and smile to think of Al, too. "Either that, or going up to Washington state, to be with the love of my life."

"Wait a minute. Wait just one minute. You can't possibly know that the love of your life is in Washington state, Brenda. Because, as you once told me: one day, when you least expect it, you're going to run full-speed and head-first into the love of your life, and end up smack on your butt with your head spinning and stars zinging and reeling. Then you'll pick yourself up, eventually, with a giddy half-smile on your face, and watch *him* pick *him*self up with a giddy half-smile on *his* face, and bingo: there he'll be."

I laugh. "What a memory you have. I did say something like that one drunken night."

"You said *exactly* that one *drugged* night. Even though I was tripping at the time, you think I could forget a speech like that?"

"No, I guess not."

"Call James. It'll be great. The guy's a real cheapskate, for one thing. I had lunch with him one day and he ordered an egg sandwich, sixty cents, and when he found out they were going to charge him five cents for a cup for water, he waited until I was done with my drink, then took my cup to get water. I mean, really. It should be dirt cheap for you to get here. At least as far as D.C."

"Yeah, ok," I sigh. "I think you've convinced me. I'll at least try to get ahold of James."

"Great. See you in Boston. You can 'pahk the cah in Hahvahd Squayah.' "

"Right, MaryEllen. Look, before I hang up, let me talk to Will."

"They're not here. Haven't seen them in days. You've got a lot of relatives around here?"

"Tons. My parents are both from big families, and everyone lives right around Boston."

"Last time I saw Will and Miranda, Will said they were going to see your Aunt Jo."

Aunt Jo: I feel a plink in my heart, like a cord breaking.

"I didn't even know she was still alive."

MaryEllen laughs. "Maybe she finally went, and took Will

and Miranda with her. Like I said, that's the last I heard from them. So come here. Then we won't have to talk on the phone. I'm only picking up odd jobs. I can't afford this."

"You're right. Maybe I'll call you from D.C. Maybe I'll just show up."

I call James, and it turns out that he's leaving in a couple of days. I arrange to meet him in Tucson tomorrow night. He sounds ecstatic to have someone to share the cost and driving. He keeps saying "Righteous."

"We gotta marathon drive," he says. "We gotta jet. *Comprende?* Can you marathon drive?"

"I can marathon drive," I say.

The way he answers my goodbye is: "Righteous."

I use exactly every coin I had brought down to use for phone calls: that seems a good sign. I go back up to Will's, thinking of Harvard Square, and MaryEllen and Sean and Will and Miranda. But when I settle down in bed, I lie awake for hours, the city lights glowing through the window above me, and all that I can see and hear in the cool darkness of Will's apartment, are the face and voice of my Aunt Jo.

31 ▩ My Aunt Josephine was a terrified

woman, terrified of noises, terrified of phone calls and of knocks on the door, terrified of doors, terrified of any room she wasn't already in, and there she was living alone in a dark and drafty house in Salem, Massachusetts, surrounded by immense oaks that scratched at the windows and moaned with the wind day and night. I lived with her for a while, when I was four. I don't know for how long. Weeks, probably. Will must have been about nine. He wasn't with me; he'd been left with another aunt. We'd been sent away because of what Will and I now refer to as our mother's "vacuum incident."

Aunt Josephine's greatest fear was darkness, so she sat up all through the night, and went to bed at the morning's light. I didn't know this, I was too young to have a clear concept of time. I only knew that when I went outside after breakfast, the neighborhood kids were being called inside for dinner.

Aunt Josephine was really my great-aunt, my mother's aunt. Life at her house was night after endless night of sitting on the oriental rug in her living room in a circle of floor-lamp light, playing with two heavy, old, china dolls that Aunt Josephine had let my mother play with when *she* was little. The only sounds were the oaks scratching at the windows behind heavy red velvet curtains, and the grandfather clock ticking loudly. Aunt Josephine sat in the corner doing needlepoint. She stabbed at the cloth for hours, without talking. I was afraid to ask where's Mommy.

One china doll was a sailor boy with a pageboy haircut, a ribbon hanging down the back of his old-fashioned sailor cap. The other was a baby with a cracked and crazed face.

"I used to tell your mother not to wash that babydoll; I told her it wasn't one of those new dolls made out of rubber like her friends had, but she wouldn't listen to me, and look what she did. She ruined that babydoll." She told me this story almost every time she brought the dolls down from the high shelf and handed them over to me. "Now *you* be more careful," she'd say.

At bedtime I'd change into my nightgown, alone in the huge, cool bedroom. Then Aunt Josephine would knock and wait for me to say, "Come in, please"—she insisted on the "please"—before she entered the room carrying a small china plate. On the plate were always the same things: two store-bought cookies, a fancy tea-type that my mother would never have bought, and one fat purple plum, so dark it was black. Almost meekly, she would set the plate on the bedside table, then quickly leave the room. I have never eaten plums as perfect as those were, dripping cold and sweet, juice running down my arm as I sat up in that tall bed in that cool room, alone.

Aunt Josephine never made me put out the light; I was allowed to fall asleep with it on. But once, just to be brave, I reached over and clicked it out, only to be surprised by beams of sunlight streaming through the blinds. I sat on the edge of the bed, sucking my plum pit, wondering if I were ever going home, wondering about the rays of light slicing through the bedroom. They showed off all the dust floating in the air. There was an awful lot of dust.

32 ◼ THE VACUUM incident:

Suddenly all the neighborhood moms were talking to me about baby brothers. Didn't I want a baby brother? Wouldn't a baby sister be sweet? I didn't understand; I had Will. *He* was my brother.

In the morning he went off to school; I didn't like that much. I always felt as if I didn't even breathe when he was gone, as if everything that happened during those long morning hours alone with my mother didn't count for anything.

I did a lot of puzzles—jigsaw puzzles. The Disney ones were my favorite: Minnie Mouse spinning through a cartoon living room with Mickey. I'd sit on the living room floor splay-legged and piece them together, one after another, then dump them out and start over. The house was quiet. Above me, my mother ironed in front of the soap operas. I would always stop playing to watch the opening of "As the World Turns"— that globe spinning through the stars made me feel that all was well.

Every day, after the soap operas were over, my mother painted her toenails while listening to records. The polish remover smelled funny. I would kneel close to her while she used it, sometimes pick up the bottle and sniff it. She'd slip two tissues from a box, fold them neatly into strips and weave them in and out of her toes before she painted each toenail, carefully, deep red.

She played only three records, over and over. I knew every word of the songs; I lip-synched to them in front of the big mirror in the hall. I rolled my eyes and clasped my hands helplessly while I sang with Peggy Lee: "My Man." "He makes me blue, he beats me too, what can I do?"

I made my voice low and gravelly for "Whatever Lola Wants, Lola Gets." But what I loved most was imitating Marilyn Monroe.

"I wanna be loved by you, just you, nobody else but you . . . I wanna be loved by you alo-wo-wone, poopoo-pee-doo, whoo!" I lay on my back and pointed my toes and waved my legs in the air. I can't imagine where I learned to do that. All I knew was that grown-up ladies did it. I didn't know why; it didn't seem like much fun. I wasn't so sure I ever wanted to be a grown-up, especially a mother.

One morning I woke to find Mrs. Vertullo from down the street standing over my bed. "Your mommy and daddy have gone to the hospital to pick out a new baby brother for you," she said.

I liked being with Mrs. Vertullo. She said good morning, and told me what we were having for lunch, and asked me what kind of game I was playing. I thought it was funny that she would talk to me so much.

After a few days my parents came home. I saw our car drive up, and I ran to the front window. My father helped my mother out of the car; they came slowly up the walk and in the front door. They were empty-handed. They didn't speak a word.

Mrs. Vertullo went home, and the house was quiet again.

It was even quieter than before, because though my mother still watched soap operas, she didn't listen to her records anymore. She lay around all day, and forgot to feed me lunch. My father had to make our dinner when he came home from work.

Then one day she vacuumed. I was terrified of the vacuum; it was large and noisy and dusty, and things disappeared into it. Whenever she vacuumed, I hid, but this time I couldn't seem to get away from her; she went from room to room furiously, doing over the same room she had just finished. Back and forth she went through the house, from one end to the other, and I finally ended up squatting in the corner of the kitchen with my hands over my ears, crying, watching her shove furniture out of the way and plunge the vacuum into every corner. She didn't stop even when Will came home from school. He watched her for a while, then he took me to our bedroom, closed the door, and had me sit on his bed and play "Chutes and Ladders" with him. Every few minutes the door slammed open and my mother came in banging the vacuum hard against the bedstead, as she got down on her hands and knees to shove the vacuum under the bed.

My mother didn't stop vacuuming until it got dark and my father came home from work and made her stop. He told my brother to fix us peanut butter sandwiches for dinner, and he led my mother by her elbow into their bedroom. Will let me eat my sandwich in front of the TV, then told me to go to bed even though I hadn't had my bath.

Late that night I woke; the blackness around me was filled with a blood-curdling wailing. I thought it was our dog; I thought he was dying. "Moffy!" I screamed, and ran to the bedroom door, but Will's voice rang out. "Stop it, Brenda! It's not Moffy!"

I'd never heard him sound so scared; I was afraid to ask him what was making that noise. I hid under the covers though my fast hot breath was making it too stuffy under there. I heard the phone ring a few times, then I slept, and in the morning Mrs. Vertullo was there again, getting Will ready for school. I was glad that I was going to spend the whole day with Mrs. Vertullo, but at lunchtime my father came home with Will, and had us pack up our clothes. He let me put mine in my mother's fancy makeup case. I packed quickly because I was afraid he would change his mind.

We drove to Aunt Iris and Uncle Vic's and left Will there, and I felt sorry for him because they pinched cheeks, hard, when they said hello, and called you a big baby if your eyes teared. It seemed that they only laughed when they had played a joke on someone that really wasn't a funny joke at all.

My father left me with my great aunt Josephine. She met us out on the porch, thin and thin-haired and smiling in her tight-lipped way, and they talked above me while I pushed the heavy porch swing back and forth. Then my father drove away, leaving me on the front porch of that huge dark musty house in Salem, Massachusetts.

HIGHWAY 40, EAST

33 I SWING OFF the Greyhound in Tucson and there is James; I know it must be him although I only saw him a couple of times running a forklift at the apple distributor's and couldn't remember exactly what he looked like. He is skinny and long-haired, wearing an oversized fatigue jacket with no shirt, leaning against a station wagon packed to the gills, a bright orange U-Haul trailer hooked behind. He's parked right where the buses pull in, and already a harried station worker is heading toward him.

"Hey, righteous, cool it, I'm on my way out," he's telling him as I walk up. Then, "Brenda! Sugar Face, Saving Grace, let's blow this state." He opens the door for me, and I hoist in my pack and then myself.

"What *is* all this junk?" I ask him. The back of the station wagon is crammed with Mexican border town garbage: black velvet paintings of Jesus in agony, and Elvis in agony, plaster skulls, dozens of piñatas already sunbleached and beat up, leather belts tooled with MEXICO, studded with fake turquoise.

"Cool, huh?" he asks. "The U-Haul's full of this stuff, too."

"But, why?"

"They'll pay a fortune for this stuff back East." His grin spreads even wider. "I'm gonna trade West Coast junk for East Coast junk."

I laugh and shake my head.

"Righteous," he says, and pushes back his long, wet-looking

hair. He starts the car with a broken-muffler roar. "Gotta get our grub," he says.

"When are we leaving?"

"Leaving? We've *left*. We've left, and this car stops for gas and nothing else until we hit D.C."

"Oh, jesus, James. I've just spent thirteen hours on my butt in a Greyhound bus getting here. I thought I was going to have some time to recuperate."

"Nope. This is the cruisemobile, and we're cruising. As of now." He goes just a half a block before he pulls into a Safeway parking lot, brakes, pulls out his key, and is out his door in one movement. Almost before I realize it, he's halfway across the parking lot. I sigh and follow him into the store.

He runs down an aisle and whips up a loaf of bread without breaking his stride, then swings down another aisle. He seems to have a master plan here, so I leave him and amble over to the produce section.

"What kind of apples are these?" I ask the produce man. "I mean, what grower?"

"Beats me," he says, but heads toward the cooler, so I follow him. James comes out of nowhere, and jogs past without stopping or even looking at me, on his way to the apples.

The produce man pushes open the swinging door and I follow him in. "All kinds," he says. "Sunny Maid, Red Rooster, Cold Hills. We get every kind there is in here." Boxes are stacked from floor to ceiling, but I don't see that familiar label.

"You ever get any Juan-of-a-Kind?"

"Nope. Never heard of them."

When I come out of the cooler, James is at the cash register, signaling to me. All he has on the counter are the loaf of bread, a jar of peanut butter, and a carton of milk.

"MaryEllen told me you used to cashier at one of these places," he says when I get to the register.

"*Did* you?" the young cashier asks me. She looks like she's straight out of high school. "*Where?*"

She seems so interested. I remember those quiet times when there were few customers, and I actually had a chance to speak to anyone about anything. How precious that was.

"San Diego."

"Really?" she asks.

"Did they have all those brands of cigarettes lined up behind you like they have here?" James asks.

"Sure." I shrug.

"Oh, these," the cashier says, running her fingernail along the variety of boxes. "Sure are a lot of them, aren't there?"

"Well, you have a nice day, now." James winks at her. "What'd you say your name was? Lacy? Crystal? Desiree?'"

She giggles, gives him an oh-you-kidder wave of her hand. "I told you, *Nancy.*"

Outside, James opens the ice freezer, pulls out a bag of ice, and puts it in the grocery bag, though I hadn't noticed that he'd paid for ice at the register.

He unlocks and opens the U-Haul door, and I don't know what's keeping all that border town junk from tumbling into the parking lot. All the same kind of stuff is crammed in there, along with a stand-up cooler. He dumps the ice in the basket at the bottom of the cooler, sets the carton of milk on a tray. The other two trays are scattered with aluminum foil packets. They look like a bunch of leftovers. That would be just like James to bring a bunch of leftovers all the way across country.

Back in the car, he unzips his jacket. Apples and bags of M & M's tumble out.

"Righteous," he says, "the way you distracted that produce guy and that chick at the register. Really righteous."

"James," I whine. "*Don't* do that to me. Don't make me an unwilling accomplice to your crimes."

"Cool," is all he says, and smiles. He thinks I'm kidding.

He pulls a butter knife out of the glove compartment, wipes it on his pants, then begins spreading the bread with peanut butter, laying the pieces side by side on the front seat.

"We don't stop for food. Not rest-au-rank food. Milk we restock on at gas stations." He licks his fingers, picks up the receipt. "Two sixty-five. That's, one thirty-three you owe me. And, let's see, apples, about, oh, eight cents apiece . . . twenty-four, three times fifteen for the M & M's, forty-five plus twenty-four is sixty-nine, and one thirty-three . . . uh, two . . . oh two. And three seventy for gas. Uh, uh, five seventy-two."

He's looking right at me as if waiting, as if he doesn't want to keep a list the length of the trip, so I dig around in my pocket and pull out a five and a one. He stuffs it in his own pocket and doesn't mention change. He goes back to spreading peanut butter.

"You can give me the twenty-eights cents later," I tell him.

"Righteous. Now, we don't stop for anything but gas. If you gotta pee, and we're not due to get gas, pee in a cup and throw it out the window."

"That's easy for you to say." I laugh uneasily. I'm not so sure he's kidding.

When half the loaf is spread, he clamps a plain piece down on each buttered one, and packs the sandwiches back into the bag.

"Fourteen sandwiches," he says. There is one heel left. He rips it in two, stuffs half in his mouth and hands the other half to me. "Fourteen sandwiches, six apples, six bags of M & M's. So you have seven sandwiches, three apples, three bags of M & M's to split up over the twenty hours however you want."

The twenty hours. The words sit before me like a billboard. *"What* twenty hours?" I ask, though I know what his answer will be.

"The twenty hours it'll take us to get to D.C."

"James, you're crazy. I've been across this country a few times; there's no way you can make it in twenty hours. Look, where's the map?"

He pulls it out. "Oh-fficial Triple-A U.S. Map. Check it out." He points to a square on the mileage/time reference chart. "Albuquerque to Washington, D.C., thirty-seven hours and eight minutes. And those estimates are for old farts with pea-bladders wobbling along at fifty miles an hour. Now, look," he points to the map, "I drive to El Paso by four a.m., you take us to the border of Texas by ten, then I hop the cruisemobile onto United States Interstate Number Four-oh and we don't stop until we've pulled into the garage at the White House. 'Ger-*ald!*' I'll say. 'How's that slice?' Righteous. Let's jet." He starts up the car and off we go. "Now, Bren, we drive six-hour shifts. Six driving, six keeping the driver company, six driving, six sleeping, six driving, seventy miles an hour, two days, and righteous, I'll be rollin' in my sweet baby's arms."

We marathon drive. James likes to talk, but I don't encourage it. If I hear the word *righteous* one more time I'm going to jump out the door even if I splat on the pavement like all the bugs splatted on the windshield.

At two in the morning, I ask him if it's ok if I sleep for the two hours before my shift is supposed to start.

"Yeah, now you mention it, we really should start out with the passenger-sleep-shifts first."

"*Now* you decide that."

I wake up groggily to find us stopped at a gas station, James pumping gas. The gas station lights are all the more stark for the desert blackness around us. I sit up, thinking I'd better go to the women's room while I have a chance. I wonder if I'm going to need a key. I don't see an attendant anywhere. Maybe he's cleaning the bathrooms.

Suddenly, James throws open his door, cranks the ignition,

jerks the car into gear and we're rolling before he even picks up his foot or closes his door. We bounce across a gravel area, flinging gravel and dust, then bump onto the pavement, the trailer swaying wildly behind us.

James slams his door. "Whoo-ee!" he hoots.

I cover my face with my hands. "God damn, James." I look back at the station. Still no one in sight, but the attendant will only need to catch the slightest peek at us from a distance in order to identify us, a goddamned station wagon pulling a bright orange U-Haul trailer down an empty desert road.

"Righteous! Eight sixty worth of gas. You owe me four thirty."

"How about this for an idea, James. Next time you decide to pull a stunt like that, *I'll* go in search of the attendant myself, and I'll pay the whole eight fifty."

"Eight sixty."

"Eight sixty. God damn, James. I want to get to the East Coast. I don't want to be spending Christmas Eve in jail in New Mexico. I don't want to be spending Christmas Eve in jail anywhere. For your future reference."

James grins at me. "Four thirty, darlin'."

I pull out another five. "Now you owe me a dollar."

"I'm keeping track. And it's ninety-eight cents."

An hour later, an hour that I haven't slept through, it's my turn behind the wheel. I tense up at every set of headlights that comes up behind us, thinking what a fool, what a conned sitting duck I am; I'm going to be stopped, and blamed; I'm going to end up in jail.

We speed over the state line; I've never been so happy before to enter Texas. I still have an hour left on my driving shift. I'm tired from lack of sleep, and exhausted from worry, but I'm relieved; the driving's easier now.

After a half-hour, I stop for gas. I wake up James so he can stretch his legs and pee.

"Where are we?" he mumbles, scratching his tousled head as he shuffles across the blacktop toward the men's room.

"In Texas already. You're owed a little more sleep before your shift."

Back in the car, James crashes to sleep in the same position he left, almost as if he hadn't gotten up at all. I keep glancing at him as I pull around a detour and back onto the freeway. I try to imagine who would love him. Obviously, his girlfriend that he is on his way to pick up and bring back to Tucson. Katrina is only a junior in high school, and from what I can tell, what's going to happen is a ladder-to-the-second-story-window elopement, without the eventual marriage. The closer I pull Katrina to us, the more I worry about her. I feel like an accomplice in another one of James's crimes.

Already the sun is high enough in the sky to not shine in my eyes anymore. That's a relief. Driving into the desert sun is miserable, even in winter.

I roll along for a long stretch before a jolt runs through me at the sign, Welcome to New Mexico, Land of Enchantment.

New Mexico. New Mexico! It finally gets through my dazed mind that I've been heading *west* for the last half-hour, that I'm back in arrest territory, that I've added at least an hour of useless driving to our neverending trip. If James wakes up now I can expect anything to happen. And the next place I can turn around is god-knows-where.

I drive and I drive, feeling like I'm driving myself right into some copper's waiting arms. The sun behind me glares on parallel lines that run on through the desert forever with no breaks or crossings or cloverleaf bridges. How could I have been so stupid to be glad when the sun was *behind* me? I drive and I drive and I drive. How ridiculous and helpless I feel, pressing the accelerator pedal, speeding us in the wrong direction.

Ok, I think, calm down. We haven't gone that far. It's never as long as it seems. Check the odometer. There'll be a turn-around spot in a mile or two. It'll just *feel* like ten.

Ten miles later there's still no turnaround in sight. I take my foot off the gas, slow down to almost a stop. James stays dead asleep.

The median looks a little tricky. There might be a little drainage ditch, foot or so deep, at the bottom. Hard to tell. But I'm not going any farther in the wrong direction; I know that much.

There are no cars nearby. I ease off the pavement and down the slope. Bumpy, but so far so good.

Then I'm heading uphill, breathing easier. Until I feel the trailer catch on something, see the word "U-Haul" tip past the rearview mirror, hear the crashing sound of all that junk shifting and falling inside the trailer. I take my foot off the pedal. The trailer stops in its half-tipped position, doesn't go all the way over.

"MY DRUGS!" James screams, and I jump so violently that my head hits the ceiling. He's sitting up, facing the back window, his face ashen. "My drugs, oh sweetjesus help me, my drugs, my drugs."

Of all the reactions I expected from him, this was not one of them.

He throws open his car door, falling to the grass and scrambling on all fours to the trailer like a crazed madman. "My drugs! My drugs!"

The cooler is tipped over and when he opens its door, I see that the aluminum foil packages are floating in the ice and water at the bottom. He pulls the packages out, and they're labeled, jesus, they're *labeled*: MDA, 10 grams; coke, 6 grams; psilocybin mushrooms, 1 lb.; LSD (windowpane), 150 tabs. James is shaking the water from the packets, laying them out in a row on the bumper, opening them, exposing their contents right out here on the median of a New Mexican freeway, and cars in both directions are beginning to slow down.

"James, for god's sake, look what you're *doing* here." But he doesn't look what he's doing, he doesn't see anything but the drugs in his trembling hands.

"Oh," he moans. "My drugs. I was going to trade all this for the best junk." Now I realize what kind of *junk* he was talking about when he mentioned earlier trading West Coast junk for East Coast junk.

A westbound pickup truck, back full of gawking kids, pulls over, stops, and a short-haired Good Samaritan cowboy gets out, brotherly concern all over his face.

"James, jesus, look, will you?" I start tossing the packets into the jumble of Mexican stuff, but James grabs both my shoulders and shoves me away.

"Keep your cotton-pickin paws off *my drugs,* Brenda Bradshaw!" I look up at the cowboy. I can't tell if he's heard that or not. He's clomping closer.

A big eastbound rig pulls over, kicking up gravel and dust. As calmly as I can make myself appear, I pull my pack out of the car and run toward the rig.

The driver has hopped out of his cab. "It's nothing," I say. "Tow truck's already coming. Can I get a ride with you?"

"Sure," he says, then puts his hands on his hips and looks confused.

"I, uh, I was just riding with him, and uh, he's not such a nice guy. You know."

"Oh, all right then, hop on in."

I'm not a good liar, in fact, I'm a horrible one, and now I sit next to this good-natured salt-of-the-earth trucker feeling like a scummy criminal.

The truckdriver, Mark, is going all the way to Philadelphia. Hour upon hour he pulls the road beneath us in a big generous roaring way. He's one of the world's steady-Eddies. He doesn't talk much; he chews gum and doesn't offer any to me. I know he'll be glad to give me some if I ask for it. I can tell that he's big on Live and Let Live.

He pulls Amarillo past us, then Oklahoma City, Little Rock, Memphis. Somewhere along there we stop at truckstops for lunch and dinner. We talk a little then, about family, about food, pleasant small-talk to pass the time. Just outside of Nashville, around midnight, he pulls into a truckstop motel. "I believe in the idea of sleep, myself," he says.

"Is it ok for me to stay in the cab? I have my bag with me."

"Ok by me. You can use my room to clean up in after I'm done in the morning."

I sleep well, high and safe in that miniature motel room. In the morning I'm wakened by Mark's light rap on the door. He hands me the motel door key without a word; I take a quick good hot shower. We're off as the sun begins to rise on the road; we head up into the snowy Appalachians. The day flies by. I don't need anything, and Mark needs nothing from me. Not even pleasant conversation. The sun rides across the whole blue expanse of sky, and sets again; we keep riding on through the night.

I fall asleep and wake up when Mark jiggles my shoulder. "End of the line," he says. I sit up, rub my face and eyes hard. We're in a lot, brightly lit with eerie yellow buzzing lights, behind a huge warehouse, other rigs lined up around us, a few of them pulling away or pulling into place. He gets out, so I do too, on shaky legs. I pull my pack down, shoulder it, then just stand in the parking lot for a long while trying to get oriented. I see Mark walking away.

"Mark! Thanks a lot."

"Don't mention it. My pleasure."

I stand there, just stand there, for what seems like forever. I'm somewhere in or close to Philadelphia; I know that much. I take a few steps, stop, turn, walk in the other direction.

I don't even know how to get out of this lot, never mind know where I'm going to go next. Then I see Mark walking toward me.

"You need a place to sleep? Security guard says you can sack out on the couch in one of the lunchrooms, just for tonight, if you leave by seven."

"Great. Thanks."

I follow him through a maze of hallways. "See you," he says, as the security guard shows me into a lunchroom with about ten tables and a couch.

"I'll wake you by seven. Don't get into any trouble, little lady."

I plunk down on the couch. The guard's footsteps fade down the hall and all seems well. Two days before Christmas. I'm healthy, I'm not in jail. And I'm only four hundred miles from Sean and MaryEllen, and from my brother Will.

Suddenly I laugh out loud. Poor James, whatever happened to him? He didn't even know he was heading the wrong direction, in New Mexico, yet. I stretch my tired muscles gratefully along the length of the couch. And Katrina. Katrina right now must be in her own bed, safe and sound under her parents' roof. I suppose it was me who did that, without even trying, who saved Katrina so much heartache. Maybe I have, probably I have. Hopefully I have.

34 A BIG green-and-brown camouflaged army truck honks, pulls onto the shoulder, and stops. I look around. It certainly can't be stopping for me. I turn my back to it, stick out my thumb again. Two, three insistent honks blast out. The truck's reverse lights come on, it backs up to where I'm standing.

I open the door.

"Hop on in, and welcome!" The driver looks too young to be in the army, too frail to be handling a big truck like this. He barely looks old enough to have a driver's license; out on the street, I'd have guessed him fifteen, tops.

I say, "I didn't know army trucks could pick up hitchhikers. Civilians."

" 'Scuse me, ma'am, but I'm a member of the United States Marine Corps, and I can do whatever I *damned* well please, 'scuse the French, ma'am."

At least, that's what I think he's said. His Southern accent is as thick as blackstrap molasses.

I climb in gingerly. Something's not right.

"I'm Brenda."

"Randy, ma'am." He offers his hand; his handshake is tight and tiny and remarkably sweaty. "Randy Lipkiss."

I nod to him, then turn to the window to hide my smile. Randy Lip Kiss? "Where're you headed?" I ask.

"Headed to my mama's for Christmas. I hate the North, I hate the damned Yankees, and I hate the goddamned marines. 'Scuse my French."

I don't know what to say to that. We rumble along for a long while, then I offer, "I'm from California." His look lets me know that as far as he's concerned, if you're not from the South, you're a Yankee.

We stream under a big freeway sign. Boston: 239 miles. I take in a big breath, sigh it out, and smile.

Suddenly, Randy slams his fist on the dashboard. "Damn! I ain't never gonna make it home with only this much gas."

"Where're you supposed to get gas on these long trips?"

He screws up his mouth at me like I'm stupid.

"Oh, I guess at a marine base, huh? Or if they're letting you use a truck to get home in, do you have to buy the gas yourself?" I'm thinking, yeah, here's the shakedown. He's going to want money to buy gas.

"I don't think I can exactly pull this sucker into a Texaco station now, can I? 'Cause they didn't 'xactly let me use the truck to get home in. They didn't even give me leave to go home."

"Ran-dy!" I whistle. "You're AWOL?"

"That's what they call it. Away With Out Leave."

"Absent without leave, Randy. I was brought up in the air force."

"AWOL, either way. I'm gonna eat right and sleep right for the first time in five weeks where I ain't considered a stupid redneck."

"And you stole this truck? You stole a U.S. Marine truck?"

"Borrowed it. Just to get home in, now. I'm bringin' it back."

I sit there and let it sink in for a while. AWOL. AWOL in a stolen United States Marine vehicle. It's kind of funny in a way. I wonder how much trouble I'll get into if we get stopped. Doesn't seem likely that anything will happen to me. Randy, on the other hand . . .

"You must be really homesick."

"I miss my mama so much I can't stand it no more." He has tears in his eyes.

I want to stop at a phone booth, call up the marines and say, hey, remember that enlistee, Randy Lipkiss? Well, it was just a joke. Just a bad mistake. Then I want to take him by the hand and not let go until I deposit him on his mama's doorstep.

"Where's home?" I ask him.

"Waycross, Georgia!"

"But where's your mom now?"

He eyes me suspiciously. "I don't know anything about what kinda crazy ideas you Californians have, way out there in that land of *fruits* and *nuts,* but where I come from, home is where your mama is."

I sit for a while and puzzle over this, wondering what cultural bridge I have to cross before I can understand why he's driving north on his way to Waycross, Georgia. And then I remember: Welcome to New Mexico, Land of Enchantment.

"Randy, Randy, Randy," I say in mock exasperation. "You're going the wrong *way*. You're headed *north*." I laugh. "You're getting deeper into Yankee territory by the minute."

"Are you shittin' me?" he yells. His face has flushed instantly. "You're shittin' me? Jesus Fuckin' H. Christ," and sudden beads of sweat form on his upper lip and forehead, he gets a fevered look in his eyes, and I realize too late that this isn't a case of homesickness, that this boy is insanely desperate to get to his mama, that nothing will stand between him and his mama; I watch in horror as he stomps his boot on the brake, throws his skinny body onto the wheel trying to get onto the exit ramp that is already past.

"No!" I scream as the weight fishtails behind us, the windows fill with fast white streaks and the whole unstoppable monstrous mass of us skids slick as air on air. We tip in sickening slow motion, my stomach leaps into my chest, and just at the balance point, just as it is really going to happen, jesus, Brenda, it's going to *happen*, the Marlboro Man smiles at me under bright lights, leaning calmly against a barn door, I love him, save me save me oh save me. I shut my eyes to it, and it comes, crashing, ripping metal, wet, wet everywhere, shattering glass my blood screaming my bones screaming heart screaming my head smashed, pressed, compressed. Then the strange silence.

Am I dead? Am I dead? I begin to make out little noises, someone panting, sobbing, me, I think. A window handle turning. A voice, Randy's, saying, "Holy shit." I open my eyes.

White. White! Sparkling white, pristine white, oversized shavings of snow all around me cold and wet, no red at all, no *red*. My head wonderfully uncompresses, I feel an icy scraping across my cheek and turn to see the muddy bottom of Randy's boot disappear through the open window above me.

I'm hanging in my seatbelt, the windshield shattered into icy cobwebs, but still in one piece. My hands are trembling so badly I can hardly undo the seatbelt latch, and just as I do, a body drops through the window into the cab, a bearded bear of a man begins talking to me gently; I am looking straight at him but not seeing him somehow, he asks me questions, This? This? Can I breathe? Can I move? Do I hurt? Can I stand? Through stages I am lifted up to the outside, a spinning group of faces stare at me expectantly. Randy is pacing, kicking the snow, shouting, "They're gonna lock me up and throw away the key! They're gonna forget they ever put me in jail! I ain't never gonna see my mama!" A young couple is following his pacings, shouting over his shoutings, "What's in the truck? Just tell us what's in the truck!" I sink into a trembling mass on the cold snow; the bear man sits beside me, lifts me onto his lap and leans me into him. "Hell, I don't know," Randy finally says. He waves his arms toward the truck. "Shit. Could be a fuckin' A-bomb for all I know."

The couple looks at me. "I don't know either," I say. "He's AWOL. From boot camp. He stole the truck to get home to his mama's for Christmas."

Randy is kicking the snow, spraying it in bright arches around him. "I'll never see the light of day again. Jesus Fuckin' H. Christ."

Up on the road, against a glowing orange dusk, rush hour traffic is slowing with gawkers, but no one else is stopping to help. All the people who did are standing in a semicircle, hands in pockets, watching me and Randy, who is now sitting in the snow, hands clasped behind his neck, head between his knees. They are all waiting for what happens next in an accident, their moment to be important, anxious for it to happen, the sirens, ambulance, mostly waiting to tell their stories, "The whole thing just went into a skid and clipped the billboard . . . ," the police bent over their notebooks, nodding.

"You know," says a man to Randy, "you could run. I mean, hell, I would. Maybe you get back to the base, they haven't even noticed you were missing. I've already forgotten what you look like. If you get what I mean." The other people in the semicircle are all, surprisingly, nodding in agreement.

"Naw," Randy says. He doesn't even look up. His thin voice comes from the depths of his hunched shoulders, his bony hands. "They'd find out. They're gonna throw me in jail and throw away the key. Jesus Fuckin' H. Christ."

It suddenly occurs to me that running is what I should be doing. Having been brought up in the air force, I know I don't want to mess with those military types. They wouldn't be rough or anything; it'd just be all that paperwork involved. I get shakily to my feet. I seem to be ok, really; I walk around and flex things, roll my head around on my neck. I gingerly ask the man who's been caring for me if he'll get my pack out of the cab, which he does. Nothing has happened to it, either.

I walk over to Randy, squat next to him, put my hand on his back, on his uniform which is wet with sweat. "Randy?" I ask. He doesn't answer. "Thanks for the ride. You take care of yourself." I heft up my pack, which seems to weigh tons now. "I really have to go," I say to him. He nods his head, but doesn't look up. I say faint thank yous to the group, then start a slow trudge up the embankment, my boots squeaking in the snow. My legs shake and wobble beneath me until I finally sink down, sucking in the icy air.

"Come on." The bearded man is suddenly beside me, lifting my pack off my shoulders. "The only place you're going is to the hospital."

I hold up my hand, shake my head, too out of breath to answer.

"Oh, come on," he says, goodnaturedly. "My treat, ok? Just come on."

He picks up my pack with one hand, helps me up the hill with the other. The accident is quite a dramatic scene from above: a few small trees knocked flat, snow shaved in a clean swatch past the clipped billboard to the green camouflage truck, lying bent on its side. Beside it, the circle of people, hands in their pockets, looking cold, and in the middle, poor poor Randy Lipkiss, crouched over, crying.

"I'm Danny," the man says as he helps me up into the cab of his refrigerated truck, and hefts my pack up after me. "Here." He hands me his handkerchief. "You've got mud all over your face."

I roll my eyes, shake my head in disbelief. "That's where Randy stepped on me to get out of the window." I wipe at the crusty mud as best I can. "By the way, I'm Brenda. And thanks. Thanks a lot."

"You sure got yourself into a mess," he says, as we rumble down the road.

I shrug. "At least I'm out of it already."

"Not if you've got a concussion, you're not. And I don't suppose you've got any friends around to watch after you."

"I do, as a matter of fact. They're near Boston."

"Good friends, I hope. I mean, Boston isn't exactly spitting distance."

I smile. "Good friends."

He brings me to a hospital emergency room, and of course the first thing they want to know is my financial status. "I'll take care of this," Danny says. "You just call your friends." He disappears into a side room.

Suddenly I feel exhausted, and very alone. My right arm is throbbing like mad. I roll up my sleeve. My arm's coloring up nicely, all right, from being thrown into the truck's metal door. I fill out the endless forms at the front desk. Then I ask, "Is there a pay phone around?" I cover my eyes with my hands. Please, a phone. Sean and MaryEllen. Please; please.

The emergency room is busy. I practically have to push my way through one particular group of panicked people to get to the phone. There are really a lot of upset people sitting around. I dig out my address book, take a deep breath, dial MaryEllen. As the phone rings I start planning what I'll do if there's no answer. I'll be fine. I'll get a cab, a motel room, I'll rest. Everything's ok.

But when MaryEllen's voice answers, I break apart, sobbing the whole story out in one release, listening with a huge hurting lump in my throat as MaryEllen calmly reassures, "We'll be right there. We'll just put on our coats, and we'll be right there." This is of course, not exactly right, I realize after I hang up; they are hours away. I drop myself onto a couch in the waiting room.

When I leave the examining room, Danny is waiting for me. "Doc says I'm fine."

"You'll live to make more mischief, huh?"

I laugh. I pull my wad of money out of my pocket. "I don't know if I'm going to have enough, but I promise I'll send the rest if you'll give me your address."

Danny holds up his hands, puts them behind his back. "I told you, my treat. How often does a person get to be a hero? And two days before Christmas, too?"

"Can you just give me your address?"

"Sure," he smiles. "I'm Danny. I'm from Chicago. You can remember that, right?"

I just smile at him for a while, stand with my hands in my pockets, rocking back on my heels. "Yeah. I won't forget you."

"Fine. So you're okay, right? And did you get ahold of your friends?"

"Yes. They're on their way. You've got to get going, don't you?" Every time the emergency doors open, I can hear the refrigeration unit on his truck in the parking lot rumbling away.

He stands for a while with his mouth skewed up in indecision.

"Your friends are coming. Are you sure?" He eyes me suspiciously.

"Danny, I'm sure."

"And you're going to be ok?"

"Because of you, I am, Danny."

"Ok, Brenda." He raises his hand with a sad smile on his face. "Bye."

"Bye." I watch him as he plods out the door and across the parking lot to his truck.

I walk back to where my pack is propped against a couch, and plop down gratefully. It's going to be a long wait.

After a minute I realize that I'm in the midst of people who are waiting for news about someone named Jonesy. I pick up that he was in a car accident, I pick up that it was Jonesy's fault. On the circle of couches next to our circle, sit the friends and relations of the person Jonesy hit. The two groups exchange weighted looks as they pace and sit and talk. A man comes out from the back and joins our group. He is pale, drawn, his skin actually a little gray. "His arm is off," he says. "He had it out the window when the car rolled. They're trying to save it."

"Jesus," a woman says, and starts crying into the chest of the man sitting next to her.

We begin our long wait, with time stretching and contracting. I am bound up in the energy clutching this group of people on these couches and chairs; I'm worried sick about Jonesy's arm.

I get up after a while, pace the room, go in the bathroom and pee. In the mirror, under wobbly fluorescent lighting, I look like the rest of the group, pale. In the canteen I buy a can of beef stew from a machine, heat it in the microwave. It tastes like flavored starch. Jonesy is still in surgery, no word. I'm so involved with this group that when a woman named Marian goes home to put the kids to bed, I wave goodbye to her along with everyone else.

I am so worried about Jonesy that I'm confused, for a second, when I see MaryEllen and Sean sweep in, jovial, joking. They passed the truck on the interstate; it's still there, was that it?

"Omagod, Randy *Lip*-kiss?" MaryEllen shouts. "Really?"

Sean whistles, points to my purple arm. "Really attractive," he says. Right there in the waiting room they wrap me in a blanket they have brought, hot from MaryEllen having held it in front of the floor vent of the Rambler all the way here.

"So, besides that," MaryEllen asks, "you're ok, huh? You know how I always was concerned about that bod of yours." Sean holds a thermos of hot coffee. He knows me. He's pouring a plastic cupful even as we shuffle, the three of us, through dirty slush; there is the Rambler, Sean's good old beat-up Rambler right here in this crazy hospital parking lot. I crawl into its friendly back seat, onto the torn upholstery, and try hard to keep my eyes open and talk a little with Sean and MaryEllen, but it feels so good to give in, to set that cup down on the littered floor, to collapse deep into the cavern between the seat backs as the car rumbles my head, and Sean and MaryEllen mumble in the front, and laugh a little, and mumble some more. And soon I don't even know that I'm flying down the road.

35 ◼ WHEN I WAS fifteen years old my parents moved to San Diego and stayed there, but before that we moved eleven times. The air force was always transferring my dad. We moved from Virginia where I was born, to Massachusetts, Florida, San Francisco, back to Virginia, Washington, Virginia again, Texas, Hawaii, Maryland, Los Angeles, and San Diego.

A few years ago I marked it out on a map. The map was inked all over, criss-crossed. I looked at the map and it suddenly occurred to me that I didn't remember making any of those trips. I had dropped down the East Coast, flown the Pacific twice and made seven full sweeps of the U.S., and I couldn't remember a mile of it.

Later Will told me that every morning that we were traveling, mom knocked me out with her Valium. She called them "motion sickness pills." She always had a lot of Valium around. Other times she called them "muscle relaxants," "sleeping pills," "diet pills." I guess she gave us "motion sickness pills" to keep us from whining in the back seat, the way kids will. Will said he had figured out what they were early on, and just pretended to take them, then he'd lay low and quiet in the back seat and read.

We covered about twenty-six thousand miles. Some of it was in the air, but there were probably twenty thousand miles of pavement that streaked beneath me as I snoozed, as I dreamt it all away.

At night in the motel room, Will would often read to me the exciting parts of the book he'd been reading all day. Will read to me a lot. I had a book of nursery rhymes that I toted around with me everywhere, I even slept with it. I still have it, too. When I read it I can still hear Will's little boy voice. He used to put his heart into those rhymes. This was my favorite:

I had a little nut-tree, nothing would it bear
But a silver nutmeg and a golden pear;
The king of Spain's daughter came to visit me
And all for the sake of my little nut-tree.
I skipped over water
I danced over sea
And all the birds in the air
Couldn't catch me.

36 "WE'RE AT the old homestead," MaryEllen whispers, waking me. "The new old homestead."

I pick myself up groggily, fumbling the blanket around my shoulders, and open my eyes and ears and throat to a different world, that good coast world, heady, clean, thick ocean air, a windy seaside pinging of fittings on a boatmast. I shuffle behind Sean and MaryEllen down a narrow cracked sidewalk, through the gate in a picket fence, up to the door of a scaled-down shingled Cape Cod house, a regular old fisherman's cottage. Inside is one cozy room, half the kitchen area taken up by an ornate footed stove. Everywhere are cubbyholes, windowseats, half-round windows and exposed beams; a narrow, precarious staircase bends around one corner up to a loft that is not much bigger than the mattress and cardboard boxes of clothes and books that are stacked at its foot.

"Pleasant dreams," Sean sings out softly as he and Mary-Ellen head back down the stairs. I lower myself onto the rag rug that's beside the mattress, tangle myself into the blanket and drift back into blissful sleep which I waken from by the pounding of flamenco dancing.

Flamenco dancing. I open my eyes to an eerie shaft of light shining up from the floor, and remember: Sean and Mary-

Ellen's loft. Castanets are clacking, there is a rhythmic stomping, an "Ai, ai ai!" I crawl to the edge of the loft, hang my head upside down. A man and woman are flamenco dancing with great flourish next to the stove; MaryEllen sits on Sean's lap on a kitchen chair, watching.

MaryEllen spots me, smiles, jumps off Sean's lap and jogs over to the stairs.

"I forgot to tell you, Will and Miranda are gone."

"What do you mean, gone?"

"They've split. Gone. Vamoosed. To the other end of the world, if you ask me. Someplace named Creedmoor, North Carolina. To Miranda's parents' house. Hmmm, hmmm, hmmm . . ." She sings, "Come on and marry me, Bi-illl . . ."

I sit up. "You mean, gone, and not coming back?"

"They didn't know you were coming for sure, Brenda. And those two . . . My, my. Little lovebirds. Believe me, you wouldn't want to have been around them anyway. Disgusting," she says as she goes back down the stairs.

"They're gone," I say out loud, as I drop back onto the rug. It doesn't matter; nothing matters but sleep. The castanets speed up impossibly. There could be an elephant show going on down there; Will and Miranda could have blasted off to the moon; now there is nothing so important as sweet sleep. I nestle into the rumbling rag rug and grab that sleep again, grab that sleep; it's so so easy.

37 🖼 I SLEEP my way through the night and the next day and most of the next night and day, and then it's Christmas Eve and we head out to a Christmas Eve party.

"This is going to be wild," Sean says. We're in the Rambler on our way to somewhere on the Cape. The party is at Rage's house; he's another overeducated welder, a workmate of Sean's, who plays guitar in a band called Zog Agog. The band is going to be there, playing frenzied rock versions of Christmas carols. MaryEllen and Sean have sprayed their hair green for the event, and they're wearing red clown noses. I've got on a gold bowler I've borrowed from MaryEllen.

The party is wild, the room hot with sweaty bodies dancing to "We Three Kings," the line "field and fountain, moor and mountain," being repeated in a chorus again and again and again until the whole room is jumping to it, me too; a picture falls off the wall and shatters, seconds later, the Christmas tree falls over. Rage has his shirt off and is dancing around with his guitar, his sweaty chest tangled with flashing tree lights, and the drummer is swinging his arm full reach, slamming his drums with a plastic pink flamingo. I dance out of control until I'm about to fall. People in a wild frenzy are destroying the Christmas tree now, draping each other with lights and garlands and ornaments. I reach up. My head is covered with tinsel. I don't know where the bowler went.

I dance into the kitchen and find Sean and MaryEllen there. Their red noses are gone. The music stops, and Rage comes straggling in out of breath, plugs his string of lights into the outlet next to the refrigerator, opens the refrigerator door. He takes out a carton of orange juice, slugs the whole thing down.

When he's done, Sean introduces him to me.

"Ah!" he says. "Ah! A California girl! Um . . . Come here, California girl, I have someone you need to meet." He puts his arm around my shoulders, unplugs himself, and leads me from one room to the next, searching. "I've just met him myself, tonight. He's just visiting, too. And you two," he says solemnly, "belong together. Ahm, there he is." My eye catches onto this beauty of a boy across the room; I am hot with blushing by the time we reach him. "Maine," says Rage, "meet California. California . . . Maine."

There's a strange thing that happens to me only in the absolute heights of lovemaking: my jaw becomes electrical. But here is this boy just *smiling* at me, and my jawline is short-circuiting. I have to reach up and rub its length with my knuckles.

We are staring at each other, not saying anything, grinning wide-eyed for the longest time. I'm holding both his hands though I don't know how or when that happened. He reaches up, brushes my hair back onto my shoulders, runs his electrical thumb along my bottom lip. "Yes?" he suddenly asks, and when he kisses me, I almost fall over. We kiss and kiss, smile and kiss. "Yes?" I ask him, and he starts to laugh, and I start to laugh. He grabs my hair in two big bunches, draws my face to his oh deliciousness we kiss and kiss, laugh some more. I touch the corners of his lips with my fingers, my tongue, lips, I kiss his chin, his Adam's apple, I simply must kiss this man's Adam's apple, nothing in the world could keep me right now from kissing this man's Adam's apple, the tender hollow next to it; he brushes my cheek with his fingers, with his lips, we rest our forearms on each other's shoulders and stare at each other some more. People push their way around us; it doesn't matter, we kiss and kiss, I could drown in these kisses, be buried in these kisses. "Yes?" he asks when we stop for air, and he takes me by the hand, both of us laughing and laughing, down the hall, the hall is too long, I have to stop him, push him to the wall, kiss him some more, we have been too long apart. "We can use Ernest's room," he whispers to me, backs me into a room, shuts the door and oh my Maine boy, where did you ever learn to do that? And *that?* I want to run my tongue on every inch of his sweet skin, there is licking and biting, sucking, teeth on hipbone. He sees my purpled arm, groans in sympathy, presses his lips to the bruise, then moves his mouth onto mine. A bead of sweat tickles down my chest to my belly, and there's no laughing now. No laughing.

Oh, no laughing. Then, slowly, I am realizing the room around me, my breathing slowing, I am spinning in a languid descent back into the world, the room; I hear party noises outside.

He is here again now, back in the real world, kissing me again; I reach for his hands, rub them on my slick thighs, and we settle, melting slowly together into sleep.

I wake to a tapping at the door. "Jack! My Maine man! You in there?"

He clears his throat. "Oh, yeah, yeah."

"You're Jack," I say to him, and he whispers, "Yes," and kisses me.

"Listen, bud," says the voice through the door, "I hate to break up the party, but we've really gotta take off."

"I'll just be a minute." He looks at me. "I hate having to do this. I hate having to go."

He turns on the bedside light, which is luckily a dim one. While he dresses, I pull on my shirt and underpants, but stop there and sink back onto the bed. I'm feeling wonderful. I don't want to leave the room.

"Beauty," he says to me. I sit up. He brushes my tangled hair off my face, stares sweetly into my eyes, at my lips. "Merry Christmas," he says. Then he is gone, and I am crawling back into my bed, my chest vibrating hugely with a satisfied sigh.

"Jesus, it's Brenda," I hear MaryEllen say. I open my eyes to Sean and MaryEllen's silhouettes in the doorway. There is still some party action going on behind them. "We decided you left hours ago with that guy you were so shamelessly dryfucking in the hallway, tsk, tsk. Move over. So was that the love of your life? And where'd he go, already?"

"He's gone back up North to no doubt make some woman in Maine very, very happy." I sigh, contentedly. "Naw, he's not the love of my life. Well, maybe in the fourth dimension."

MaryEllen takes off her pants and flings herself into the bed next to me. For a second, I'm startled: I'd forgotten about the green hair. "I am *exhausted,*" she announces. "Ernest went home with the woman next door and said we could sleep in his room, thank god. I couldn't drive home now." Sean tiredly drops his pants, shoes, pulls his shirt over his head of green hair, crawls into bed on the other side of me.

"Night, M.E.," he says. "Night, Brenda."

"Sean!" says MaryEllen. "I need a smackeroo on my smackeroo."

They kiss over me, then plunk down heavily. We tangle our limbs together and fall asleep.

A bright light shines in my eyes; I am *so* tired of being woken. "Go away," I say. "Let me sleep." In a second I am sitting upright, heart slamming in my chest as I hear a woman's fuzzy voice over a police band radio. When the light, a flashlight, moves to MaryEllen's startled face, I make out in the doorway a huge cop, gun in his holster, his scary voice: "Looks like I hit the jackpot here. A *ménage à trois.*" He slides his flashlight beam back and forth between the three of us, pausing on Sean and MaryEllen's green heads. "One earthling and two aliens. Very kinky."

Sean leaps out of bed, and with two large steps the cop is in the room, has flung Sean face down onto the bed, and is snapping handcuffs on. "You wanta just cool down, son? I'd ask you to keep your pants on, but it looks like I'm too late for that."

"What the fuck is going on?"

"You're under arrest for disturbing the peace. Where's your pants?"

MaryEllen surprises the hell out of me by starting to cry; I wish she wouldn't because I'm right on the very edge of crying myself. My heart is banging around in my chest. The cop is *big* and has a *gun,* MaryEllen and I are half-naked and Sean is in handcuffs. I see another cop leading another guy in hand-cuffs down the hall.

The cop moves out to the hall, shouts, "Officer Layton? Couple of ladies in here," then says to us, smiling nastily, "and a gentleman. On Christmas Eve, my my my." Sean has finally managed to maneuver his pants and shoes on, and the cop starts to lead him away.

"Hey! You mind if I get my shirt on? It's a little cold out-side."

The cop drapes Sean's shirt over his shoulders. "They brought the whole goddamned SWAT team," Sean shouts to us from the hallway.

"Officer Layton will be here for you ladies in just a minute. Don't go away," the cop sneers.

"Jesus," MaryEllen says, as we rush to pull on our clothes. A woman cop walks in sheepishly. "Hi there." She closes the door behind her. "My name's Christie, and you didn't hear me say this, but I am really sorry. And Rasmussen out there is a son-of-a-bitch. Are you ready to go?" she asks gently. "You're under arrest for disturbing the peace."

Outside a half-dozen other women are waiting with a male cop. The men have already been taken away. "That's all of them," Christie says. They both sigh and shake their heads as they load us into two police cars. "Helluva way to spend Christmas Eve," he says.

On the way to the station, Christie tells us about the other atrocities the son-of-a-bitch Rasmussen has done, though this one takes the cake, she thinks. *"Handcuffs,"* points out MaryEllen, "he put my boyfriend in handcuffs. It's not ex-actly like Sean was threatening him."

Christie laughs. "Probably thought that was a loaded gun he had in his shorts. Oh, lord," she sighs, "Merry Christmas, ladies."

At the station we are brought to the women's cell. I can

hear the men in the distance chanting, "Cof-fee, cof-fee," then laughing. I hear a voice that I recognize as Rage's shouting, toughly, "Yeah, copper, I'm some kinda bad dude. I disturbed the peace. And you let me outta this clinger, I'm gonna do it again, too."

We in the women's section are in a pretty jovial mood ourselves. This is all such a bad joke, after all. We have to put our personal items in large envelopes, signing the envelopes on a line labeled: Prisoner. We have to take off our shoes and belts, get fingerprinted, go down to the basement one by one to get our picture taken, full-face and profile. They have me hold my number up under my chin. 026359. I smile.

When I get back to the cell, one of the women is crying. Christie is leaning over her. "My mother is going to die if she ever hears about this. She's probably waiting up for me right now. I want to go home."

"Look," Christie says, "can you tell her you're spending the night at a friend's house?"

"Rene, tell her you're at my apartment," one of the women offers.

Christie tells some men who are talking in the hallway to be quiet. She stands on her desk to cover the loudspeaker with a towel, and we all try to not laugh while we listen to Rene lie to her mother, a sweet Christmas Eve lie.

Then all of the paperwork is over, and half of us are seated in the open cell, half in the office; we are drinking coffee, we are all punchy from lack of sleep, giggling over everything. I close my eyes and try to transport myself mentally to where Jack must be, his sweet smooth body comfortably resting in a warm bed. I smile.

"How did this happen anyway?" a woman asks.

"Neighbor called in to complain. Rasmussen went up to the door, paced thirty feet back, and could still hear the stereo. County ordinance on noise control. Thirty feet."

"How could *we* possibly have been disturbing the peace, though? We were in *bed*," MaryEllen says, indicating herself and me.

"Yeah, I guess you should be arresting Rasmussen for disturbing *your* peace." It isn't until the laughter dies down that I realize what she's really said: disturbing your piece.

Rasmussen walks in and everyone gets quiet, Christie shuffling papers around on her desk. He's wonderful, Rasmussen, the cliché bad cop; still, I'm afraid of him. That's real.

"Officer Layton, you want to tell me what these prisoners are doing out of their cell?"

"Well, as you can see, sir, there really isn't room for all of them." She's trying to look confident, somewhat defiant, but she's not carrying it off very well.

What she's said is true, though. There's only one one-person cell here, one bench to sleep on, a seatless john with no handle for flushing. I remember now, having read about that once, that officers have to check through shit for contraband before they flush the toilet from outside the cell. And I'll be damned, there it is, it's really true.

"Well, just make room. I want all the prisoners in the cell."

"Yes, sir," she says, and when he turns his back, gives him a look: son-of-a-bitch.

This is really uncomfortable now. The party's over. Five of the women are sitting sullenly elbow to elbow on the bench, three of us are sitting on the floor. The cell door is closed.

"How long do we have to stay here?" a woman asks.

"I'm afraid until morning. Eight or so. Five, six more hours. We won't be able to get ahold of a judge before that."

We sit there quietly now, shifting. Occasionally we can hear shouting from the men's section of the jail. I feel endlessly weary.

After a while, MaryEllen lets herself out of the cell, which they have at least left unlocked. She leans over Christie's shoulder, they mumble for a while, Christie looking concerned. MaryEllen leaves the room, I hear a toilet flush; when she returns, Christie hands her a cushion off a chair to bring back with her into the cell.

"Whoa," I say. "How do you rate this special treatment? What'd you bribe her with?"

"It's because I'm *pregnant,*" MaryEllen says. "You haven't even noticed?" It's true; when I look closely I see the little half melon.

"You can be a witness at the wedding." I'm still reeling from the pregnancy announcement; now I begin reeling from the wedding announcement. "You're not kidding, are you," I say.

Far off in the men's cells, singing begins: "Silent Night." They begin wailing it as a joke, but soon their voices soften, lower, meld together like a choir. Soon we women join in with our high voices. I reach out, hold onto one of the bars, lean my forehead against its coolness, close my eyes. "Round yon virgin, mother and child, holy infant so tender and mild, sleep in heavenly pe-eace, sle-eep in heavenly peace."

The heavenly peace is shattered by MaryEllen. "Hey! Y'know what? When I was little, I thought the line was: Round, young virgin!" She cradles her own roundness in her hands, throws back her head, stomps her feet, and laughs in that raunchy way of hers.

38 ◪ OUR ARREST CHARGES get thrown out

before they ever get thrown at us. In the jail parking lot, Sean and MaryEllen hold and kiss each other as if they're being reunited after six months of separation in Siberian work camps, not six hours in a small-town jail. We go back to their

house and sleep through Christmas day, get up groggily
Christmas night and manage to cook up a Christmas feast.

The next morning Sean and MaryEllen kidnap me into the
car to take me to my Christmas present. "We've gotten you
something you really *need,*" MaryEllen says.

They stop at a house tucked between a supermarket and a
billboard. A hand-shaped plywood sign posted on the lawn
reads: LADY MADONNA. PALMS READ.

"Here." MaryEllen hands me a twenty. "We figured she
ought to just *know* that you were coming, but we called ahead
anyway. Just in case you're a hard nut for her to crack. Maybe
she won't be able to see through you." She shoves me out the
door. "Go, Brenda!"

I take a few steps, then laughing and shaking my head, turn
back to the car, but Sean is making a fast getaway, backing
the Rambler full speed, flinging gravel. At the end of the drive
he stops, and MaryEllen rolls down her window. "We'll come
back for you when you're fortunate," she yells. They pull
away, leaving me standing stupidly next to the plywood hand,
holding a twenty.

I walk up to the stoop, wipe my feet on the mat. A sign is
tacked to the front door: COME IN. I open the door. In the
vestibule hangs a black velvet painting of the Virgin Mary,
ringed with flashing Christmas tree lights. I stand for a while,
shuffling my feet and clearing my throat. At last I call out a
"hello?"

"Come in," a woman's voice says, close enough to make
me jump. Then there is a click, and I see her illuminated by
the crystal ball before her, an on-line electrical switch in her
hand. I step into the tiny living room. I can just make out a
chair, a couch, a TV on a stand in the corner. The woman is
sitting behind a card table; I sit on the folding chair in front
of it.

She is middle-aged with long dark hair and the expected

gold hoop earrings and bandana. "I am Lady Madonna," she says, with some attempt at mysteriousness in her voice. She smiles at me, then suddenly rocks back in her chair, throws back her head and shrieks, "Customer!"

A sullen, pretty girl of twelve-going-on-twenty pushes in through a swinging door. Even now, in the dead of winter, she is wearing shorts and a Harley-Davidson t-shirt and gold sandals. "Mo-om," she whines, rolling her eyes.

"Customer!" the fortuneteller says again, impatiently, in a tone of voice that every mother uses with every teenaged daughter. The girl reluctantly pushes back through the door, which I can see now is the way to the kitchen, rolling her eyes at me as she does. I can't imagine what this Lady Madonna wants her daughter to do. I want to follow the girl into the kitchen, tell her that whatever it is, she doesn't have to do it on my account. But in seconds she returns carrying a cardboard box that is rumbling and scratching and mewing. "Take a kitten," the fortuneteller says. The girl tips the box before me for a better look. Six, eight kittens, all tumbling around, clawing, screeching.

"I can't take a kitten. I don't live here. I'm just passing through."

"Take a kitten," the fortuneteller insists. "You need the responsibility. It's one of your major problems. You shirk responsibility."

Her daughter sets the box down, lifts out a squalling fat-bellied gray kitten and dangles it before me. It swipes all four paws pathetically in the thin air.

"I'm not taking a kitten."

The fortuneteller sits and stares at me for a while, biting the corner of her lip. I stare back at her. Finally she sighs. "Go ahead," she says to her daughter, who leaves with the box. "You change your mind, you let me know," she says to me. "You need the responsibility."

"Now," she says, in a getting-down-to-business way. She puts her hands flat on the table and smiles at me as if expecting something. I don't know what she wants of me; I think crazily of just asking her, Al? Or *Brenda's Quest?*, but she grabs my hand and begins examining it in the light of the crystal ball. She runs her fingers along the lines, presses the fleshy muscles. "Mound of Venus," she points out to me, and then says, "There is a twin."

I almost jump out of my seat, because Al *is* a twin. There's that twin brother of his, Rolly, who still lives in San Diego. The fortuneteller smiles. My heart is pounding like mad.

"You are a twin," she announces confidently, and I drop back into my seat.

"Oh, no. Not me. This guy, Al. Who I was going to ask you about. He has a twin brother."

"No! You! *You* should have been Al's twin. If you weren't so stubborn. You were stubborn even before you were born." She is explaining this to me in a tone of voice as if I am just stupid, as if anyone could see all of this but me. "You were to be his twin, but you insisted that you wanted to be him, not his brother. And you fought and fought, refusing to give in, and while you were fighting, another boy was happy to step in and be his twin. And they were born. And you were left in limbo. And you're still in limbo. You were lucky to be born at all. By then no one wanted you. Isn't that right?" She leans forward over the ball; the light plays off her face. "Isn't that right?" she demands, and I'm thinking, what a cheap shot, to play off everyone's worst fears. And at the same time, I'm thinking, Will did. Will wanted me.

"You're such a fool." She shakes her head. "You should have been Al's twin." She eyes me with disgust. "Foolish and stubborn and irresponsible," she spits out, in the same way she spoke to her daughter. In fact, I'm sure she's called her own daughter foolish, and stubborn, and irresponsible.

She rocks back in her folding chair, sighs deeply, rubs her forehead: the universal exhausted overworked woman.

"So, what else do you want to know?" she asks, suddenly friendly. I just sit, too muddled to speak or move.

"Love life?" she asks. "Most of you young girls want to know about your love lives."

I just nod my head.

She peers into her ridiculous crystal ball with great concentration. I stifle a snicker but some of it escapes anyway. She ignores it.

"He lives out West," she says. "A place with an Indian name."

"Spo-*kane,*" I say, and I realize that I've whined the word and rolled my eyes just like her daughter did.

"Spokane," she says, as if trying out the sound of it. "No . . . Someplace else."

"Ok," I shrug. "Cheyenne, Wyoming."

"Yeeeeeeesss," she smiles. "That might be. And there are animals."

"He's a cowboy?" I ask, incredulous.

"That might be. Twenty dollars." She clicks off her crystal ball, stands up, takes the bandana off her head. I stand up and pull Sean and MaryEllen's twenty from my pocket and hand it to her.

"Merry Christmas," she greets, as she walks me to the door, though it's the day after.

"G'bye," I answer. I squint at the sunlight. The Rambler is sitting in the driveway like a dream come true, Sean and MaryEllen's faces grinning through the windshield.

"Christmas present number two," MaryEllen starts as I get in.

"Please, MaryEllen," I interrupt, "I don't think I can stand any more Christmas presents of that caliber. You are ever so kind. Thanks but no thanks."

"But this is *your* Christmas present to *us*. Be our witness, ok? We found a justice of the peace working today."

"You're getting married right now?" I ask, delighted.

"Sure, why not?"

Sean starts up the car. "So what's your fortune?" he asks.

"The love of my life is a cowboy in Cheyenne, Wyoming."

He whistles. "No shit. Yippee-yi-yo-ki-yay." And all the way to the wedding we harmonize: "HOME, HOME on the RANGE, where the DEER and the ANtelope PLAY ... where seldom is HEARD, a discouraging WORD, and the SKIES are not CLOUdy all DAAAAAY ..."

39 ▨ SATURDAY MORNING Sean gives Mary-Ellen and me a ride to the Civic Center. There's a show called "The Magnificent Jewels of the World," surprisingly popular, the thing to see in Boston this winter, and MaryEllen has a job for the day hawking programs. She set up the job a couple of weeks ago; there are no openings left now, but I decide to go along to keep her company. Sean's going to the shipyard to put in overtime, worried about cash with the baby coming, I guess.

Sean pulls over to the curb and I've waved goodbye and am across the street before I realize that MaryEllen is not with me. She's opened Sean's door and is sitting on his lap with the softest look on her face; he says something and she laughs and they just look at each other. It feeds my heart to see scenes like that. There I was hurrying along like a blind ant thinking things like; dirty slush, it's *freezing* out, what crowds!, all kinds of useless garbage, and something simple like this happens to set everything straight.

MaryEllen pins her solicitor's license to her coat, then picks up her box of programs from a trailer. There are other hawk-ers, jostling for position, most trying to be among the first to hit the crowds coming from the parking lots. They are yelling things like, "Souvenirs, here!" and "See the Hope Diamond! Over two hundred dazzling photos!" They straddle their heavy boxes of programs, and shove a program into people's faces as they pass by.

We follow the crowds for a few blocks, leaving the other hawkers behind. MaryEllen chooses the perfect spot, giving people enough time to turn the corner of the Civic Center, be shocked by the long line, and, just as they reach her, have it sink in that they'll be standing, cold and bored, for a long, long time.

MaryEllen doesn't set down her box of programs. She hefts it around on her hip. She paces, just a few steps away from the oncoming crowds, so that they have to come to her. She doesn't say a thing about jewels. She sing-songs, not so much like a hawker, but like someone having a great time pretend-ing to be a hawker, "Feel *good* about your*self today!* Help *send* a *girl* through *col*lege." People like that. MaryEllen really does have that kind of look, that spunky All-American look of a girl working her way through college, against all odds. The programs are four dollars, and not only is MaryEllen pulling them out of the box so quickly that they're sticking together, stuffing wads of bills into her pocket, but an occasional person is telling her to keep the change from their fiver. Her box is soon sold out, and we return to the trailer.

Some of the other hawkers follow us back to her selling spot after seeing MaryEllen pick up her second box. It doesn't cut into her business, though. There's a different crowd wait-ing in line now, and this time, MaryEllen unbuttons her coat even in the cold, juts out her rounded belly as best she can, pats it with her wedding-ringed hand, and smiling beatifically, chants, "Line forms here, folks, line forms here. Baby needs new shoes, baby needs new shoes." Some people laugh out loud, charmed. The line *does* form there. The other hawkers, hopelessly yelling, "Nefertiti's crown! Glossy pictures!" eye MaryEllen with disgust. I think she must be used to that by now: people being pissed at her for doing things better than they can.

Lunchtime we go to a diner and get sandwiches. I get a cuppa, MaryEllen asks for water. Our booth has one of those small jukeboxes, still stocked with Christmas music. I throw a dime on the Lennon Sisters' "I'll Be Home For Christmas," to groans and hisses throughout the diner. MaryEllen laughs, dumps bills on the table to count.

"Oh!" She stops counting. "Is this bad luck?"

"Naw," I tell her. "That's in gambling. You never count your money while you're sitting at the table. It's just for playing cards." I'm thinking that I never heard it being bad luck to count money between races at the track. In fact, I did my share of it, standing on the ticket-littered blacktop, shuffling through bills. I add, "It's certainly not bad luck to count money you've *earned.*"

"Sixty-eight dollars," MaryEllen announces. "That's all profit, too. Shit. Are you ready to go? I've got to get back to business."

While she's throwing on her coat, I pull a bus schedule from my pocket. "You go on ahead, MaryEllen. I'm going to take a bus back. You know, it's kind of cold. And boring for me."

She shrugs. "Take my cash back?" she asks.

I sit alone with a refill, flip through the selections on the jukebox. I love jukeboxes like this. I love everything about them, the typewritten cards, the greasy red buttons, the way the metal pages click together. I play a Beatles song, "Long Tall Sally." I listen in on the conversation in the booth behind me. A woman is talking about house slippers.

I take MaryEllen's money back to the house for her, throw it on the table. I myself have only $120 or so to my name. I pull out my money and count it. $112.47. Worse than I thought.

The house is the usual quiet peaceful cave. I pick out a book to read, sit in the windowseat. *Two Years Before the Mast;* I've read this book before. I love this book.

At the end of chapter six are these words: ". . . we continued sailing down the coast during the day and following night, and on the next morning, January 14th, we came to anchor in the spacious bay of Santa Barbara, after a voyage of one hundred and fifty days from Boston."

January 14th. This is the 3rd. *I* could be arriving in Santa Barbara by January 14th, easy. The spacious bay of Santa Barbara, sun setting behind the whalelike humps of the Channel Islands, barely visible in the haze. Cool sand under bare feet.

Out the window, Sean and MaryEllen walk along behind the picket fence, through the gate, up the walk, then burst through the door with cold wind and conversation.

"I'd *sell* them first," MaryEllen is saying to Sean. "I wouldn't have them growing all over the house with no place to *go.*"

"M.E. wants to start a sprout farm," Sean says to me as he takes off his coat, scarf.

"Damn!" MaryEllen pulls a wad of fives and ones from her pocket, adds it to the pile on the table. "That's farm money right there."

Her idea is to grow sprouts in waxed cardboard boxes stacked all over the house, and sell the sprouts to grocery stores and restaurants. "All they need is seeds and water," she explains, "not even any sun." It sounds good to me. It takes five days for sprouts to grow, and I'm sure she'll have a thriving business in a week. I'm remembering the way she used to hammer nails at the sites we worked together: Blam! once to set them, Blam, Blam! to knock them flush.

"God," I say, "now you're going to be hustlin' produce men."

The night turns unusually cold, a record cold, we hear on the radio before we all turn in for the night. The house is drafty, the heating system bad, so when I'm trying to settle in on the couch, chattering under all the blankets and coats I can find, and Sean comes down to say I'd better sleep upstairs, I'm up in a flash. All the heat in this house drifts upstairs.

I settle down on the rag rug next to their mattress, cover myself with the blankets and coats. I have the coats on the bottom of the stack, next to me. I've always liked sleeping under coats.

I'm ready to go back West. Maybe Lucien is back, putting the finishing touches on *Brenda's Quest*. I close my eyes and the ship sails gracefully before me, *Brenda's Question* trailing behind. But then Martin's sullen face flashes up, and I jump.

I shake his picture out of my head. Al. I'll think of Al. I remember the way his eyes can look so innocent, and his smooth lips so wicked, at the same time. I remember how he'd said, all those years ago when I stood in the doorway of his basement apartment, "I want to marry *you*." Then, for some odd reason I get a picture in my head of a scene that happened way back in high school. I'd spent lunch with Al in the art room, next to a huge papier mâché sculpture of a woman. Al was fighting tears while we talked. I reached out and held his hand. He'd thought Gloria, who was his girl-friend at the time, was going to marry him, but now he knew he was losing her.

The bell rang. I followed Al outside, and there was Gloria. She didn't see Al.

I was only a sophomore then; I was just a girl. Al was a senior. I remember distinctly the look on Al's face when he walked up to Gloria, and I remember distinctly the thought that occurred to me at that moment: Al is a man. He reached up and put his hands on either side of her face, startling her; he drew her face to his and kissed her with a wanting I had never seen before, while I stood close by, watching.

The rustlings are unmistakable, hand rubbing skin. A sharp intake of breath: MaryEllen. Covers dragging across the bed, one of them rolling atop the other, satisfied "ohs" there in the blackness, inches from me.

I roll onto my belly, cover my ears with my hands, clamp my eyes tight. I want to jump out of my skin. I concentrate on the dusty smell of the rag rug, but Sean and MaryEllen are too loud. I rise onto my hands and knees amid a blackness full of half-crazy moans, gather the coats and blankets in a bundle, crawl over to the stairwell.

When I'm halfway down the stairs, MaryEllen's laugh rings out. "Why, Brenda Bradshaw," she mocks, "whenever did you get so shy, my shrinking violet?" She laughs again, and Sean laughs. I can't think of a snappy comeback, not one goddamned word of a witty reply. My face feels like a hot coal in the icy room. I curl up in the windowseat, rest my cheek on my knees, look out the window. I'm thinking: I want a man, I want Al. I start to cry; make myself stop, angrily. It's darker than usual outside. It looks colder than usual, too, it's so clear. There must be no moon for it to be so dark and clear at once. All I can see is the picket fence, and all those stars sparkling way up there in the black black sky.

40 ◪ "THINGS ARE going to be all different, aren't they?" MaryEllen asks. She has her wedding-ringed hand on her belly, is drinking a tall glass of water. I have black coffee.

I've been around MaryEllen a lot and I've never seen her melancholy or apprehensive or regretful, not even a hint of it. Her question is packed full of those things, and more. I'm scared of it, from her.

"Naw. It's all the same thing," I answer.

"Shit," MaryEllen says. "You remember in that landscape construction job, how at the end of the day we had to go back to the shop to turn in our tools and turn in our time cards and shit, and then how we used to have to sit there and wait until the whistle blew for us to leave? And we'd all be sitting there on those two long benches with our knees lined up, and our boots lined up, and Chester spitting tobacco juice and telling those sick jokes, oh, 'Know why squirrels don't run up under ladies' dresses?' "

"No nuts," I answer for her.

"Har har," MaryEllen says. "Then that whistle would blow and we'd all rush for the gate and pound down the steps together all holding our black lunchboxes. I never thought I would miss that."

"I miss that, too," I say.

"I just felt like, like . . . now don't puke, Brenda. Like, oh, you know, like 'sea to shining sea,' like 'purple mountains' majesty.' "

"Like a fruited plain," I point out to her, "now you can feel like a fruited plain."

"Oh, *thanks*," she answers, but she is grinning. "A fruited plain," she says to herself, and sucks down more water.

"Do you remember," she asks suddenly, sitting up tall in

excitement, "that night we all dropped the acid, no, when just you and I did, not Sean, and Sean kept laughing and laughing, and we went to the ocean and we saw things?"

"You saw pillars," I say.

There had been boats on the water, their lights reflecting in straight lines from them to the sand, and MaryEllen had seen the lights as pillars. She'd said, "Light is the pillar that holds up the sky." That had just knocked me out.

"And you," said MaryEllen, "saw the ocean as molecules."

I nod. "Twice as many hydrogens as oxygens. All the way to the horizon. Past the horizon. I saw gravity, too, did I tell you? I could see the moon's gravity lifting all those molecules up."

"That night was exhausting," MaryEllen says. "And we kept waking up poor Sean to tell him those things, and he'd said, 'Wow, man, have you ever *really* looked at your own hand?' "

"And then," I say, "when it was time for us to go to work, and Sean was driving us there and we were commenting about how we were coming *down* finally, we were so glad it was happening, *finally,* 'cause of course it always seems like when you're tripping you're tripping eternally, then you said, 'Look! Galactic wars over El Cajon!' and I saw it too! All kinds of zapping and blasting in the sky. The trip wasn't over, after all."

"And then we had to grade gravel all day. And it was *hot.*"

We are both sitting there in that little house in Gloucester, Massachusetts, MaryEllen with her water and me with my coffee, and I wish like hell I could put my finger on what it is that I'm feeling right now. We sit, and sip, and don't say anything.

"I'm going to leave," I finally say.

"Well, *I* know that. You're going to Al's?"

I sit up and blink. "What makes you think I'm going to Al's? I think I'm going on the boat to Jamaica."

"I dunno, Brenda. You didn't say much about that Al character, but oh, how you said it."

"Really?"

"Sure. I mean, really, Brenda. Am I sensitive? Am I observant? Not exactly. And even *I* could hear it."

I'm stunned. "Well," I shrug, "there is *something* there." We sip our drinks some more. "I might go to Al's, sure," I say, nodding.

Late that afternoon I take the bus into Cambridge, and in bookstores and coffeeshops and laundromats, tack up three-by-fives asking for a ride to the West Coast. The West Coast, is all I ask for, maybe that will decide it for me. On Sean's old portable I've typed, ASK FOR DALE so they won't know if I'm a man or woman, so someone will call only if it doesn't matter to them.

I put up cards around Harvard too. All the buildings there look like churches to me. It feels strange tacking up notecards there.

When I get back, MaryEllen is out. Already I start organizing my backpack, even though I probably won't get a ride offer for a month. When I find my address book, I page through to Al. I don't give myself a moment to think about it, I go to the phone and dial.

It rings in a strange distant way, then there is a recording. *The* recording: "The number you have reached is not in service at this time and there . . ." I slam down the receiver, "Damn!" I shout. I grab up the phone book, flip through to the area code section. "Spokane," I tell the information operator. "Al Righetti."

"The number for Alfred Righetti, attorney, is 273-8169." Fine. I cross out the old number, write down the new. Fine. I hang up the phone. I sit back in the chair, holding my address book in one hand in a solid grip, and I don't call Al.

41 ▨

FOR A WHILE there in San Diego, right af-
ter MaryEllen and I had gotten laid off from our jobs, and
before I started working the track for Will, I took the bus up
to La Jolla every day, and took the stairs down the cliff so
that I could swim around the Scripps Institute pier. There
were other piers, in fact there was a pier right at the end of
my street in Ocean Beach, but lots of people fished off them.
Only the scientists at Scripps fished off this pier, and not
often.

There were always a few surfers, so I'd watch them for a
while. Then I'd throw off my shirt and shorts—I always wore
my suit under my clothes—and I'd wade in, finally diving into
the startling cold of the first foamy breaker.

I'm one of those lucky people who bob like a cork, bob
like a boat. I think I could swim forever without getting tired,
if I had food and water and it wasn't too cold. Swimming out
through the waves the length of the pier was easy.

But there was something about rounding that farthest piling. All of a sudden I'd start thinking about sharks. It's really
ridiculous that I'd start worrying then; if a shark wanted to
attack me, it could do it as I passed the second piling, it could
do it as I was *wading,* for that matter. But reasoning has nothing to do with self-induced terror, and it really was terror, to
be sliding up and down big rollers over deep dark water,
knowing there was a whole world down there, sharks, sharks
too, of course, and me. Whatever was I doing there, messing
around in a world where I didn't belong? I'd find myself
thrashing in a roundabout way, trying to look in all directions
at once through black water, looking for that flash of sunlight
on cold blue sharkskin I would someday surely see. I'd start
hyperventilating until my chest ached, I'd become lightheaded, then I'd finally break into a panicked swim back to

shore, counting the pier pilings out loud god, god, because when I got to ten, around ten, a wave would almost always come along and pick me up and speed me back to the shallow water, where I could stand, and wade back to the beach on shaky legs. I'd be crying a little, too. It's really strange, crying, when you're already all wet.

I'd lie on the hot sand and watch the surfers some more. Soon I'd feel dry and lazy, a smooth breeze would sweep across me. I'd warm up, then get hot; I'd be able to see my pulse beating in the skin of my stomach.

Then I'd take the bus back home. Almost no one rides the buses in San Diego, the system is inefficient, the city too sprawling. Sometimes I'd have the whole big bus to myself as it rumbled down the coast, the sun lowering to the ocean. And the next day, at noon, I'd take the bus up to La Jolla again, take the stairs down the cliff and dive into that first cold breaker, beside that long pier.

42 🖾 OF COURSE it sounds too good when I get wakened by a phone call ("Dale? Is this Dale?") first thing the next morning, me heavy-lidded, stuffed up and groggy, and this girl on the line, chipper, friendly; she saw my card on the ride board at Harvard, oh, please, would I do her a big favor and keep her brother company all the way to Santa Cruz? I can hardly believe this success so soon, and while the girl talks I clear my head with a picture of Santa Cruz, sweet green Santa Cruz, stands of sky-sweeping redwoods, fields of brown cows teary-eyed, bored, and ruminating, plodding through the new grass that rolls all the way down to the crashing gray Pacific. The girl is heaping it on: her brother is a nice guy, he is a businessman, rich, a *businessman,* he'll pay for everything,

restaurants, hotel rooms; he's terrified of flying, and she told him she'd go along and keep him company but now she and her boyfriend have made up and she doesn't want to go, and her brother is so mad, would I please, please go? "... And I told him you're a friend of mine, ok? My name's Sandy. You'll do ok. He's not nosey or anything, just keep him company, ok? You can leave this afternoon, right? Around one?"

Sean and I hug long and sweet before he leaves for the shipyard, me saying the usual corny father-to-be comments to him. I don't have much time, so I rush to the laundromat, rush back to get ready. When I'm in the shower, MaryEllen comes into the bathroom, sits on the floor.

"What're you going to do now?"

"Go to Santa Cruz."

"What are you going to do in Santa Cruz?"

"Well, y'know, MaryEllen, I really don't know. I think Santa Cruz is about halfway between San Diego and Spokane." I laugh. "Weird. Of course ..." I shut off the shower, step out and grab up a towel, "... Cheyenne, Wyoming, is along the way to Santa Cruz."

"You've got a couple of days to learn how to cowboy yodel and swingdance."

"I know how to swingdance, MaryEllen, you know that."

"Yeah, but that was the Tucson Two-Step. What do they do in Cheyenne, Wyoming? The Box-Car Box-Step?"

I laugh.

"Anyway, Brenda, thanks for letting me con you into coming all the way out here just so that you could be a witness to my wedding."

I stop drying myself, stand stunned for a moment. "Is that what you did?"

MaryEllen just grins, shrugs. She pats her belly. "I was desperation's mother."

Around ten, we go outside and sit on the front stoop. She

has just reminded me of another of Chester's awful jokes when a new white Monte Carlo pulls up to the curb, and he gets out, Sandy's brother, fortyish instead of the twentyish I'd expected, looking like he walked into a Playboy Club in 1969 and just now walked out, wearing a satiny paisley shirt unbuttoned to show off his burly chest and his gold Leo medallion, creased polyester pants the oddest shade of bright blue, short white patent-leather boots. Lots of rings. *Lots* of rings. His long sideburns are gray. Except for his dress, though, he looks like he could be anyone's uncle, apprehensive, and slightly embarrassed.

He glances at us, then walks up to me. "I'm Mac. You're Dale? How do you do?" he asks politely, and before I know it, he's hefting my grimy pack into his vast carpeted lit trunk next to his expensive suitcases, brushing dirt off his polyester pants and opening the door for me, and before I know it, I'm getting into a car that smells like an expensive new car: white leather upholstery. Mac turns the key, the engine hums; heat blasts into my face from a climate control panel, color-coded cool blue to raging red. He slides the stick into drive. Outside, through tinted glass I see MaryEllen standing on the curb, drifting away from me, with her mouth open, hand halfway up in a bewildered goodbye, and I'm sure that through the tinted window, drifting away, I must look exactly the same to her.

HIGHWAY 80, WEST

43 🗗 MAC MAKES pleasant enough, though sparse, small talk. He has a Massachusetts accent: brash and flippant, and a wry sense of humor. Right away he pulls into a gas station, the full service island, and as he gets out to head for the convenience store, says, "You can use it here, but don't worry about it cause I stopalot." I lounge on the leather upholstery and watch the young attendant slam nozzles into tanks, answer phones, collect money, wash windows, wipe his greasy hands for the thousandth time on the orange rag hanging out of his front pocket. It seems like a thousand years since I was running on autopilot like that, like I was all those days at Safeway. Some of those days, the repetition was euphoric; it seemed the world was a rhythmed, orderly place, and I was a part of that rhythm and order. Other days the repetition was just boring.

Just as the attendant finishes wiping the side-view mirror, Mac returns with two Styrofoam cups—coffee for himself, and hot chocolate for me, which almost makes me laugh out loud. This trip is going to be ok, I decide. I can hardly believe my luck.

"Do you mind, very much, if I turn this down?" I ask timidly. I point to the heater, which is blasting hard enough to flutter my hair. I don't think I should be breathing the stuff that's coming out of the vents; it smells and tastes like plastic. And I'm sweating like mad.

"Sure, if you can figure it out. I can't figure it out. I can't even figure out how to empty the ashtray." Mac slides the stick into drive, and we're off. "When the ashtrays get full on my cars, that's when I trade them in."

It seems to take forever for Mac and me to pull away from the East, to pull away from cramped, narrow-roaded New England. We fling ourselves wildly into roundabouts, only to be stopped again and again at toll booths. "Toll road" has a nasty sound to it, small and stingy. Turnpike is a little better, though even that sounds like something turning in on itself. Freeway, I love the word *freeway*. Freeway, freeway, and I lean back into the padded headrest, thinking of the West Coast rushing its way toward me, of Santa Cruz and San Diego and L.A., of that big L.A. smell of sagebrush, car exhaust, orange groves, and hand-patted corn tortillas frying in hot lard.

I think of gliding down Highway 5, past the giant letters on the hill: HOLLYWOOD. Ah, to be stopped in rush-hour traffic and sit dizzy in the glimmer of cars twelve lanes wide, that are lying in wait like a deadly snake coiled in both directions off into the obscurity of the yellow smog, in those hot dry L.A. hills. . . .

We hit another roundabout, signs everywhere, signs that show towns two or three miles away rather than two or three hundred. Damn, I miss the bigness of the West. Al lives in that big beautiful Northwest, and in a few short days I'm finally, finally going to be there with him.

Mac is right, he does stopalot. About every half-hour or so he swings into a gas station or restaurant to buy a newspaper, make phone calls at a pay booth. When he gets back in the car, he always does the same thing: throws the sports section of a newspaper on the seat, opens the glove compartment, takes out a Kleenex, wipes off his white patent-leather boots, then stuffs the Kleenex in the ashtray. At this rate, we'll have to trade in the car by Chicago, tops.

We make the smallest of small talk. We each chant a few

variations of I hope this good weather will hold out, I hope the roads will stay clear. I ask what line he's in and he says, "Sales." He asks what I study and I pull "Biology" out of my hat, hoping it's a subject he's not too interested in. He's not. I'm wondering if it's possible for me, Sandy's friend Dale, to go on like this, all the way across the U.S., chatting politely.

After an hour or so, Mac hands me a Rand McNally map book. "That's why I hafta have someone drive with me, I swear to god, I don't know what way's up on that thing. We hafta stop off in Reno for a couple of days. I hope you don't mind. Business."

"No, I don't mind." I turn to the U.S. map. "We'll take Eighty all the way out."

"Fine," he says. "That goes through Nashville, right? And Little Rock? That's the way I always go."

"No, that's Forty. That's way down south. That's way out of the way."

Actually, in the winter, I'm sure it's a better idea to take 40 until Barstow, or just past Kingman, and then go north to Reno. But I just came *out* on 40. I want to see some new places.

I look at the map: 80 goes right by Lake Erie, Lake Michigan, near Cleveland, Chicago, then spills out onto a long lonely road sprinkled with small towns: Peru, Princeton, Geneseo, and farther west, Council Bluffs, North Platte, Ogallala, Cheyenne. Maybe we'll make a stop in Cheyenne. What the hell. I imagine that love-of-my-life cowboy right now, chowing down lunch wherever it is that cowboys chow down lunch.

"You're the navigator," Mac says. Then we stream along in silence for more than an hour.

We stop at a Howard Johnson's in Scranton where Mac orders a T-bone steak. "*Very* well done," he says to the waitress. "I know, I know, the cook is gonna cringe when he hears that."

"Oh, no, sir, I'll take care of that for you. Well done. Now, what kind of dressing would you like on your salad?"

"Look, you got a rabbit at home? Take that salad home and feed it to your rabbit." He laughs. "I don't eat rabbit food."

The waitress laughs, too. She's no fool. She wants a tip. "Get whatever you want," Mac says to me. Then he buries himself behind the sports page.

After dinner Mac turns on the car stereo loud, to a basketball game. He screams and swears and pounds on the steering wheel, the dashboard, he unwraps and stuffs stick after stick of Juicy Fruit into his mouth, though I never see him spit any out. I keep close watch there in the dark beside him that he stays calm enough to keep us on the road. He has fat beads of sweat on his forehead and upper lip which he occasionally slicks back with the sleeves of his polyester shirt.

At the end of the ball game, thank god, there is a miracle six-point turnaround in the last twenty-three seconds to give Mac's team a win, and I finally start breathing again.

We drive until past midnight before Mac pulls off at a Ramada Inn, somewhere still in Pennsylvania. He comes out of the hotel office, parks in front of a room, gets our bags out of the trunk, opens the motel door. "You can have the bathroom first," he says.

Ah, of course, of *course,* here's the expected payoff, and how could I have been so naive?

"Cripes," Mac says, I guess in answer to the look on my face. "Look, I'm too bushed to try anything, ok? And whaddya think I'm gonna do, anyway, try somethin' with a girlfriend of my sister's?"

I'd forgotten about that. I shrug, go in, take the bathroom first. When Mac is in the shower, I nestle into those crisp bleached starched hotel sheets, sigh, take out Al's number and dial, listen to it ring and ring. It almost rings me to sleep before I rouse myself enough to tip the receiver back onto the cradle. Then I sleep solid as a travel-worn wanderer for the whole long black night.

44 🕸 MAC, as it turns out, is a bookie. It takes me all the way until dinnertime the next night, at a Howard Johnson's just south of Chicago, to figure this out. Mac has finished his well-done steak and his sports page and has left behind an open notebook as he's gone to the bathroom, which of course, I lean over and look at. It has a list of names: Spud-boy, Dirty Pablo, Chew, Stee, Robob; there are team names, odds, and dollars.

When he returns I lean close and whisper, grinning, "Mac! Are you a bookie, or what?"

"JesusMaryandJoseph," he swears, looking at the notebook. "Yeah, well, what the hell," he shrugs. "I keep some books, yeah," he says, somewhat proudly.

Over my sandwich and salad and Mac's well-done steak he explains to me all the bets he's taken today. After dinner I call Al from the pay phone next to the bathrooms, but again, there's no answer. I follow Mac back to the car where we listen to three overlapping games on the radio, me in charge of flinging the radio dial between them. We are hooting by the end of the third game. "Those are the biggest wins I've ever had. And all those last night, too. You must be my good luck charm. You just made me a *pack* of money. Jesus-MaryandJoseph." He throws back his head and bellylaughs. "Howzabout you quitting school and working for me? It's good money, under the table, huh? Free apartment, free phone. You just have to be home to take phone calls a few hours a day. Lots of free time."

"Yeah, and I could be sitting somewhere with *lots* of free

time on my hands. Where are you going to be when they
come along and cart me off?" He smiles, his lips tight. "On
this leather upholstery in this Monte Carlo, that's where
you'll be."

He chuckles. "You don't know nothin' if you think anyone's going to bother some small-time fry like you. They
might ask for some protection money, though," he smirks.
"You just think about it, anyway. For the next few days. You
got a few days here to think about it. Whaddya want school
for, anyway? I didn't have any school, and look at me." He
bellylaughs again. "Hell, I just won a pack of money." He
pokes my shoulder in emphasis on each word: "And, you,
din't. You college girls. Are you in school for the same reason
Sandy is? To get your M-R-S? I always told her she was studying too hard just so she could get into Harvard to nab a Harvard man. Course I didn't see her much as she was growing
up. Can you believe, there's almost twenty years between us?
What a crazy family! I grow up an only child, then when my
parents are forty, my old man gets baby crazy. Gotta have a
daughter alla'a sudden. Gets Ma pregnant, at the age of forty,
dies of a heart attack two days before Sandy's born. Jesus-
MaryandJoseph. So I come home for a year or two, to help
get Ma on her feet. That ma of ours, she's really somethin',
though. She didn't need my help. She told me to go, not to
ruin my career. I was a boxer. Light heavyweight. I was good.
Real, real good." He bites his lip. "And then she raises Sandy
alone, all the way to Harvard. And her, almost sixty." He
sighs, shakes his head, smiling. "Anyway, I got a pack of questions for you about Sandy's boyfriend. I *know* you gotta know
all about him. And I want the whole scoop."

He's caught me off guard. I think of saying, "I don't know
her boyfriend very well," but it sounds unlikely, from what
Mac's just said. I screw up my mouth.

"I don't really know your sister," I confess. "She got my
name off a rideboard."

I almost add, "My name's not Dale, either," but it seems like too much to admit to all at once. I'm not so convinced Mac is a Mac, either.

He sighs. "Oh well, doesn't surprise me," he says, which surprises me. He drives in melancholy silence for a while.

"I used to be a cop, y'know? In Lowell. I learned not to trust nobody about nothin'. I tell ya. And cripes! It was dangerous. See, all I'm doing one night is walking my beat, minding my own business picking up a little protection money, when I walk in the jewelry store and JesusMaryandJoseph there's a goddamned robbery in progress, cripes! The robbers think I'm gonna try to stop them or somethin', I don't know, I didn't have time to discuss it with them, you know? Before they start *shootin'* at me! I coulda got kilt over a few lousy bucks of protection money. You better believe I got outta that line of business pretty quick. Wasn't wort' the money."

We pass under a sign for Davenport. "Davenport!" Mac cries out. "Where the hell are we?"

"Davenport," I answer, confused.

"Florida?"

"No," I laugh. "Iowa."

"Iowas? What are ya doing to us? What are we doing in Iowas? I've never been to Iowas in my life. What's this, the Potato State? Hand over that map book. I thought you knew what you were doing. Jesus, Dale, you've got us way up by Canada."

He's flicked on the inside light, he's swerving, and shuffling the map book around; he doesn't have the foggiest idea where to look for Iowa on the map.

I take the map book from him. "Calm down, Mac. We've got all of Minnesota between us and Canada, ok? We're on Eighty. We're fine. Eighty goes right from New York City to San Francisco. From sea to shining sea. Right through Reno."

"Le-mee look at the map again." I hand it over, point to Davenport and slide my finger along 80 to Reno.

"What have you done to us?" he wails. "Look at this, will you? Look at the small print on these towns. We gotta drive through these?" He pounds his fingertip on the map. "There's nothing there! What's this: Booneville. Booooooneville. How 'bout this: Beebeetown. Cripes, what do they do in places like those, have sack races? We better stop here." He takes an exit to a motel.

That night I'm waked by Mac's hand on my shoulder, his face by my face. I fling my arm up, sit upright, defensive, but in the dim light I can see that he's already backed away, is sitting sheepishly on his own bed. "Sorry," he says, "sorry, Dale. Just checking, you know, what the hell. Sorry."

"I'm not interested."

"Can't blame a man for trying." His voice sounds shook. "Can't never blame a man for trying. Go on and get back to sleep. I won't bother you no more."

I only half-sleep, but Mac sleeps solid and heavy the rest of the night.

45 ▨ WE PULL INTO Cheyenne, Wyoming, at about eight, and Mac, shuffling the map book in his hand, asks, "Lookit: we stop here, get one good night's sleep, then make a big press straight to Reno, whaddya say? And you can drive some? Cause I gotta be at that meeting morning after next, and that's the only way we're gonna make it."

"That's fine with me; I've been wanting to drive some."

We walk down a boardwalk, past closed Western wear shops, eat at a Western steak house that has saddles at the bar instead of stools, then drive to a motel.

Mac comes out of the office with two keys in his hand. "Room one-oh-two," he says as he hands me a key. He points to the door. He looks embarrassed. "I'll meet you out here at eight. You want me to tell them to give you a wake-up call, too?"

I shake my head. "Nah. Goodnight, Mac."

I take a leisurely shower, lie in bed, turn on the TV, but there is nothing on but flashy gun shows with deaths and meanness that seem too real. I dial Al's ringing phone so many times in a row I feel I won't forget his number for the rest of my life. I pull on a flannel shirt and blue jeans, open my door quietly—I don't want Mac to get the idea that I'm heading over to his room—and look into the black night. A skyful of stars, Mac's Monte Carlo, empty gravel lots on either side of the motel. I go back inside, flop down on the bed, pick up the King James and read one of the 'begat' sections, hoping it'll put me to sleep. It doesn't. And there is still nothing on TV.

The next time I open the door, I see that one of the gravel lots is filling up with pickups. Cowboys, dozens of them, long lean cowboys in fancy-tooled pointy-toed cowboy boots are dropping themselves out of the cabs, some of them grasped by long lean women dressed in impossibly tight jeans and high-heeled boots.

I take a few steps in my bare feet away from the motel door. Above the building next door is a neon sign: Lasso Lounge, a neon lasso swooping round and round above it in the starry night.

Whooee! A swingdance bar! Nothing could feel better after sitting motionless for three climate-controlled days in Mac's Monte Carlo than to dance until I'm sweaty and about to drop from exhaustion. I back into my room, pull on socks and my clunky hiking boots—they'll have to do—then cross the parking lot to the Lasso Lounge. I laugh out loud when I get to the door. I'm going to swingdance with cowboys until I'm dizzy, and maybe after all I'll bump head first and full-speed into the love of my life the fortuneteller predicted.

The inside is dark and smoky, filled with roving eyes and

fancy belts, Michelob signs, silver-tipped boots, pinball ma-
chines, a wide-smiling bartender that I buy beer after beer
from. Then the beers are getting bought for me, I don't know
by whom. I twirl from my partner at the end of the song, reel
over to where I left my last mug of beer, tip it back; its foamy
head slides down so fast and smooth and cool. And a new fast
smooth cool cowboy shows up to spin me dizzy and silly. It
feels so good to laugh out loud. I laugh and laugh, and each
heartthrob boy I dance with I hear myself ask, "You a cowboy, cowboy?"

Then the night is over, the bar closing; "Here," a cowboy
says, handing me a beer, "drink this, it's the last one left in
the world, and I give it to you." It slides down my throat; the
cowboy looks at me appreciatively, grabs my arm; I lean into
him. Then there is the parking lot gravel beneath my crazy
stumbling legs, the cowboy's voice above my lightheaded head
says the funniest things, I laugh and laugh, my laugh is ridiculous, horsey. His truck, I think, then a sidewalk, a front
door, a key, then tumbling, panting, desperate rough gropings.
My head's spinning, stomach's boiling, I try to focus on the
lightbulb overhead, but it won't stop swooping, and he's panting, Dale, Dale, and I'm thinking I should whisper his name
back, only I can't remember his name, so while he works
himself over me I go through the alphabet looking for it:
Andy? Brad? Barry? Charles? Curt? sweat drips off his nose,
stings my eyes, David? Don? Dick? Dick, jesus, that one makes
me start laughing, Dick, Dick, or maybe Peter? and then I'm
laughing and hiccupping and he's pumping and I'm thinking
Dagwood? Ed? Eldridge? which of course makes me think
Cleaver? Beaver Cleaver? and I remember a line from the
show, where June says, "Oh, Ward, don't be so hard on the
Beaver," forget what letter I'm on and have to start over,
Axel? Buck? Conan? but by the time I come up with it,
finally, finally, of course, *Lawrence,* he's asleep beside me,

slack-mouthed and snoring, and in the dark a digital clock is flashing 3:33 3:33 3:33.

I have to shake him awake, shake him hard, and he finally rolls off the bed, stands, turns on the light. My head is still spinning the room round and round and it's full of junk, the floor strewn with clothes and underwear on the doorknob, plates of dried-up food balancing on stacks of newspapers, and the bedspread is stained, brown velvet and he, Lawrence, has a hard time zipping his pants over the roll of fat at his waist; he blows his nose into who knows what piece of clothing he's picked up, finds unmatched socks on the floor and pulls them over pale bloated toes. In the corner of the bedroom: a saddle. It takes me a while to find my own clothes within the mess. We don't talk to each other as we dress or as we pick our way over the littered living room floor, and don't talk on the drive to the motel, but as I leave the car, he says, "Thanks a lot."

"Thank *you*," I answer, just as I used to when I cashiered at Safeway.

In the bathroom as my stomach boils bitter spit into my mouth I tear the paper band off the plastic cups. I drink five full cups of sour warm motel tap water. Nothing is on TV, just fuzz. I flick from station to station, around and around the dial, refusing to believe it, almost in tears. Please, TV! I want to be numbed by TV! I lie face down on the bed gripping its corner with both hands, while it spins beneath me. Big mistake, I'm thinking, *big* mistake. A woman's fuzzy face appears on the rug, I squint my eyes to bring it into focus. It's Vivien Leigh . . . Scarlett O'Hara, in *Gone with the Wind*. She wrinkles her brow and stomps her foot as she says, "Oh, if I think about that now, I'll just go mad! I'll . . . I'll think about it *tomorrow*." And with that scene repeating itself in my head, I spin off to sleep, clinging to the bed, still wearing my party clothes: blue jeans, worn flannel shirt, and boots. Spinning off to Tara.

46 THE WINTER SUN is too bright. Must be

because we're so far north. And the air stinks.

"I heard you get in last night," Mac says. He throws his suitcase and my backpack into the trunk.

"Oh, yeah?"

"It was four o'clock." He slams the trunk closed.

He is eating gum, one piece after another, throwing the wrappings onto the ground. This time I can plainly see that he is *eating* it, *swallowing* it. It gives me the creeps. I can't help but think of the old wives' tale, that gum stays in your stomach for seven years; knowing that it's not true doesn't make me believe it any less. It's like when I'm making a salad and I cut a cucumber, I have to rub the cut end against itself until it foams, to draw out the poison. Something I learned from my mother.

"I was dancing." I point to the sign. "There."

"You came back in a car. A pickup truck, to be exact. What'd you do, get a ride from *there* to *here*?"

"I got a ride, yeah."

"Cripes," he says, but with a good-natured sneer, a roll of his eyes. "Just get in' a car, willya?"

I can't read him today. And I don't want to. I slump against the door, my eyes half-open, focused on the window. Shit. I want to blame the Boston fortuneteller for how I feel this morning, blame MaryEllen and Sean for paying her, blame Will for leaving Boston before I showed up, blame Mac for stopping in Cheyenne, blame anyone and everyone for my gurgling stomach and slamming head, my sick heart and sad soul, blame anyone and everyone but myself.

Mac's in a foul mood, too. He keeps blaming me for there being nothing between where we are and Reno. He can't get anything on the radio. He hasn't heard the results from two of last nights' games, and he's got lots of money riding on them. The small-town newspapers he's picked up report only the local high school games. He's starting to swerve around on the road as we barrel down it, his white patent-leather-shod foot pressed into the accelerator as all his attention is focused on the radio stations that he can't get in.

Lunchtime comes, but there's no place to eat. Mac streams right by a couple of two-horse towns, then it gets to be late enough that we're both grumpy from hunger, and I'm having to bite my tongue to not answer to Mac's cynical remarks.

He finally pulls off into a town that's six blocks long, mostly trailers, and stops in the gravel lot of J & T Diner around the back of a two-pump gas station.

"Cripes," he says. He sits for a while, then opens his door. "This has gotta be it, or I'll end up bein' one of those whatch-macallit, pile a bones, out there in that desert. Come on."

There are three tables with red plastic checked tablecloths, moo-cow creamers and cracked plastic salt-and-pepper shakers shaped like pigs. We sit on the ripped Naugahyde chairs. Mac picks up a grease-spotted menu, throws it down with a disgusted look.

An older woman's voice is whining in the kitchen; a man's muffled voice answers. I look at the menu. As I expected: hamburger, chicken-fried steak, fried chicken, side of coleslaw or green salad. Jell-O. The place is uncomfortably quiet. I'm afraid to shift in my seat; it squeaks.

"Cripes," Mac mutters across the table. "Whatta we gotta do to get their attention around here, squeal like a pig? Talk their language, eh?"

Finally a gray-haired woman in a houseshift, dirty apron, and fuzzy slippers shuffles into the room. "What'll it be?" she asks.

"I'll have the hamburger . . ."

"Ladies first," she interrupts Mac, and turns to me.

"Oh, uh, fried chicken please."

"Wheat toast?"

"Yes, please."

"Coleslaw or salad?"

"Salad."

"All right, now, sir, what about you?"

Mac sits, amazingly humbled. "Could I please have the hamburger. Would you mind cooking it well done."

"Fine. Wheat toast?"

"White."

"Wheat toast. It's healthier."

Mac just sits there, smiling in a bewildered way.

"Salad? Cole slaw? Special recipe, my cole slaw."

I wait for him to ask, "You got a rabbit at home?" but he doesn't, he says, "Well, then, I'll take the slaw."

"Good for you," she says, and pats him on the head. Then she shuffles back to the kitchen.

I wait for Mac to explode back to normal when the woman clears the door, but he doesn't; he just sits and raps on the table with his knuckles, and looks out the window while clanking and sizzling noises come from the kitchen. After a while the woman shuffles back with two glasses of milk.

"You need your milk," she says to Mac before he can protest. "Never too old to need your milk." She shuffles into the kitchen and back out again with our food. An old man follows her, and after she puts the plates down, the two of them settle in with cups of coffee two tables away.

"So I just don't know." She sighs hugely, a faraway gaze in her eyes, and the two of them look off into the same thoughtful distance without speaking for a while. "Kids today . . ."

"Uh-huh," the old man agrees, nodding his head. They sit a while longer, entirely motionless.

"They just want to leave home," she finally continues. "Just got to get away, so they think."

"Isn't that the truth," he answers.

It's so quiet I can hear the man's every raspy breath, and I almost jump out of my seat when he clears his throat. I'm trying to eat my chicken without making any noise at all, drink my milk by tipping the glass carefully, no slurps. I see that Mac is doing the same. Each time the woman glances over at us, Mac picks up his milk glass and takes a quick sip.

"So. They're gone. You raise a daughter, they get to twenty and they think they can just break the ties just like that, just 'cause they say they can. Don't care about their old mom."

"That's the truth." The man leans back in his chair, brings his clasped hands above him and cracks his knuckles. "Honestly it is."

"Well, I hope she likes it. 'Cause she just wouldn't listen to me."

This is when I notice that Mac's hamburger is dripping red. And he's eating it.

"So I said to her, 'Go on then, move all the way to Marron Street for all I care. Why stop at Belmont? You'll just get restless again, why not do it now?' They don't even care I got to walk all those four blocks to see my grandbabies. Kids today don't care. They're too busy being big shots."

"That's the honest truth."

"Something wrong with the coleslaw?" she suddenly asks Mac. "You don't like my coleslaw?"

"No no no. I do. Honestly. I like it." He smiles. He jiggles his fork around in the slaw, but doesn't put any into his mouth.

The phone rings, and the woman leaves the room to answer it. The man sits for a while, nodding and smiling toward us, then picks himself up and leaves too.

As soon as he passes through the doorway, Mac slides his bowl of coleslaw to me. He has a look of desperation on his face. "Eat this for me, will ya?"

I laugh. "You've got to be kidding me."

He glances wildly toward the doorway. "Eat it! Hurry up!" He honestly looks like he might belt me in the mouth if I don't do it. I glare back at him. His face softens back into vulnerable desperation. "Please."

I stuff gobs of coleslaw into my mouth, mumbling between bites, "Mac, whatever is the matter with you? What does it matter if you don't eat your coleslaw?"

"Do you mind? Do ya just mind doing me one goddamned favor?" He keeps glancing toward the door. "She reminds me of my ma, ok? Cripes, all I ask is one goddamned favor from you."

I hold my two left fingers up in a peace symbol as I shovel coleslaw into my mouth. As soon as I've lifted the last of it to my mouth, Mac grabs up the bowl and sets it in front of himself. Not a minute too soon either; the woman returns.

"Yum," Mac says, wiping his mouth with his napkin, as I sit across from him chomping on the last of the slaw. "Good."

"Good, good," she says, pleased. She pats him on the back. "Now, don't you feel better? Now, let's see, yours was one thirty-five, and yours one fifty, thirty each for the milks, ah, two eighty-five and seventy: three fifty-five."

Mac hands her a ten.

"I'll get your change," she says, but as soon as she has shuffled out of our sight, Mac mouths, "Let's get outta here."

We tiptoe to the door, then throw it open, and laughing like kids who've skipped out on the bill, we jump into his car and roar away in a cloud of dust.

47 🖾 THE SCENERY is magnificent, awe-inspiring, uplifting: lofty, snow-topped rust-colored buttes rising from a hazy snow-dusted earthen floor. I lean back and try to concentrate on all that land and all that sky instead of on my compressed heavy head, while Mac yacks away about how lousy everything is and how he can't wait to get to civilization again where people care the hell about ball game scores. He pulls off at nearly every exit looking for a newspaper, or someone who knows the scores, getting more frenzied with each unsuccessful stop.

We pass a sign: Welcome to Utah.

"Don't tell me," Mac wails. "You sent me into *Utah?* Dale Dale Dale, if there's one thing in this world I can't stand it's a goddamned Mormon." He picks up the map book, slides his finger along our route. He rolls his eyes up. "Jesus-MaryandJoseph, you're sending us right through Salt Lake City. Well, I'm not stopping."

He pulls off at every small town this side of Salt Lake City, looking for a newspaper: Emory, Echo, Coalville.

"Christ a'mighty!" he wails as he gets back into the car, empty-handed, at Wanship. "I'm going to have to drive right up to the goddamned Mormon Tabernacle, now!"

He picks an exit at random, and we end up lost on city streets. We pass a campus: Westminster College. "Look how mixed up these Mormons are, Dale, they got it all bass-ackward, these girls here get their M-R-S *before* college." Students are pouring down the sidewalks; mostly men, and with noticeable good posture. Waiting to greet almost everyone is a young woman surrounded by children.

"Ain't that cute," Mac sneers. "Norma and Norman Mormon. Mr. and Mrs. Norman Mormon, and their five normal Mormon kids. You might not know this, but according to them, God says if they have five kids, they get their own star to live on when they die. Somethin' like that. Jesus. What a crazy religion. Breed like niggers, then they don't even let niggers in the door of their church. If there's anything I can't stand, it's a goddamned bigot." He pulls over, rolls down his window. "Hey, Norman!" he calls out. I sink down in the seat. "Where can I find a newspaper?"

A fresh-scrubbed face appears at Mac's window. "Yes, sir," he says. "Right up at the next block, sir, there's a motel with a stand outside it."

"Thanksalot, Norman."

The stand has a major newspaper. "Hallelujah," Mac mouths to me, pointing to it. He has left the car running. He drops in a dime, but the stand doesn't open, it's jammed. Mac rattles the door handle, yanks on it, pounds on the box and slams it around on the sidewalk. I see the clerk inside the hotel walk around the check-in desk. He stops at the window, just a few feet from Mac, his arms crossed, frowning.

"Goddamned fuckin' Mormons!" Mac suddenly bellows, picks up the newspaper box and hurtles it toward the window. I gasp, my hands fly to my mouth, but the newspaper stand stops short of the window and lands with a crash on the side-walk. It was chained to a bolt on the sidewalk, otherwise, it *would* have gone through the window.

Mac jumps into the car and we are off with a wild squeal of tires. I glance back to see the hotel clerk blabbering into a phone.

"I don't wanna talk about it, Dale. Don't say a goddamned thing." We squeal down a couple of streets, then up onto a freeway entrance. "I gotta get outta this goddamned city. I gotta get outta this goddamned state."

I take in and release a deep breath, I look at the map. My hands are shaking. One hundred miles exactly to the border of Nevada. One hundred miles to worry that we won't be stopped and hauled into jail.

I lean on the door, my cheek pressed against the cold window. We stream past vast salt flats: lonely, lonely. I know I'm a fool if I don't tell Mac to let me out at the next town, but I'm just so tired. Outside are miles of vast, cold, flat salt. At least I'm inside, and warm, and moving toward Al. If I stop now, I may never move again.

All I have to do is last until Reno, then I can rest. I'll do nothing but lock myself in my room and watch TV for two days, then we'll be off toward Santa Cruz. I'll leave Mac at Sacramento, stay with Pam for a day or two, go north to Spokane from there. Perfect. I can even afford a bus to Spokane from Sacramento.

"What about dinner?" I ask Mac.

"Keep yer pants on," Mac says to me nastily. "I'm not stopping this car until we're outta the reach of Norman the Mormon."

I keep my mouth shut and my eyes out the window on the salt.

We stop right over the Nevada border, in Wendover. Mac finally finds a newspaper, buries himself behind the sports section as he eats his well-done steak. He isn't blowing up all over, so I know he's won his games. But he doesn't say a word all through dinner.

We pull into Reno in the wee hours of the morning. I feel like I've ridden tied to the wheel all the way from Boston; I'm so tired of moving I could scream. And now Reno. I'd forgotten that Reno is a city that never stops moving. Two in the morning and the streets are bustling. A crying woman limps down the sidewalk carrying a broken high-heel; a group of fat men guffaw, bounce off each other as they hurry into the open arms of a casino that has violet walls and violet carpets and a six-foot-tall thousand-dollar-winner slot machine. And neon does everything neon can possibly do, flashing, looping, sputtering. We pass under a sign: Biggest Little Town In The World.

We pull into the entry for the Lucky Dice Casino and Hotel. "I half-own this joint," Mac says. Sure, I think. I yawn.

But soon we're being doted over by hotel personnel, Mac's bags and my ragamuffin backpack being carried into an elevator. "I'll see you later," Mac says to me. He heads off into the casino, his step light on the blood-red carpet; he's at home.

The room is on the fourteenth floor, very posh. There is one round bed with a mirrored ceiling. I wait until the bellhop leaves before I laugh out loud. Then I sit down on the white carpeting.

"Damn," I whisper aloud. Well, I can take a bus as easily from Reno as I can from Sacramento.

I lock myself in the bathroom and take a sinfully long hot shower. In a day or so, I'll be stopped at Al's. Only a day or so more.

Just as I leave the bathroom, the ringing phone startles me. I race to it, grab up the receiver; for some crazy reason I think it's Al calling me.

"Hello?"

"Dale!" Mac's drunken voice. "Come on up here. To the lounge. In the penthouse. I got some friends here I want you to meet."

"Nah, I don't think so, Mac."

"What the hell! What's your problem? I just wanna introduce you to a few of my friends. I give you a free ride alla way across country, and you won't come up three floors to meet some friends of mine? What, you too good for me or somethin'?"

"Ok, ok. I'll be there. Give me a minute." I can tell him 'thanks and adios' there.

The lounge is tacky and extravagant. A circular room with windows all the way around, a fish pond with a fountain in the center, rotating lights coloring the fountain water.

A waitress in a sequined cocktail dress of the same blood-red color of the rest of the casino heads my way, and I figure she's going to want to know who the hell I think I am, slogging into this lounge in my blue jeans and hiking boots, but instead she smiles at me conspiratorially and whispers, "You Mac's friend? Listen, I've never served as many drinks to anyone as I've served to him tonight. See what you can do with him, ok? I can't say a thing, I mean, I work for the man . . ."

Mac is drunk and blubberingly friendly, his friends look like Mafia types. I don't want to be here.

"Mac," I say, "listen, I'm just going to be here for a few minutes; I was thinking maybe this is a good place for us to part ways. I want to get to Spokane after all, see, and I can get a bus from here . . ."

"You brat!" he shouts. "You don't think I'm good enough for you! You'll hop in the sack with some pickup from a bar, but *I'm* not good enough for you!"

My mouth drops open. That's a line from a grade B movie, not real life.

"I could pick you right up," and he advances on me, I back up, suddenly dizzy from all the flashing neon swaying in the city below, "and I could throw you through that plate glass window right there. You think I couldn't? If you were a man, I'd break your face open. You know what a cheek sounds like when it busts open? Well, I do!"

He's backed me all the way to a window, and I make a dash for it, skirting his flinging arm. He bellylaughs as I slam open the stairway door, he shouts, "Dale!" His voice echos in the void of seventeen stories as I pound down the steps hysterically down, down into the well, flinging myself around landings, my own voice echoing off the concrete walls "jesus jesus jesus ohjesus," pounding down on trembling knees, throwing open the door for the fourteenth floor. I trip over my own shaky legs, tumble onto the blood-red carpet that is printed with dizzying dice. Then I am up, sobbing, fumbling at the lock, eyeing the elevator door at the far end of the long hall while a Hitchcock audience screams in my head, "Oh, no! Don't go into that room!" I grab up my pack, my t-shirt, wheel around knowing he'll be there, looming huge in the doorway, red-eyed and rawknuckled. But there is only the empty doorway, and the glowing exit sign.

I dash back into the stairwell and wait for my breathing to slow. Mac wouldn't think of entering a stairwell. He trades in his car when the ashtray gets full. He probably doesn't even know that buildings *have* stairwells.

Mac is not in the lobby when I rush through it to the sidewalk, which is thick with bumping bodies, its own kind of hysteria. I skirt past an old woman in a brown wig who is pushing a grocery cart, its baby-seat full of canning jars of nickels, then I pass three spike-heeled giggling women, identical pink cotton-candy hair spun atop their nearly identical gum-chewing faces. And I am lost, lost—lost, tired and crazy in a lost, tired and crazy town, shuffling frantically and aimlessly like everyone around me, as if I belong, as if I, like them, had shuffled frantically onto the streets out of the womb and would shuffle aimlessly off the streets into the tomb. Never to stop. Never to rest.

I'm so pumped full of adrenaline that I walk and walk and walk, as if I know where I'm going and how I'm getting there. And why. I hope that I'm pointed northwest, because I feel like I can walk all the way to Spokane. Then I see a sign, AIRPORT, with an arrow pointing right. I walk to the signpost, grasp it, swing around it, and keep walking. I hold my breath for each car that overtakes me, thinking I might turn around to see the headlights of Mac's Monte Carlo. It's unlikely Mac will come looking for me in this direction, unlikely he'll come looking for me at all. I remember his bellylaugh—naw, my terrified face was enough of a payback for him. He's probably fallen asleep in the lounge's fishpond by now, the rotating lights sweeping past over him: green, red, purple.

The sidewalk becomes a dirt shoulder. My thumbs are stuck in my beltloops, and on the road, one after another, sets of taillights stream smoothly past me, and away.

48 ▨

THERE IS an early flight to Spokane that leaves in only ten minutes. I'll have to run to make it. The fare is one thirty-nine. I pull out all my money, loose dollars from pants pockets and pack pockets, and put it on the counter. Only ninety-seven dollars and some change, and the tears I've been fighting suddenly break. "How close can I get to Spokane?" I sob. How close to Al, I almost cry out loud.

"That same flight stops in Seattle before continuing to Spokane."

It costs eighty-nine fifty, I have only eight dollars and some change left. I dash the length of the airport and onto the plane. Within minutes I'm sitting in the reassuring hum of the plane, my seatbelt snug. I take the flight safety instructions from the pocket of the seat before me, and read that my seat cushion doubles as a flotation device, as we float over the hazy desert.

"OrangejuiceSpriteTabCoke?"

The stewardess is dulled, and I am grateful beyond words to her for her dullness as she passes me an orange juice with her pale hand, enameled fingernails.

"Oh, *thank* you," I say with such sincerity that she glances down at me, disturbed. Orange juice in a stemmed plastic cup, sweet orange juice, healthy and clean. Peanuts in a shiny packet. I tip my head back gratefully into my seat.

I'll call Al as soon as I get to Seattle. He'll be glad to drive six hours to pick me up. He'll be ecstatic. I'll see those soft brown eyes of his all the way across the crowded airport lounge, he'll run to me and his hug will seem to last forever. Then he'll drive me home, to his basement apartment at the end of the road.

The plane hums monotonously. We'll be landing in an hour, and until then, I am being taken care of, and all is well.

49 🏵 AT THE AIRPORT in Seattle, I collect my pack, then make a beeline for a pay phone. Al must be at work by now, so I call the directory operator on the hunch that he'll be listed at a law firm. Sure enough, he is: Blumenfeld, Jones and Righetti. Then I almost fall over when the operator gives me the number. It's the same number I'm already holding in my hand: 273-8169. The number I was dialing all those *nights* for all those weeks wasn't his home, it was his *office* number.

"Do you have Al Righetti's home number, please?"

"I'm sorry, it's unlisted."

I slowly hang up the phone, stand for a long time while things sink in. Then I have to feed in a handful of my precious coins before I can hear Al's office number ring.

"Blumenfeld, Jones and Righetti."

"Let me speak to Al, please. Righetti. Mr. Righetti."

"I'm sorry, he's out of the office for the rest of the day. May I take a message?"

"When will he get the message?"

"He generally calls in for his messages at the end of the day. If you leave your name and number, he'll return your call tomorrow morning at the latest. May I have your name?"

Before I can think, I've said, "Brenda Bradshaw," but then I don't know what to say for a message. Of course I could leave the pay phone number, but I don't want to hang around the airport hoping he'll call. I feel absolutely desperate; I can't stand the thought of waiting anywhere for any length of time. I have to see Al, I have to get to Spokane. On the other hand, I only have six dollars.

"I'm an old friend of his from San Diego. Could you give me his home number?"

"I'm sorry, I can't give that out to anyone."

"Look, we went to high school together. Wheeler High." I sing some of our alma mater to convince her. "Nestled in a fer-tile val-ley, glor-yus to our view . . ." I laugh. She doesn't. "See, I'm over here in Seattle, and I thought I'd surprise him. I know he'll be just ecstatic to hear from me." I pause, but she doesn't offer anything. "I don't know what to do now."

"I'm so sorry, I really do sympathize with you, but I almost lost my job giving out his number once. I mean, Mr. Righetti is a criminal lawyer. I can't give out his home number to *anyone*. If you can give me your hotel number, I'll see what I can do about finding him, though I can't promise anything."

"No, no, that's all right. Just tell him I'm coming. That's all."

"You're coming? That's the whole message?"

"Yes. Goodbye."

I sit in the airport lounge for a while, then I go out to the sidewalk and check out the hotel buses. One thing about airports: they're not designed to be walked away from. Finally I mingle in with a group of geologists who are on their way to a convention at the Hilton. As the bus whisks us away the man next to me says to a man across the aisle, "So, Steve, what's the latest on pseudo-proto-dolomitization?"

When we get to the hotel I hop on a city bus and ride around deciding what to do next. I'm filthy and sleepy from having walked all night to the airport in Reno. I don't have money for a Greyhound ticket; I don't have money for a hotel. There is nothing in this world for me to do but keep moving toward Al.

We pass Seattle University, so I hop off. I go to the cafeteria, examine all the options looking for the most volume at the least price. I finally settle on the hot lunch special. Two dollars, but I'm absolutely famished. I talk with as many students as I can, passing the word around that I'm looking for a ride to Spokane. Finally a girl comes over and tells me her father is going as far as Ellensburg this afternoon. I follow her to a pay phone while she calls him to set it up.

"Bye, Dad, love you." She hangs up. "His name is Phil; he's a cool guy; you'll like him. He'll meet you over here by the phone in a half-hour or so."

I get on the phone, try Information again for Al's number. It irks me to know Al's number is sitting right in front of the operator when she says, "It's unlisted." I was hoping to find an incompetent operator this time, who would give it out by mistake.

I get change at the cafeteria. In my hand I hold two dollars in bills, and two dollars in change. All my money. I cringe over each coin I drop in, dial Al's office. He's still out, has not called in. I tell the secretary that there is no new message, and I hang up.

Suddenly I feel like calling someone to remind me that I'm not totally rootless in the world. Will. Can I even find Will?

I try his old number in San Diego, expecting no answer, or maybe a recording that the phone's been disconnected. I'm surprised when an operator answers the ring, rattles off a new number for him, and hangs up. I repeat the number over and over under my breath until I get ahold of another operator to ask her to make a collect call.

Miranda accepts charges. "Oh, yeah, yeah, Will and I are getting along right fine. Took him home to meet my family and all. Creedmoor, North Carolina, that place is something else. I've done a bit of changing since I left Creedmoor, and I guess it shows. All my nieces and nephews had a fight over who was going to take me to school for show-and-tell."

"Is Will there by any chance?"

"Oh, he's here, all right. He's just indisposed. Sleeping, I imagine. I could wake him. I don't know what shape he'd be in to talk to you."

And then I hear it in the background: Crystal Gayle.

"What's wrong with him?" I almost shout.

"Oh, nothing wrong with him, really. He's just been holed up in the bedroom all day. He's been working real hard. He landed an amazing contract downtown, a whole office building that's getting a complete gutting. It's big-time. We've hit it big-time here, fast. I'm singing, too, over at La Paloma on Harbor Island." She wails along with Crystal Gayle, "It's been too lo-ong a time, with no pe-eace of mind, and I'm ready for the times to get better." A shiver runs through me. "You ought to see this place we've got. In La Jolla. You got a pen? Two fifty La Playa."

"Two fifty La Playa. I can remember that."

"It's really classy. Things are going great with us. How are things with you?"

"I don't know yet. I'm in Washington State. I may not be coming back. I may be moving to Spokane."

Miranda whistles long and low. "Things are going pretty hot with that old beau of yours, huh?"

"I don't know. I haven't seen him yet." I know it sounds ridiculous; I don't care. "You just tell Will . . . you just tell Will to take care of himself, and I'll let him know where I am as soon as *I* know where I am. And tell him I'll come back to San Diego whenever he needs help."

There is a long pause, then Miranda says, "There's nothing wrong. There's nothing he needs help about. And if he did, Brenda, I'm here."

I mumble goodbye, still feeling uneasy. A fatherish looking man is in the lobby, glancing around. I greet him, and introduce myself, and follow him to his car.

Phil is a doting father who actually swells, physically swells with pride when he speaks about his daughter. I'm enthralled by him, warmed by him, as his station wagon hauls us up up up the snow-laden Cascades. Our pleasant lazy conversation runs from the Grand Canyon to hydroponic gardening to sea chanteys. I know a lot of sea chanteys, I tell him, and he begs to hear them.

I laugh. "You don't know what you're asking for. I have one lousy voice."

"I'll take you up on the bet that mine is worse, but I'll sing the choruses if you'll be my chanteyman. Come on, this hauling up mountains is hard work."

So we sing: "The *Flying Cloud*," "Rolling Home," "The High Barbaree," "Bell-Bottom Trousers":

> *"When I was a serving maid down in Drury Lane*
> *My master was so kind to me, my mistress was the same*
> *Then came a sailor, fresh from the sea,*
> *And he was the cause of all my misery.*
>   *Bell-bottom trousers, coat of navy blue,*
>   *He can climb the rigging as his daddy used to do."*

We sing "Time to Leave Her," "Stormalong." Then when we're all warmed up I start into my favorite, and our two voices blend in that magical way that voices do, sometimes.

> *"Oh Shenandoah, I love your daughter,*
> *A-way, you rol-ling ri-ver!*
> *I'll take her 'cross yon rolling water.*
> *Away, away! I'm bound away!*
> *'Cross the wide Missouri!"*

When the last verse dies out, we sit for a long time in silence as the Cascades wind their way above and below and around us with their snowy beauty.

"I used to want to be a singer," he finally says, so quietly I can hardly hear him. He keeps looking straight at the road. "Oh, nothing fancy . . . street singing, maybe, Irish tunes, sea chanteys, for loose change." He smiles. "I'd forgotten all about wanting that." He looks at me in an admiring way that makes me want to blush. "Thanks for reminding me I wanted that."

Before long we pull into Ellensburg. I thank Phil heartily. I don't know what time it is. I run to a gas station, change my last two dollars. It's after five! Shivering, I go into a booth, slide the door shut, drop in the coins. The phone rings and rings and rings. "Damnit, Al," I whisper. "It's me, Brenda. Pick up the goddamned phone, Al. It's Brenda."

When I hang up, my coins jingle down one by one, like a win in a slot machine. I step out of the booth onto the icy sidewalk, hoist my pack. The winter sun has already disappeared. I can't reach Al tonight. I have two dollars in my pocket. I can't think of anything to do but keep trying to get to Spokane, even if I have to sit outside Al's office door all night. I walk a few blocks to a warm diner, drop one of my precious quarters on a cup of scorching black coffee, and do something I thought I was going to be doing two months ago. I pull out my notebook and my marker and at long, long last I letter a sign: SPOKANE.

50 ⬛ I STAND with my thumb out in the darkening dusk until I'm afraid I'm going to fall asleep standing up. I can't be more grateful when a worn-out red VW bus stops for me. The driver is young with a headful of loose curls and a wide-open smile, a dimple creasing the length of one cheek.

"Not going to Spokane," he says in reference to my sign, "but this is a terrible thumbing spot. I can at least drive you to a better spot, if you don't mind a short stop along the way." I nod and smile, throw my pack into the van and follow it in. He holds out his hand for me to shake as he pulls the van back onto the road. "Name's David," he says.

"Brenda Bradshaw."

He asks where I'm traveling from and I tell him San Diego. He asks how long it's taken me to get here and I surprise even myself with my answer of two months.

"I got sort of sidetracked," I add.

I wait for the obvious remarks about a woman traveling alone, and whether it's been scary, but he doesn't say anything. I appreciate that. It's nice to not have to explain myself to at least one person.

He is on his way to a parking lot to finish up the last round of his job. "Anyone," he says, "can get a job as a parking lot attendant in Washington in January."

David works at a few lots all over Ellensburg, the kind that have locked boxes at each space for payment. He pulls into a lot. Diamond Parking, reads a sign over a small shed that has windows on all four sides.

"This'll take about fifteen minutes," he says as he unlocks the shed. "You can stay here to keep warm." He kicks the side of a small paint-spattered portable electric heater, and it starts up, glowing orange, fan blowing. He has carried from the van a plastic quart milk bottle filled with water—the same type of water container that I carry. He pours some water into a pot, dumps coffee grounds right into that, sets it on a hotplate, then goes outside.

I sit on a three-legged stool stomping my boots next to the heater. I watch the fog of my warm breath for a while, then I pretend to smoke a cigarette, blow the smoke out in sophisticated ways, a childhood game I've never grown tired of. Through the dirty window I see David undoing locks and collecting envelopes from boxes, stuffing them into his pockets, blowing into his cupped hands. A few times I notice that there are no envelopes, and he walks once around these cars, examining the bumpers and looking through the windows. When he's covered the lot, he walks to the corner and with a great scraping racket drags a fifty-gallon drum over to a car and chains it to its bumper. By the time he gets back to the shed I'm feeling toasty and comfortable. His clothes are emanating cold; cold is glowing off him like off a block of ice. The water has just hit a rolling boil.

"This is my end-of-the-day reward." He pours the coffee into two stained white mugs, dancing away from spilling drops. "I sure hope you like this stuff. It's Turkish coffee. Strong, and you have to be careful about the grounds. Don't be too cavalier about how you down the last half of the cup." He smiles his nice smile. I'm still on the stool and he has propped his long self against the wall. "I don't know why I like this dirty old shed so much. Maybe because it sits here empty all day until I show up."

I love the coffee, of course. I'm such a coffee fiend, especially on the road. It's hard not to be, since all the cars in America run as much on coffee as they do on gas.

"That's quite a ticket you write, there." I point to the barrel.

David smiles wryly. "They have to call the boss to get unbarreled. It's one of the joys of this job—when people don't pay, I get to be judge, jury, and executioner all at once. For instance, that car I just barreled had two bumper stickers, a John Birch Society one, and one that said, 'Insured by Smith and Wesson.' If it's an old car, worn tires, I don't barrel them. Baby seat in the back, don't barrel 'em. They've got enough to worry about. And then there was one yesterday that had a pair of red kneesocks and a worn-out paperback of Emily Dickinson poems in the front seat. I couldn't barrel that."

We finish our coffee, leave the cups on the shelf, and climb back in the van. Soon we come to a well-lighted entrance with a Shell station and a FastMart. "This ought to be a better place to get a ride. I can take you twenty miles farther if you want, but there's nothing around where I live, no lights or hotels."

"Well," I pause. I just can't stand the thought of stopping. "Would you mind taking me that far? If I don't get a ride, it'll be better for me to be away from town, because I just sleep outside. I like sleeping outside. I've got this great sleeping bag . . ." but it all sounds like such blah-dee-blah to me now; give me a fifty and I'd be cozy between two clean sheets in a Holiday Inn watching an old Natalie Wood movie—*Splendor in the Grass* would be nice—calling room service, steam drifting out of the bathroom from my hot shower. But I only have two dollars and maybe, if I'm lucky, some forgotten raisin bread dried crisp from Mac's heater. And my quart jug of water, which will be frozen tomorrow morning when I wake up stiff and dirty, with a headache and a bellyache, on the icy ground. Fine shape *I'm* going to be in when I finally get to Al's. I'm going to look like a street urchin who needs saving from the big, bad world.

"I like sleeping outside, myself," David says. "I go out in the field behind my house. Like a kid, with a blanket tacked up for a tent. Not too often in January, though," he laughs.

I squint into the darkness. "What's the land like around here?"

"Desert."

I remember now the conversation I'd had ages ago with one of my first rides. Hard to believe it was only two months ago. I'd said, "It seems funny for there to be desert in a state like Washington," and he'd said, "More deserts in this country than anyone knows. Deserts everywhere."

We rumble along for a while. I watch David, barely lit by the light from the speedometer. I always like watching people drive Volkswagen vans. They lean on the wheel and half-smile in a friendly, peaceful way. The van rattles and sways—comforting, like a creaky porch swing.

"Brenda?"

I wake up, confused. "I'm sorry," I say, rubbing my eyes. David's van is stopped, idling on the gravel shoulder. "I've hardly slept the last two nights. I'm sorry."

"This is the turnoff for the house." Just ahead, in the headlight's glow, I can make out the beginning of a gravel road to the left. "You want to get out here?"

"Yes, this is fine, thanks," and I'm fumbling with my pack, thinking: Ask me to stay on your living room floor, oh, please ask me to stay.

"I've, I've got this great box of macaroni and cheese at the house. You know, Kraft? With the packet of dried-out fluorescent orange cheese?"

I have one hand on the door handle and the other grasping my backpack. "I love that stuff."

He smiles his smile again, dimple creasing the whole length of his cheek, as he turns to the left, gravel flying.

51 "THAT HOUSE!" I gasp. His headlights are hitting an old two-storied farmhouse, standing alone and slightly lopsided between two massive cottonwoods. "When I'm traveling, I see one or two of these a day, and I always wonder who lives in them. They seem so lonely. And so peaceful."

David nods. "It does something to people to drive past a house like this—see the kitchen light on at dusk—on sunny days see sheets hanging on the line. I've thought about that a lot, how this house right here does something to hundreds of people a day. Sometimes I feel like I'm doing something important in life just being here to turn on the kitchen light."

The inside startles me. There are the big rusty radiators,

graying wallpaper, and creaking pine floors, but not the original furniture I crazily expected. The large entry hall is empty; we pass a bedroom with a mattress on the floor, neatly made, an open sleeping bag for a bedspread. Next to the bed are wooden shelves stacked neatly with folded clothes, a couple of paperbacks. His room seems strangely intimate in its sparseness and order.

In the living room, beside a window, sits a drafting table. And drawings. Hundreds of drawings taped on the walls all around it: charcoals of roadrunners, jackrabbits, watercolors of bighorn sheep. And coyotes, lots of coyotes, in mid-turn, mid-leap.

"You draw!"

He just smiles, pleased, pulls an "Encyclopedia of Mammals" off the shelf, picks up a couple of children's books from a table and gives them to me to look at while he cooks in the kitchen. Illustrations by David Kerrigan.

"And short-order cook at the Plaza when the students show up in September," he yells from the kitchen. "When the place is busy for the first few months before the students figure out how to make Kraft macaroni and cheese."

I page past tarantulas rearing, a scuttling Gila monster, a leaping salmon, mouth ajar.

"The Plaza is the sort of place that keeps their saltines stacked in fifteen-year-old Tiparillo boxes under the counter."

A swaying gibbon, a myna bird just alighting on a vine. And then I realize what is alike about all these drawings: the animals look startled, not in fear, but in awe.

David brings out two bowls and also a blanket for me because the house is chilly. We settle into two old comfortable overstuffed chairs; with the same movement we swing sideways to hang our legs over the chairs' arms. Over dinner I talk lazily about some of my travel adventures. David doesn't seem disturbed; he doesn't question me about danger, doesn't make any comments about how brave or foolish I am. It feels good to be looked at like a regular person.

Through the window above his drafting table, in the distance, I see lines of headlights slide past.

"How long have you lived here?"

"Three years."

I look around at the windows within my sight. "Oh. I thought maybe you'd just moved in. You don't have any curtains."

"No one to look in, except from afar. It's like what we were talking about earlier; all these people drive past, and they see me shuffling around inside. It's ok with me. I think it makes them remember. Home. Or what home once was to them. Or what they once wanted their home to be."

"I just had a driver say something like that to me. That I reminded him of something he once wanted. I reminded him of something he'd forgotten he'd wanted."

David's mouth is slightly open in a half-smile, and it seems almost as if he is leaning toward me, though he's not; he's still slumped in his chair.

"Well," he finally says. He picks his feet up high, gracefully rocks out of the chair, gathers up my bowl. I wrap my blanket around me and follow him into the kitchen while he starts to do dishes.

"What's in Spokane?" he asks, and something about that question jolts me to the core. The word *what*. What will be in Spokane for me? At first I don't know how to answer, then I realize how innocent David's question really is.

"A friend. It's rather a mess. He's moved, and I don't know where, and I only have his office number—I can't seem to find out his home number. So I can only get ahold of him during office hours. Which I haven't been able to do yet. Do you have a phone? I'll make a collect call."

"I'm sorry. I don't."

He puts the clean bowls on the shelf. We return to the living room. "I have some drawing I need to do tonight. I hope you don't mind."

"Of course not." I slump back into the comfortable old chair. With familiar ease, David climbs onto his stool, chooses some pastels, and begins sketching. I pick up one of his books, open it at random.

On the page, a hawk wheels above me. The only background is blue sky, yet I know the hawk is hovering over a mountain: I can feel the hot breeze that is ruffling its feathers; I can smell sagebrush. High desert silence is ringing in my ears. The hawk is staring right at me, caught in a precise instant of alertness—almost a look of recognition. Amazing. How does David *do* this?

"David?"

He looks up, his face flushed. He is holding a stick of charcoal in mid-stroke, startled by my break into his world. I stand up to look at his work. More coyotes, dashing off into the night.

"I'm sorry," I say. "Go on with what you were doing."

He does. I drop back into the chair. David sweeps the charcoal over the paper almost feverishly, the muscles in his forearm twist and flex. I close the book, drop it gently to the floor. In the distance, cars hum past. Some of them going to Spokane.

I wake to David calling my name quietly.

"Brenda? You might be more comfortable if you stretch out." On the floor is a nest he has made of blankets and sheets, my sleeping bag, and the sleeping bag he had on his own bed. Even some towels. Probably everything he owns.

I drop gratefully onto the pile, pull out his sleeping bag and hold it up to him. "At least take this back. You're going to need it."

"I'll be all right. I have a blanket." He takes the sleeping bag from my hands and lays it on top of me. We exchange shy goodnights. He asks if I want the hall light left on, but I say no. He shuts it off and goes into his room.

I close my eyes, try to conjure up Al's image, his delicious combination of innocent eyes and wicked smile. But he won't appear. I try to remember his voice, his hair.

I sit up, feel around in the dark for my backpack, unzip the side pocket and pull out Al's letter. I know what it says. "Brenda! I've passed the bar exam at long last and I'm ready to start living again. Visit me. Visit me. Visit me. Al."

I grasp the letter in my hand, lie back down.

"Goodnight, sweet Al," I whisper. "See you tomorrow."

52

I WAKE EARLY; my first thought is that I'm covered with Reno lounge dirt. I shiver.

David is nowhere to be found. I search the downstairs, call loudly up the stairwell. His van is still parked out front. Then I catch a glimpse of his lone lean figure, walking off over the rolling grasslands.

I take a long hot shower. I know one thing: when I step into Al's law office today, I don't want to look like something that's just wandered in off the street. Even if I have. I step out of the tub, smudge the steam off the mirror with my hand. I look so tired. My clothes sit in a pile on the floor. Disgusting. What would a forensics expert find on them? Dirt from a curb in Gloucester, fried chicken grease from a diner in Wyoming, beer from a Cheyenne bar, leather-tanning chemicals from a late-model Monte Carlo, particles of red carpeting from the Lucky Dice Casino in Reno, and that particular sweat that is caused only by fear.

I dig around in my pack. One dirty t-shirt, two dirty pairs

of socks, two dirty underpants. Everything else is in the filthy pile on the floor; I'd been wearing it all because of the cold. The only clean thing I have is the skirt I've been saving to wear for Al. Such a ridiculous piece of clothing to have carried with me all this time. I have no clean shirt to wear with it, anyway.

I hear David in the house, stick my head out the door. "David?" He comes down the hallway. His hair is blown into lovely wild curls around his face. "Do you have a washing machine here?"

"Yes. An ancient relic. It works. No dryer, but if you hang your clothes outside, they'll be dry by noon. It's cold out, but sunny and windy. You're welcome to stay and do that if you like. I'll even be here. I don't have to barrel anyone today." He smiles.

"Thanks." I close the door, look at my clothes. What filthy thing should I wear now; what will have to go unwashed? I sigh.

"Brenda?" David's voice startles me; he hasn't moved from the door. "You want to wear something of mine while you wash your things?"

His clothes feel great—worn jeans that I have to roll up twice, wonderfully stiff and scratchy from being line-dried, a large soft cotton shirt. I curl up in the chair and page through David's animals, examining each in detail, while the round-barreled washing machine chugs slowly in a room off the kitchen. Soap smell mixes with the smell of the oatmeal bubbling on the stove.

David goes outside and comes back in with a load of wood, starts a fire, dishes up breakfast, and we eat. All the while, we don't say a word. The silence is intoxicating.

The washer stops. David carries our bowls to the sink. I get up, pull my clothes out of the washer piece by piece, run them through the wringer. It's surprisingly hard work to pull the wringer handle round and round, but the work feels good.

I go out the back door with my clean clothes in a cardboard box; the screen door slaps shut behind me. I squint into the morning sun that is shining through cottonwood limbs onto the wraparound porch, step with clean bare feet across the cold porch onto the icy ground, and begin hanging the clothes. Steam rises from the laundry in the box. A bird streaks across blue sky, and in seconds is gone. And always, in the distance, is the hum, the call of the road. By noon, I'll be gone.

I go back inside, sit on the floor before the fire, hold my feet up to warm my soles. David is at his table, drawing, surrounded by his animals, looks of awe.

"What's upstairs?" I ask. My voice surprises me—sweet and languid.

"It's empty. It's nice up there. You can see a long way." He seems distracted. "You should go up there and look around. It's nice up there."

The stairs are appropriately creaky, the darkened gray garlanded wallpaper scattered with brighter gray squares at the landing, ghosts of what must have been wedding photos, first-grade teeth-missing photos, an eight-by-ten black-and-white glossy of a bright-eyed boy in a starched navy uniform.

The upstairs sitting room is a glorious high-ceilinged wonder of sunlight and shadow. A black-and-white photo of a baby hangs in an old black frame on the wall. I walk over to it; each step I take creaks. The picture was taken by someone inside a boat, facing the open hatch. The baby is in a makeshift highchair—a rope tied around the uprights of the ladder. It sits on a step, hands out, leaning forward earnestly, its sweet baby-bird-mouth open, eternally ready to receive a spoonful of food which is being eternally offered by a young, graceful hand. Outside the hatch, a boom is just visible, some sail, loops of line, a few clouds. A salty breeze seems to blow right through the hatch, past the baby, and out the picture to where I'm standing. I stare at it for a long while, barely breathing, drinking in all the details.

Finally I turn away and go into the back bedroom. Empty, but the closet is full of hangers with the ends bent down to make them smaller: a child's room. The baby in the picture? I walk to the window, lean on the sill, looking out to the free-rolling hills. The crib would have been here. I can imagine a young mother pacing this room sleepily, late at night, mumbling lullabies to her restless baby. I pace, myself, back and forth, then go down the hall to the next room.

The view from the window is sliced with bare cottonwood limbs. In the summer it must be a moving curtain of green, the room no doubt cool and breezy, filled with the soothing flutter of leaves. On the wall opposite the window is the ghost of an oval mirror. This room faces west; a girl standing here, looking at her reflection in the setting sun, would have seen her face surrounded by the glowing halo of her hair.

The next room, the sunrise room. The parents', I think. Cottonwood limbs fill the window here, too, making a bright pattern on the floor. I walk to the window, look out at the grasslands, at the small piece of road visible. East, to Spokane. I cannot for the life of me remember what Al looks like.

Then the front room, and this one a mystery. The floor creaks loudly. It's on the south side of the house, the floorboards probably dried and shrunk from the hot square of sun shining all day through the window. A venetian blind is raised flush to the top of the sill. I stand at the window, forehead pressed to the cool bright glass, giddy from the height. It's one of those old generous windows, the top molding past my reach, bottom sill pressing my shins. I feel I could float out, the way I float so naturally in my dreams. This room faces the road. Who would have had this room? What did it mean to them? Before the venetian blind there were probably lace curtains. I try to imagine the person who must rarely have left what was then the farm, standing here looking out on a road that was forever reaching out like long arms over the rolling hills to the east and west.

Tacked inside the closet, a 1962 calendar from White Star Laundrymat in Ellensburg. A blond-haired boy and girl kneel, faces tipped to a glowing light, eyes shut peacefully, hands folded in prayer. Printed below them: "Faith and Grace."

I cross back to the window and lower the venetian blind, which clatters and squeaks all the way down. The slats have been turned shut, but at my eye level, two of them are bent inward. Someone had peeked secretly through this closed blind, then. I raise the blinds back up, then sit crosslegged before the window, head resting on my folded arms on the sill, watching the cars glide by in each direction. I doze in the hot hot sun. Faith and Grace. Faith and Grace. I dream that I am dancing in a barn. The barn is lofty, smelling of dirt, but there is a gleaming new wooden floor down, and mirrors, and a ballet barre. I dance to myself in the mirror: *jetés, ronde de jambes, glissades.* Then I leap, hang in midair for that one golden second, tattered skirt swept behind me, fingers taut before my face, dramatic, hurt, and wronged. Beams of dust-filled light strike the floor all around me. Al and I are married, in the dream. We own a large house, the barn, a lot of property. I still can't remember what Al looks like. I love the barn.

A noise wakens me. Slowly I relinquish the toe shoes, the barn. I sit confused, the bright, dirty windowpane inches from my eyes, and try to imagine what the noise was. I feel hot and dopey. Then I remember David below, slowly pull myself up, and walk downstairs on shaky legs, past crystal doorknobs, past high windows full of bare limbs, past the family of ghost-pictures on the landing, down, down.

David has just come in from outside. He has his jacket on, his hair is windblown. I smile sleepily at him, walk to the window, look at the lines of cars passing each other in different directions. My clothes are flapping on the line.

"I fell asleep upstairs."

"I know. I sat up there with you for a while, and read some.

There's something about that room and that window. I've fallen asleep the same way, before."

"What time is it?"

"Late. Almost three."

Almost three. My heart plummets to the floor. Too late, too late.

"Are you thinking of leaving?" David asks.

On the word, *leaving,* I suddenly, finally, picture Al, Al's face, crystal clear, his smooth lips, the line of his jaw, his brown eyes locking on mine.

I shake my head in amazement, turn; there is David, dimple dipping into his cheek.

"Good!" he says, mistaking my head-shaking for a "no." "Good!" He nods, his curls fly; light seems to fling off them into the room. "I just brought my drawings down to the mailbox. So we can do anything now. We could . . ." He grins sheepishly. "I work, I draw. I walk. I've almost forgotten what else there is. What would you like to do?"

Go to Al's, I'm thinking. But if I go now I'll have to sit outside his office door all night. "Is it ok if I draw, some?"

"Yes," he answers, simply. He goes to his drawing table, pulls out a huge sheet of clean white paper, smoothes it, tapes it down. He shoves the stool out of the way with his foot and we stand next to each other, working on the same piece of paper. I can only do crude, cartoony stuff, but I'm not embarrassed; I draw and draw, filling up my side of the paper, not noticing time passing. A man's face, a stick-and-square for a pipe coming out of his semicircle smile, a curlicue of smoke whirling out. A lollipop tree with scribbles for nests. David and I talk without pausing in our drawing. I don't even look at what David is doing on his side of the paper. "Did you go to school to learn to draw?" "Naw, I was alone a lot as a kid and I taught myself." I draw a **v** over a circle: a baby bird with its mouth open. Over it, a mother bird dropping a squiggle line of a worm into its mouth. "I filled up books of my own studies, starting when I was about ten. Then," he chuckles, "I made a list of all the things I knew about drawing. There were twenty-five rules. When I came up with twenty-five I thought I'd discovered them all. Like elements on the periodic table, I guess." He puts down his stick of charcoal, holds up his blackened fingers, and reads in the air, with mock seriousness, "Rule number twenty-five: The objects themselves are not as important as the spaces between them."

53 🎴 D A V I D makes spaghetti, and we eat with the same comfortable silence as at breakfast. Then he gathers the bowls.

"Allow me," I say with mock grace, take the two bowls and two coffee mugs from his hands, and start to wash them in the sink. The warm soapy water feels good. "Do you know anything about that picture upstairs? Of the baby? It's a wonderful picture." I begin drying the dishes, setting them carefully on David's bare shelves.

David smiles sadly. "That's me."

"That's you? You were on a sailboat."

"I was *born* on a sailboat."

"Are you kidding me? Born on a sailboat." I shake my head. I fold the dishcloth neatly, hang it on the rack. We return to the living room and slump into the same two chairs.

"I lived on that boat until I was ten."

"I'd love to live on a boat for a while. I might, still."

David nods, says, "Everyone should for a while, at some time in their life."

"I've never been out on a boat far enough where I couldn't see land. I've always wanted to. In high school, I used to go to the beach, wade in, and start swimming straight for the horizon." I hold my arm straight out; I can see that horizon. "Well, I always hit the kelp beds before too long. So I'd stop and tread water and look back at the beach. The cliffs would only look like a thin white line, even though they were thirty feet high. And teeny-tiny people; I could barely see them. I'd bob around, all alone out there. I loved being all alone. I used to hold onto a fat stem of kelp and close my eyes and just float on my back out there, for a half-hour or so." I have my head tipped back, my eyes closed, arms out. I'm remembering one especially hot day, hot dry Santa Ana winds blowing, floating out there in those salty swells, with Al. He held onto the kelp that day; I held his hand.

I open my eyes; David's dimple is creasing his one cheek.

"Why did you live on a boat?" I ask.

David shrugs, laughs a little. "I've never known how to answer that. It's just where we lived. My dad owned a small company. Had a few offices. One in San Luis; we'd dock in Morro Bay for that. One office in Seattle. Once I was in school, we docked in Seattle for the school year. But otherwise, where we sailed depended more on weather and seasons than anything else. My dad had just set up his life that way. He was pretty old when I was born."

"Raised on a boat," I say again, in disbelief. "I was raised on air force bases myself. I always thought it was strange that people lived in the same house, in the same town and the same state, year after year. A place that they owned, their very own house."

"I always wondered why people lived in houses. In fact, for a long time, I didn't know that people lived in houses at all. Until I was about five, my dad says, I used to ask people, 'What's the name of *your* boat?' "

I suddenly remember: *Brenda's Quest. Brenda's Question.* I ask, "What *was* the name of your boat?"

"*Rose,*" he says, in such a way that I can smell it, the salty breeze, the spicy petals. "That was my mother's name."

"Was her name. She's not alive?"

"She died when I was ten. We were docked in Puerto Vallarta. We had a little scooter on board, a shiny blue one, that we used for running errands wherever we were docked. My mom was out on it, getting groceries, and she went out of control on a curve, hit a rock, got thrown and hit a tree." He sighs. "My dad and I went down to the morgue. It was just a trailer, really. My dad wanted me to see her body, but I wouldn't do it. I just wanted to remember her the way she was. My mom was so . . ." he squints his eyes, says with conviction, ". . . pretty."

Pretty: a word a ten-year-old would use to describe his mother.

"We were sure she was going too fast. She always liked to speed on that scooter. Whenever I rode with her, I clutched onto her waist and jammed my face into her shoulderblades. I could never look down at the road, it was such a blur. I was always scared to death."

"It's funny to think of someone's mom speeding around on a scooter."

"She was young. She was only seventeen when she married my dad. He was thirty-seven. When she died, she was only twenty-eight. Twenty-eight—that's how old I am now." He shakes his head. "My dad put me on a plane to Seattle to live with my Aunt Kathleen, while he sold the boat and settled some things. He sailed *Rose* to L.A. and sold her there. Then he came back to Seattle and bought a house. He never remarried. I don't think he's ever sailed again, either."

"Have you?"

"Yes, lots. But I haven't even stepped on a boat now for about five years."

"Why not?"

"I live here. It's not near the ocean." He shrugs. "I like it here. I'm happy with where I am and what I'm doing right now."

I remember the picture: the baby's mouth reaching out, wanting and patient at the same time. I remember the slender hand, ready to offer the spoonful of food. "Do you have a picture of your mom?"

He shakes his head. "The summer after we moved to Seattle, my dad had to go to San Luis for a while. Things were all different—there wasn't a boat for me to live on; he wouldn't take me with him. I was really mad at him for leaving me for that month, but funny thing was, I was even more mad at my mom, then, for leaving me forever. Anyway, one night, I collected together all the pictures I had of her, and burned them out on the back patio in my aunt's Weber Kettle. I probably would have burned that one that was upstairs, but my dad had it. He gave it to me a few years ago. When he was visiting. He lives in Florida now."

"Have you drawn her?"

He just drops his head, shakes it. We sit around in silence for a while, then we both get up and start preparing to sleep. I pick up my nest from the corner and unroll it on the floor.

"Oh! My clothes! On the line!"

"You can get them in the morning."

We pass each other in the hallway, shuffling to and from the bathroom. When I'm ready to shut off the light, I hear the shower turn on. I go to the door. "I'm calling it a night, David. See you in the morning."

For some reason, I get the feeling that he is stock-still in the shower, that he is waiting for something else to happen. It's almost as if I can feel him holding his breath. I stand outside the door for what seems like forever, trying to imagine what more I should be saying to him, but I don't know what it can be. Finally I shut off the light and lie down.

After a while, David walks across the hallway to his bedroom and closes his door. Suddenly, I find myself wide awake. Now, this is really strange, because I can sleep anywhere, under any circumstances, when I *want* to. Once, I fell asleep in a speedboat, sitting up. I've never understood when people say they envy how I can sleep; I don't see what the skill is. I can't sympathize with their insomnia. But here I find myself, in a friendly, safe, comfortable place, and for the first time in my life my brain is refusing to shut down for the day, my eyes refusing to close. What *is* this, I wonder. Well, of course, I slept all afternoon. I hear a rustling in David's room, a click, a sliver of light slices from under his door. I can see stars out the window, hear an occasional car pass on the distant road. Al is only one hundred and fifty miles away. David coughs. His light clicks off. I close my eyes, try to conjure up Al's image: his smooth lips, brown eyes. But I've lost it once again.

I finally sleep, and I dream of David. He's standing in a field, saying something to me, over and over, the same two words, only I don't know what the words are. He smiles, he repeats them with infinite patience. I examine the words. Yes, they're English. Yes, I can hear. Yes, David is speaking loudly enough, and clearly enough. Still, I just don't know what the words are. I walk up to him, put my eye right up to his mouth. He doesn't seem to mind. "Welcome home," he is saying. "Welcome home."

I wake. A dim square of light appears on the wall, gets brighter; the sound of a truck approaches. David appears in the hallway, wrapped in a blanket.

"Are you asleep? It's Deeker!" he announces happily, as if I should be excited, too.

He goes back into his room. Outside, the engine stops, truck door slams. There is a stomping on the porch, a bang of the front door swinging open.

"Loner! Wake up, old man! Ollie-ollie-oxen-free!" A large

figure stomps up the hall, face wide and bearded like a lumberjack's. "Lon-*er!*" he yells into David's doorway, then enters.

I hear them laughing and talking, though I can't make out the words. Finally the hall light comes on. David, dressed now, walks into the dark where I am, leans over me, says quietly, sheepishly, "I suppose you're awake?" Deeker pushes past, squats, holds out his huge hand.

"Brenda? I'm Deeker; how do you do? Get up! Get dressed! *Meteor* showers!"

He heads for the front door. David leans over me again, his hands on his knees. "I'll bring an extra blanket for you. You want to come along?"

"Of course."

Alone in the cold room, laughing, I pull on David's cold clothes, my boots, sweater and jacket, then bound down the hall, slap through the screen door and fly down the porch steps thinking I'll have to catch up with them. But they have been waiting for me beside the porch.

We head across the field behind the house, crunching through the frozen grasslands, wrapped in blankets. The sky rains stars above us. Finally we stop and lie down, me in the middle. We are all three shivering violently in the icy night air. We scoot together for warmth, but we can't seem to get warm, so we get up again, joking and shoving, rearrange the blankets so we're all lying on top of one blanket and under two. We rustle this way and that, complain loudly about who's stealing all the blankets. And then, finally settled in, the whole of huge black space opens before us.

"Oh! Look at that one!"

"There! That one! Two, there!"

"Three! Three at once!"

I can't make my wishes fast enough; my falling-star-wishes are making me dizzy with wanting so much, so fast.

"The coyotes are watching the *sky* fall in!" David shouts. I think of coyotes, the look of awe, tarantulas rearing, jackrabbits transfixed.

"Catch one!" Deeker yells, and we play a game of catching stars like falling leaves, our six pale hands flashing across the black sky.

"Here," David says. "One for you." He presses a star into my hand.

I remember MaryEllen on the bed that night at the apple ranch, quoting Cochise: "They roam over the hills and plains and want the heavens to fall on them." I feel blessed.

"That's Orion," I point. "The Hunter. His belt is made of Mintaka, Alnilam, and Alnitak. My brother Will taught those to me when I was four years old. And there's Gemini. The twins."

We lie quietly for a long while, being blessed by gifts from the heavens. Deeker finally stands up, wrapped in his blanket. "I'd have to say Gemini has things together. If I was a star wa-a-ay up there, *I'd* want a twin." He scratches his beard. "That was a great show. Peak is over, though, and I've got to get to work in a few hours. Brenda . . ." he nods toward me. "Loner." He stands above us for a few seconds, his breath billowing. "Next time." I can hear his boots in the crunchy grass all the way back to the house, then his truck start up and drive off.

David and I are bundled together in one mass; I can barely tell where I end and he begins. We could be a rock, we could be grass, the earth itself.

"My brother, Will, says that we're made of the stuff of stars. That everything that we're made of, a long time ago, shot right through a star. Sometimes I feel like I can remember it—speeding through space, burning." I feel silly now, to have said that, but David nods his head.

Suddenly I'm exhausted. A few last stars fall, and the next

time I look, the sky is becoming light, and the Milky Way has shifted in the sky.

David and I are spooned together. He stirs behind me. "Look," I say, "the Milky Way's been spinning above us."

I'm stiff, so stiff I think I'll never move again. I tell David about Will, how he was always outside at night with his head tipped back. I tell him the story about Will in the Peanut Gallery of the "Howdy Doody" show, and when I get to the part about the giant Tootsie Roll bouncing across the stage, we laugh and hoot together in the frozen grass. I can't see David where I'm lying, haven't seen him yet since I've woken, and it's almost as if I'm having a grand time just telling stories to myself. I explain about the spot in space. I tell about the list that I made when I was ten, of things to do in my life, and about Lucien, and *Brenda's Quest.* I even tell him about living with my Aunt Josephine, right down to how juicy the plums were. I talk about everything but Al.

We get up when the sun hits us. We tease each other about how scruffy we look. I comb my fingers through my knotted hair, pinch my cheeks, rub my eyes. The sun is bright and clear, the air icy, like it was the morning Al and I got up to see the sunrise together. No . . . it was the sun*set* we saw . . . the milk was so cold, the car hood so hot.

I shake my head to clear it, then David and I walk back to the house, our four boots trudging together through the crunchy grass.

54 ◈ BACK INSIDE, David starts the oatmeal bubbling on the stove, and I go out with the cardboard box to collect my laundry. The sun is hovering low in the crisp, clean air. A perfect day to travel in, a perfect day to start over

in. I bend the stiff, cold clothes into the cardboard box, go into the house. David is at his desk, drawing. I go into the bathroom, take a shower, reluctantly pull on my cold clothes and fold David's into a pile. For the first time it occurs to me why he's so conservative and neat with his possessions, of course: he was brought up on a sailboat.

David is sitting on his stool turned sideways from his drawing table, staring at his drawing pad in his hand, pencil grasped in his other hand resting on his hip. I think he has heard me come in but he doesn't look up. I lean against the doorframe, hands in my pockets, one boot atop the other, and wait. He raises his pencil as if to add something, brings it down. He glances at me critically, adds a few dark strokes, then holds out the pad, his eyes narrowed, no smile, but his dimple creasing the length of his cheek anyway. The drawing is *me*, me as I've never seen myself before, eyes wide, mouth slightly open in a sudden gasp. Full of awe.

"It's me," I say stupidly.

"Last night," David says. "You last night." Then he laughs suddenly, loudly, infectiously, and says, a little embarrassed, "You right now."

I don't know what to say. "May I keep it?" I finally ask shyly.

He takes it from me, looks down at it for a long time without saying anything. "I'd like to keep it. If you don't mind."

I shake my head. David spoons out the oatmeal, and as usual we eat without speaking. While he does the dishes I pack my clean clothes neatly into my backpack. It feels so good. Everything in order; I'm clean, my clothes are clean. I fold each piece of the nest I've been sleeping on, stack them on the chair. I set my pack upright in the middle of the room. David walks into the room and looks at it.

"You have to go now?"

I nod. "I do."

"All right."

He carries my pack for me down his gravel driveway and across the highway. He sets my pack down on the shoulder, then surprisingly, crosses to the other side of the road, turns, and stops.

And there I'm standing in my muddy boots, heels in the dirt and toes on the gray pavement, the road stretching out forever in both directions, and on the other side of this road stands David, the whole bleak landscape behind him, lone house between two ancient cottonwoods, the bright gray horizon behind him, him shivering with his hands jammed in the pockets of his open jeans jacket, his shoulders bent forward like folded wings, and he is smiling, but there is something wrong—no dimple, his smile has no dimple, and he is nodding his head slightly up and down, up and down, as if answering a question, except I haven't asked anything of him, and he finally says, a fog of warm breath coming out with each word, "You make people remember what they once wanted."

He turns and walks away, he doesn't stop or look back, and finally I hear his screen door slam in the distance.

I remember with sudden horror and urgency that I didn't ask him about what he'd said to me in the dream. I know beyond the shadow of a doubt that he knows what he'd said; I know I could ask him and he could explain it to me. I want to run back up his road, and ask him.

"You are crazy, Brenda," I say aloud. "It was a goddamned dream." There are no cars on the road yet, it's early; I stand in silence shifting in my boots. I want to cry. "I've got to get to Al's," I say, out loud.

David's screen door slams again in the distance. My heart starts pounding in my chest. But David doesn't come down the road. I don't know where he is until I see him hanging a sheet on the line between a cottonwood and the house. Then he stands in front of it, raises one arm high, and full-arm, waves goodbye. From this distance he looks strangely fragile. I wave back to him, full-arm. Everything is so quiet; my ears ring. Then I hear a car in the distance. The car draws closer. I don't put out my thumb, I stand on the road facing David's house with my arms hanging loose at my side. The car passes me, slows, pulls onto the shoulder, and sits, idling. Two light beeps. I pick up my pack, trudge to the car, and get in.

55 ◩ WELCOME to Spokane. I chuckle out loud.
"What's that?" the driver asks.
"Nothing. Just something I was remembering."
Everything looks amazingly familiar, right down to the ice on the trees. I know every detail about this city; I could get out of the car right now and find my way to Al's basement apartment. Except Al doesn't live there anymore.
We brake for a red light, and there, across the intersection is the gas station I made a midnight stop at five years ago while trying to find my way to Al's. "I'll just get out here," I tell the driver. I step out onto the icy sidewalk, hoist out my pack. "Thanks for the ride. Good luck with your girlfriend. Everything'll probably work out just fine."
The light changes; I jog across the intersection, drop my pack to the pavement and step into the phone booth to look in the directory. Blumenfeld, Jones and Righetti: 5626 3rd Ave NW. I swing my pack over to the gas station window and slide my finger around on what is probably the same map, yellowed now, taped inside. I'm feeling wildly tragic and romantic and solid, just like I did five years ago. Al's office is downtown, not too far away; maybe a couple of miles. I skip

and slip down the icy sidewalks, grinning; I feel dizzy and silly.

And then suddenly there's the waterfall, the river smashing right through as if this weren't a city at all. I run to the railing, lean far over, letting the icy mist rise into my face. I laugh out loud, "Yi yi yi yi!" I trill into its plummeting depths.

Market Street, Independence Avenue; I feel good, fresh: the lonesome traveler come home. I start to hit the downtown area, people in business clothes bustle past at a good clip, with purpose. They glance at me, askance.

Outside the cities, when you're trudging along in your hiking boots with a pack on your back, people eye you with a type of respect, even, occasionally, with envy: you're a gypsy, a vagabond, an untamable romantic. In the cities, you're just another homeless bum. 'I'm on the *road*, not in the *streets*,' I want to explain to each woman who crosses, high heels clicking, to the far edge of the sidewalk when I pass.

Then suddenly I'm outside Al's modern tower of an office building. I throw my head back and squint up at its height like a country bumpkin. The double entry doors open and close; people rush in; I time myself and slip in the doors, like skipping into a moving jumprope. The red carpeting in the foyer reminds me of the stuff in the Lucky Dice Casino. Next to the elevators are droopy plants. I stop like a stalled car, people jamming up behind me, then skirting around. I'd never, honestly, imagined what this awkward part would be like; in my dreams there'd only been me on the road, then that one magic moment when I would see Al; when in one smooth movement he would draw me into him and bring me home. I'd never imagined standing in slush-covered boots with a travel-worn backpack, in a building so new it smells like wet paint, the whole of the business world rushing around me.

The directory board says that Al is on the seventh floor. I shove my hands in my pockets, jingle around my two dollars of quarters. I feel like I have only two dollars' worth of everything left: guts, spunk, nerve. My whole being is running on a handful of loose change.

Forget the elevator; I head to the stairwell. It's nicer in here, alone; I bound up the stairs despite my pack. Seventh floor. Panting and sweating, I push through the door. Outside Al's office I drop my pack off my shoulders, lean it on the wall, wait for my breathing to slow. Then I'm through Al's office door, asking the receptionist for Al. Everything is sparkling and wobbling.

"Mr. Righetti should be in any moment. Would you care to take a seat?"

"No," I answer, a little too loudly, back myself through the door, and stand, bouncing on my heels, in the hallway. A few men pass; I study their faces. Maybe I won't recognize Al; maybe he's changed.

But the elevator door opens, and people spill out, and there among them is Al, walking toward me, looking sweet and silly and too young for his suit. "Al," I mouth; no sound comes out. He looks up with a start; his soft brown eyes lock onto mine with an almost audible click. "Brenda," he mouths back, and I remember in a rush that lifts and twists me like a whirlwind why I traveled ten thousand miles to get to him, the line of his jaw. And now he is only a hallway length away. I want to call out, to run to him, I remember now, I *love* him; I bite my lip to keep from laughing out loud. But I'm in my worn jeans and stretched sweater and all around him are his colleagues in well-tailored business clothes and newly shined shoes, thoroughly engrossed in conversation, so I only smile at Al and walk toward him as normally as I can manage.

Al's trying to communicate something wildly with his eyes, I don't know what. Maybe he'll walk right on past me, maybe he won't acknowledge me at all. But a few feet away he surprises me by saying, "Brenda!" as if noticing me for the first time. I'm trying to decide if it's ok to hug him, to touch him, I so need to touch him, when he grabs both shoulders of the woman next to him and shoves her between us like a shield.

"Brenda, good to see you. I'd like you to meet my wife."

I'm smiling, he's smiling, she's smiling, I think I'm smiling, my lips seem to be stretched comically wide: yes, that's a smile. "How do you do?" I say. Wife. Wife.

She laughs a little, says with great ease, "Absolutely fine, thanks." She half-turns to Al, says goodnaturedly, "So it's come to this already? My *wife?*" She turns back to me. "I do have a name; it's Nicole."

The other people have gone into Al's office, so the three of us are left in the hall. I'm grappling around my muddled brain for something to say; my face aches with the strain of holding onto my smile, my heart aches with the strain of holding in a gasp, a drop of sweat trickles down my side to my waist. I am painfully aware of my shabby clothes, my pack leaning against the wall; I feel childish and foolish. Wife.

"Well," I say. When I swallow, as casually as I can, it hurts. "You're newlyweds?" I ask stupidly.

Nicole breaks into a radiant grin. "One week," she answers.

We stand, all three grinning intensely. You would think we were getting our picture taken. "Well. Congratulations."

"Thank you," she answers.

I turn to Al, formally. "I was just in the area," I say, "and I thought I'd drop in and say hello. Hello."

"It's good to see you," Al says again.

"Uh, well, I should be going. Nice to have met you." I back away with a small, awkward wave, trip over my bootlace on my way to the elevator. Then I remember my pack, and turn around in time to see Nicole point to it and say, "What's *that* doing here?"

Al opens his office door, ushers her in, then catches my eye over his shoulder and mouths, "Wait."

The hall is empty. I lean against the wall, bite back tears, shake my head and half-laugh. Wife.

Al's door swings open. He rushes to me, then stops, arm's length away. He reaches out his hand to me and I almost take it, until I realize that he's showing me his wedding ring, not in the backhanded, flitter-fingered fashion I'd seen women do, but with his palm up. For a while, we both peer into his cupped hand as if he's holding something precious and interesting, something like a baby bird still too young to fly away. He smiles shyly, as if he'd hand it over to me, what his marriage means to him, if he could. Then he puts his hand in his pocket.

"Jesus, Brenda, you look great," he says, drinking me in, grinning, now, with a true grin. Tears well up in my eyes and sit there. I rub them away; they well up again.

"Al. You got married."

He nods. "It happened pretty quickly." He looks embarrassed and proud at the same time. "Nicole was in town on a job interview and she had a rental car and it broke down and I happened to be walking past." He laughs a little at the memory. "She looked so pitiful, she just didn't know what to do, stranded out there on the side of the road. I'm thinking of writing Avis to thank them for giving her a lousy car."

I drop my head, snort slightly at the irony of it. "I hitchhiked here alone to see you. Hundreds of miles."

Al's smile turns a little sad. He dips his head. I rub away the wells of tears; they come back.

"I didn't think you were really just in the area."

"Naw, come on now, Al, of course not. I only came here to see you." I kick at one boot with the other. I laugh. "I was going to sail to Jamaica on a wooden ship with a pirate named Lucien. He has gold teeth." I run my fingers along my teeth.

"You're the only person I've ever known who would say something like that and mean it. You mean it, don't you?"

I screw up my mouth, nod yes, shrug.

"You're a different breed, Bren."

A different breed. That's what Lucien called me. I wish, right now, that just for a little while, I didn't have to be a different breed. "Do you remember that note you sent me, asking me to visit? 'I've passed my bar exam at long last and I'm ready to start living again.' I've still got it. Right here in my pocket."

"You never came," Al says. "But then if you had, I never would have met Nicole."

"I'm glad for you," I say. "I'm so glad for you." I'm afraid my tears are going to start spilling over. I blink faster and faster.

"Brenda."

I lean back into the wall, take a deep, weary breath, thinking about all those miles and miles and miles. "I don't know why it took me so long to get here. It doesn't matter now, anyway." I'm feeling sorry for myself. I hate feeling sorry for myself. I can't even look at Al, I have to stare at the carpet.

"Where are you going now? Don't hitchhike anymore, Bren. Please don't."

"I don't know. Back to San Diego, see my brother. I'm kinda worried about him. I think he might need me to help him out." I feel so tired, weary right down into my muscles, right down into my bones. "Al, can I borrow some money? Just to get back to San Diego with." He is already pulling notes out of his wallet. "I don't know, somehow I ended up with only two dollars in my pocket."

"It's a gift, Brenda," he says, handing over some bills.

"I knew you'd say that. I'll send it back as soon as I get to San Diego."

"I knew you'd say that."

"Well." I look down at my pack. For the first time ever, I can't stand the sight of it.

"Let me help you with that," Al says, then, as he's hoisting it onto my back, "it's heavier than it looks."

We stand together in the hallway, stare at each other and breathe and swallow. "Remember? . . ." I ask, "Remember how I said, 'Even though I won't marry you doesn't mean I won't love you madly, always?'"

He smiles shyly and nods. I nod, too. "I'm glad," he says.

The elevator door opens and I get in, and I suddenly remember the fortuneteller saying all that stuff about how I was supposed to have been Al's brother. There's no time to tell Al about all that, now. "I'll see you in some future life," I say.

"I love you, too," Al mouths, as the doors close.

At the Greyhound station I opt to get on a slow bus that's leaving now rather than wait until tomorrow for a through bus. I plod down the aisle, finally find, with great relief, two empty seats. I plunk down and stare out the window at the side of another parked bus. What was it that Al said, five years ago? "Just think of it, Brenda, there we'll be for the rest of our lives, coupling and uncoupling like two boxcars in the moonlight on a legendary, neverending stretch of great American railroad." I remember how he ran down the street, shouting, "Brenda! Put me on your list! Put me in as fifty; put me in as thirteen." As I drove away. As I drove away.

"All right, folks," the busdriver swings into his seat up front; the whole bus rocks. "No smoking cigarettes, cigars, pipes, marijuana, or any other substances, legal or illegal. No radios. This is the bus to Seattle with connections to Portland, San Francisco, L.A., and San Diego, and all points between that you have never seen before and will hope to never see again." The doors slam shut, the bus rumbles, jitters. The sun has not even set on the day, and already, I'm pulling away from Spokane, Washington.

HIGHWAY 101,
SOUTH

56 ◼ FIFTY-SIX HOURS and ninety-seven stops later, the bus pulls in and then out of Cardiff-by-the-Sea, Solana Beach, Del Mar, and La Jolla before its final stop in San Diego at eight o'clock. I get off, collect my pack, step over and around all the bums passed out at Horton Plaza. I'm glad I have somewhere to sleep tonight.

I manage to catch one of the rare buses going to the coast. It turns south, though, at Sunset Cliffs Boulevard, so I hop off, walk north past Ocean Beach Park. Lots of people are yelling in the big field . . . a soccer game going on in the dark. I cross the bridge that goes over the dry San Diego riverbed. The red light blinks on the top of the Sea World tower a half-mile away. It feels good to be following a route I know so well: through the bushes to the frontage road along the marinas, across the bridge, under the row of pines running through Vacation Island, over the bridge to Mission Beach, around the bay. Lights shine on the water like pillars. Then it's up Mission Boulevard past the head shops, turn in a walkway between a row of beach cottages, to the boardwalk. I trudge along, ocean sounds on one side, beach house sounds on the other, and bikes and skateboards and barefoot people all around.

Lucky for me, Tug's Bar is still serving its Friday night fifty-cent spaghetti dinner, even though it's after nine. I balance my full paper plate and my beer to sit on the wall. This feels just right: hot garlic bread, cold beer going down, stiff ocean breeze in my face.

Then I keep going up the coast, up to where the houses get more and more expensive, some with security signs: Armed Response, hanging on their wrought-iron gates. I take a guess at where La Playa might be, and eventually I walk onto it.

I can hardly believe it when I see Will's place—a small and classy old Spanish-style apartment building with courtyards, gardens, a fountain. Either Miranda has made a hit at the La Paloma, or Will's renovation contract is even bigger than Miranda made it out to be. I walk through the archway into their courtyard and right away hear my brother singing, and see his shadowy figure through the window.

Will's got this great voice that he never uses. It's only good when he really belts it out; when he sings at a normal volume, it's wobbly and unsure. I remember watching him sing with his seventh-grade class a song called "Mrs. Murphy's Chowder." It's a song about what's in her chowder: "cowbells, doorbells, balls, bats, and Democrats"; Will just loved that song. When he'd wailed out that one word, chOOOOOW-DER, it seemed like he could have swallowed up the whole of his seventh-grade class.

Later he grew self-conscious of his voice, I don't know why. So right now when he's really belting out this Beatles song, "Please, Please Me," I know he must be feeling pretty great about Miranda. It's an especially hard song to sing, the way it goes way down on the "Whoa, yeah, like I please . . ." and way up sweet and high on the "yooooou," but he's hitting all the notes right on target, knocking me out he sounds so sweet and silly.

I lower my pack by the front door and sidle up to a window. Miranda is right there on the couch, punching on a calculator, balancing a checkbook. Will's in the kitchen drying a glass, and singing. I lower myself onto the dirt in the bushes under the window, leaning my back against the rough stucco wall, and settle in. Will sings until the song ends on that long drawn-out high note, starts another Beatles song, "Long Tall Sally," which is a challenge, too, a really hopping song. He ends it with final, simulated guitar chords, and Miranda laughs.

The phone rings. Will's voice: "No, not yet. Listen; I have your address, though. As soon as I know where, I'll drop you a line, ok?"

Al. It's got to be Al, checking up on me.

"Oh, I don't know . . ." He laughs. "You're beginning to talk me into it, though. Maybe I'll get a thirty-two now rather than a twenty-eight."

Al?! Whatever was I thinking of? Will's talking with someone about some supplies he's ordering or something. Whatever was I picturing . . . that Al would toss his Nicole out into the Spokane snow in his desperation to get me back? I almost laugh. Jesus, Brenda.

Through the window, the familiar and mundane have never sounded so precious: Miranda coughs, glasses ping, silverware clatters, a chair creaks, water plops in bursts. I feel suddenly tired, in a good way, in a relieved way. I settle back against the wall.

Here I am back on familiar territory, home turf, where I can knock on a door of a home where I belong, at least belong to more than anyplace else. It would seem as if I'd be dying to get into the light, onto a clean soft couch, with walls around me and people I know. Only I don't feel at all desperate about it, which surprises me. I drop my head onto my knees and drink all the noises in. Things sound good in this house; things sound fine.

Finally I crawl over to the side of the apartment, unroll my sleeping bag in some hibiscus bushes. The narrow window of sky above me is silver with the reflection of city lights, not at all like the jet-black openness pinpointed with stars at David's. It's hard to believe it's the same sky at all.

The night is winding down early in this area. There's the

everpresent city hum, but not many nearby noises from the houses and apartments. The light goes off at Will and Miranda's. I lie on my back, my jacket for a pillow. I drift in and out of sleep. The city hum slows down, softens. I love the dead of night in cities. It calms me to think of all those hundreds of thousands of people lying down, dreaming like babes; me, too, just another one of the babes, resting peacefully.

In the morning I don't knock on Will's door; I put my toothbrush in my pocket, leave my pack hidden in the hibiscus, and walk down to Pacific Beach to the Open House Coffee Shop. I brush my teeth in the bathroom, untangle my hair with my fingers, before eating breakfast. The teenaged daughters of the Armenian cook are waitressing. They're good waitresses; they'd rather be elsewhere on this sunny Saturday morning, so they're not smiling, but they're not sulking either. As usual, they're carrying themselves with a great deal of foreign dignity, which is nice to be around.

Some of the benches have been recovered with new Naugahyde since I was here last. This building was once a surf shop, then a used bookstore, an A & W, and a frozen yogurt place before becoming Open House Coffee Shop. Over the years I've been a customer at all those businesses; me and this building go back a long way. That's about the closest you can get in Southern California to a sense of continuity, to the pull of your roots, to a brush with history.

After breakfast I walk back most of the same route I walked last night: along the boardwalk, around the bay, crossing bridges over slow-moving water and fast-moving Saturday morning beach traffic until I'm rounding the nursery next to Kelly's Boatyard.

Brenda's Quest takes my breath away.

She sits high on her scaffolding up against the blue sky; her bowsprit points to the sea. She's oiled and painted, her brass shining, her standing rigging in place. All she needs are her sails and her running rigging, and to be set in that ocean where she belongs. She is looking grander now, I'm sure, than she has ever looked in her entire life.

In gold letters, *Brenda's Quest* winds across her curved bow.

I see all of this through the fence. I'm still ten feet away. The dogs aren't barking; I'm far enough. "Hel-lo!" I call out, my hands cupped around my mouth, like a sailor on the open sea. "Lucien!" There's no answer. After some thought, I call, "Martin!" No one. Then I remember how you call out to get the attention of the people who live on the boats in the free anchorage. I cup my hands around my mouth again, throw back my head. *"Brenda's Quest!"*

I take a couple of steps closer. The dogs start up their frenzied barking. At the far end of the boatyard, the man I met earlier jogs down a ladder from a deck. "Hi," he greets me, as if we were old friends. He's rubbing his big, greasy fingers on a rag. "Lucien says to tell you he's coming back in about three weeks, around the fifth or so, and expects to see you then."

"All right, thanks," I answer, simply.

"See ya, Brenda," he says, startling me by remembering my name, but then I realize he's been looking at *Brenda's Quest* for weeks now.

I walk back to Will's. It'll be good to see him; to make sure he's really all right; Miranda, more likely, will be home. It'll feel good to take a nap on their couch, anyway. I start to cross the bridge, and suddenly I feel it: I'm pulling the riverbed beneath me. I'm in my spot in space; I'm as solidly in my spot in space as I've ever been.

I remember Will and I, one night; we were just little; we had that little-kid intensity about us. "Nothing can knock you out of your spot," Will said to me. It was late, his face was glowing in the dim light from the nightlight. "Watch." He swung his pajamaed legs over the side of his bed, stood up.

Then he threw both his legs out from under him, landed hard on the floor. "What did I do?"

"You fell, down, Will'am."

"Nope. I picked up the world."

I get to the other side of the bridge, but the feeling doesn't stop, as it often used to. I'm still moving the world around me. I have never felt so blissfully balanced.

No one is home when I show up, but Will's skateboard is beside the stoop. It wasn't there earlier. I sit down on the step: I pick up the world. I lug off my boots, pull off my socks, shove them into my pack, then get out my notebook and pen, and write.

"Will, I'm back. I borrowed your skateboard. See you at dinnertime. Brenda."

I place the note behind his screen door, pick up his board. I ride a few blocks to the base of Mount Soledad, then, cradling the board under my arm, I start pushing Mount Soledad down, under my two bare feet. Right and left, I push until at last there's nothing left above me to push down; nothing above me but that precious blue sky.

57 ◪ Mount Soledad: Mountain of Solitude.

Downhill of me are bulldozed sagebrush, tumbleweed, eucalyptus, their roots exposed. Around the ripped landscape, bulldozers lie unmoving in the sun like so many oil-slicked bodies on the beach, soaking up energy for the coming week of work. First thing Monday morning, they'll be ripping and scraping again.

This part of the mountain is being smoothed and sculpted, covered with developments called "Willowdale" and "Forest Greene," names that have nothing to do with the land. I don't think developers see ridges, mesas, bluffs, and peaks. I don't think they see canyons, gorges, gaps, and glens. What they see are humps and holes. They push the humps into the holes. Then they cover up all the flatness with houses, roads, fences, driveways, patios, pools, and hottubs.

I take a few steps off the pavement, onto the churned-up, hot dirt. I sit down; the soil cradles me. I lean back on my elbows. From this position, it looks like there is almost nothing between me and the ocean. There are my blue-jeaned legs, bare feet, mounds of red soil, then vast legions of distant sea, a gray horizon. The sun's heat ripples off the soil; the pungent smell of the sagebrush is soothing. I lie back, nestle my head onto the soft dirt.

Brenda's Quest. Fittings will ping, the hull will creak. I'll winch lines, trim sails, teach myself to steer by the stars. I'll keep watch through the night; at the first touch of dawn, I suppose I'll have to cook for gold-toothed Lucien and sullen Martin and myself, before I'll be able to drop off to sleep in that clammy, creaking berth. It's hard for me to imagine the salty dampness while lying here in the sun, my bare feet baking in the dry heat. I feel now like I felt a few days ago at David's, in front of the fire, warming my soles. David's clothes were rough, clean and dry.

What was the name of David's boat? *Rose.* Rose: her hand forever offering. David caught forever, in a moment of patience and wanting, on a boat forever floating. And I was caught forever by David's hand, with a look of awe.

So what now? MaryEllen always said, when in doubt, make a list. "What's Important in Life. 1) Adventure; 2) Love." No, when I made that list at the apple ranch, I crossed out "love," because love could be encompassed in adventure, could be the biggest adventure of all. "What's Important in Life. Adventure."

It seems forever since I last saw MaryEllen. I count back

the days to when I left their fisherman's cottage in Gloucester.
Nine! I sit up tall, count again: four days crossing the country, two days with David, one day doing a U-turn in Spokane,
two rumbling down the West Coast on the bus. Only nine.

I stand up, step onto the hot black pavement that slopes so
smoothly and steeply down Mount Soledad. Nothing moves.
Mountain of Solitude. I look out to the ocean. There are only
a couple of sailboats far out there, close to the horizon. I smile
to think of *Brenda's Quest* pressing through the swells, *Brenda's Question* overturned on her deck.

I roll my board back and forth under my foot. To my right
is a newly paved cul-de-sac. I step onto my board; the mountain slides up behind me, my hair flies. I lean, slowly turn
the mountain in a circle, then in a tighter and tighter circle,
before I throw out my arms and spin the earth into a blur
beneath me.

I walk back to the top again, stand on my board, unmoving,
looking down the long, steep expanse of winding road. I could
really pick up some speed on that road. "You could kill yourself, too, Brenda," I say out loud. Still, I have never felt so
blissfully centered and balanced.

A hawk wheels over me, hovers. It looks down at me in
that precise moment that David captured in his drawings; a
look of recognition and awe. "David," I hear myself whisper,
aloud.

I throw my legs forward, the board begins to roll, the
mountain slides. I head for the far left of the road, lean into
a tight curve, head for the right, swing into a tight curve; it's
as if the mountain and I are dancing a slow one together. The
mountain slides and sways, I press my hips toward it, slowly,
again and again and again. Finally the smooth, new, black
road becomes well-used gray. I've gotten low enough to where
houses and cars are. I jump the board onto the sidewalk, do
some hotdog stuff in the bright sunshine.

Then I'm leaning lazily into the corner of La Playa. The board clacks rhythmically over the sidewalk lines.

Will is standing in his front yard, barefoot, with his hands in his jean pockets. "Brennnnn-da," he sing-songs, like he used to when we were little. His broken-toothed smile melts me. I kick the board up into my hand; Will hugs me in that solid and simple way as only a brother can. "Come on in."

My pack is lying on the living room floor. "That looks like it's been some miles," he says. We sit down at his table and he pours me some coffee. "Where've you been?"

"Around. Around the world, it feels like. Twice. How was Creedmoor?" I ask.

"Miranda's family was great; gracious and polite in a way I've never seen before. Real Southern Hospitality. The little cousins all liked me. They all said 'Ain't.' 'Ain't his accent cute?' North Carolina is nice. But you know, if they took out all the churches and mobile home parks, it'd be a virtual wilderness. Oh, by the way, I have your money."

He goes to a drawer, pulls out an envelope and hands it over. It's full of bills.

"What's this?"

"It's the money you gave me to go to the apple ranch with. The stuff you won at the track. Thanks."

"Will, I *gave* you that money."

"Fine. Ok, consider that you gave it to me. You told me you'd help me out, and you did, and now I'm telling you that I'll help you out, and I will."

"Just a minute," I say. I put my hands up, look off to the side trying to unmuddle my brain. Who's helping who out, and didn't I come back here to take care of Will?

"Anyway," he adds, "I don't need it. I'm doing really well. Miranda's doing really well."

"I can see, that, Will. Look at this place; it's beautiful."

I glance around. Nice furniture, plants, a new, high-tech

stereo. Quite a collection of albums, Miranda's, I guess, except
for the album on the top, the Crystal Gayle.

"Kirby had a crush on her," Will says.

"What?" Kirby.

"He had a crush on Crystal Gayle. He used to go wild
whenever she showed up on Radio Saigon. Remember the
picture I have of the two of us? He sent a copy of that picture
to her in a letter. I don't know if it was just the way Kirby
was smiling in that picture, or if it was what he wrote—well,
you remember how sincere Kirby was—but anyway, she actually wrote back, promising to go out to dinner with him
when he came home. He carried that letter with him all the
time; it seems like I was always catching him rereading it."
He drops his head and shakes it. "Poor old Kirby," he says.

Kirby Renfroe ended up as bones and teeth rolling in the
surf; he ended up as a name on a plaque. Maybe, after all,
that's all I ever need to know about what happened to Kirby.

"David called," Will adds, simply. He didn't say, "Some
guy called, I think his name was David or something, who is
he?" He said, "David called," as if we both knew him. "He
called a few times. I talked with him for a long while a couple
of nights ago. About sailing, mostly. I like him. I like him a
lot. Seems lonely, though." He picks up his coffee cup, puts
it in the sink.

"Lonely? No, I don't think so. Alone a lot, maybe. But not
lonely. He's . . . you know . . . well, not *lonely.*"

Will sits on the floor, pulls on his steel-toed boots. "Well,
look, I'm off to do some work; feel free to make yourself at
home. We've got a nice patio."

After he's gone, I change into shorts, lie down in the sun
on a webbed lounge chair on the patio. I can hear the patter
of the fountain out front, the wind rustling palm fronds high
overhead, the pinging of fittings on the mast of a catamaran
that's sitting in the yard next door. I take a long drink from
a glass of ice water. I'm stopped; I can't believe I'm stopped.

Soon I go inside. My pack is lying as it was before. I sit on the couch and look at it for a while. Then I smile and sigh, pull on my boots and jeans, and hoist it up onto my back. I leave a note: "Will. I'll write you when I get there. Brenda."

Then I step outside, and start pulling toward me what I need.

A Note About the Author

Sharlene Baker was born in Chelsea, Massachusetts,
in 1954, and was raised mostly in Hawaii and California.
She now lives in Durham, North Carolina, with her daughter,
Chelsea, and her son, Nathaniel.

A Note on the Type

This book was set in Garamond, a typeface
originally designed by the famous Parisian type cutter
Claude Garamond (1480–1561). While delightfully unconventional
in design, the Garamond types are clear and open, and
maintain an elegance and precision of line
that mark them as French.

Composed by Creative Graphics, Inc.,
Allentown, Pennsylvania.
Printed and bound by Fairfield Graphics,
Fairfield, Pennsylvania.
Designed by Mia Vander Els.